Folly

DRAGONS OF THE CROSSROADS BOOK 2

LORI SALTIS

VAGABOND TALES

I dedicate this book to Jennifer Gagliardi.
May our mutual folly yield great results.

Penny

I'm at the Auld Sod and the last person I expect to see is Lennon.

Literally, the last person.

As usual, I'm performing on stage with my family for the pleasure of Sharpers, Strowlers, and the Upright Man. No, not Kingfisher. Bridie's brother, Christy, found out what that bellend had done to us and flew from Dublin to San Francisco in a fine rage to challenge him for the position of Upright Man. What a glorious bout that was, watching Kingfisher getting bounced and trounced about the ring until he wound up bloody and unconscious at my uncle's feet. I cheered myself hoarse. Even thinking about it now makes me smirk.

As is the way with Strowlers, Kingfisher was sent packing and Uncle Christy took over the San Francisco Nest. Couldn't be more ideal for my family, right?

Yeah, right.

Christy is sitting at the exact same table that Kingfisher used to leer at us from. Beside him is his wife, Auntie Joanne, who, unlike poor Doreen, is the acknowledged and honored Mother Bird of our Nest. She's holding a red rose, bought for her by Uncle Christy for no particular reason. They're surrounded by their children and generously buying drinks for the entire pub. It'd be the *craic* if it weren't for the presence of yet another Likely Lad.

Among Strowlers, a Likely Lad is a young cove coming into his own. He's got his first trailer and is ready to travel apart from his family. The only thing stopping him is want of a wife.

I think you know where this is going.

Since I turned eighteen, Uncle Christy has taken every opportunity to parade me before whatever Likely Lad has blown into the Nest that week. Or is it the other way around? Doesn't matter. Before a marriage can be arranged, I give a flat-out no. I'm sure most of them say the same because I'm naught but a sour bitch when it comes to their ilk. Christy hasn't given up, but that's his problem.

My problem is I'm in love with a memory. When we first returned to San Francisco, I thought I saw Lennon everywhere, around every corner. I searched so many faces and never found his. I should be over him by now, but I'm not. I never will be. I don't want to be. Mum thinks I'm stubborn and that's why I won't move on.

Thing is, she's right.

Tonight's Likely Lad has a name I refuse to remember. He's all freckles and whiskers, and carries a banjo. Nice touch, but it's not going to fetch me. He wants to sit in with us for our second set and Bridie can't refuse with Christy sitting right there, giving her stink eye because of my cold shoulder. I refuse to dance accompanied by an unknown musician who'll be looking up my skirt from behind. I pick up my ukulele and stand behind him, so he can't see me without turning and being obvious.

While he tunes his banjo, I pipe up, "How about we start with 'Unfortunate Lad'?"

Bridie shoots me a warning glance, but Kai smirks and says, "Yeah."

Likely Lad looks over his shoulder. "Same tune as 'Streets of Laredo', right?"

I shrug as if to say, 'everyone knows that,' because everyone does and I'm so not impressed. He starts plucking out the opening melody and Bridie joins him on her violin. I strum my ukulele while Kai steps up to the microphone to sing.

> *"As I was a-walking down by St. James' Hospital,*
> *I was a-walking down by there one day,*
> *What should I spy but one of my comrades,*
> *All wrapped up in flannel though warm was the day.*
> *I asked him what ailed him, I asked him what*
>   *failed him,*
> *I asked him the cause of all his complaint.*
> *It's all on account of some handsome young woman,*
> *'Tis she that has caused me to weep and lament."*

'Streets of Laredo' is about a cowboy dying of a gunshot wound, but 'Unfortunate Lad' is about a rake dying of the clap. I sing along to the chorus with gusto.

> *"And had she but told me before she disordered me,*
> *Had she but told me of it in time,*
> *I might have got salts and pills of white mercury,*
> *But now I'm a young man cut down in my prime."*

Likely Lad is a pretty good picker, which adds another dimension to our sound. Uncle Christy isn't stupid. Even if he can't fetch me with this particular lad, he can draw in Bridie with musical talent. The song ends and Likely Lad glances back at me with a twinkle in his blue eyes.

I smile. I can't help it. He's not a bad sort and it's not his fault he's being thrust upon me. Then I chew my lip. I can't slip up and show him even an ounce of interest or Christy will pounce.

"How about some Pogues?" calls out a woman from the audience

Bridie turns to Likely Lad with a smile. "Do you know any Pogues songs, Conor?"

He nods and starts strumming the melody to "A Pair of Brown Eyes."

I suck in my breath. Of all the Pogues songs, why did he choose that one? It's about a battle-scarred soldier who lost his love, a brown-eyed girl. Now he roves the streets of Dublin in search of a pair of brown eyes. I know the feeling. When we returned to San Francisco, I did the same, wandered the streets hoping to find those brown eyes that had warmed with laughter and froze with anger. But, as in the song, those eyes weren't waiting for me to return.

The penny whistle is a key instrument in this song, so Bridie steps aside, yielding to me the microphone next to Kai. He strums his guitar and sings while she plays the squeezebox. I close my eyes as my fingers work the intricate chords of the bridge, which I love. It sounds like a bird calling to her lost mate. When I finish, I gaze out over the audience, who are swaying along to the melancholy tune. At the front of the bar, near the door, I spot a pair of round sunglasses, Lennon-style.

My heart lurches. I gasp and blink in case the bright stage lights are playing with my eyes. The crowd shifts and I can't see him anymore. Bridie plays the opening to the next verse with more emphasis and I realize I missed my cue. I jam the penny whistle into my mouth and bungle the first few chords before picking up the melody again.

I spot the glasses again on a young man with dark hair. He could be Asian, but it's hard to tell. Could it really be Lennon?

No, impossible. Right? It's been two years. Would he remember the name of an obscure pub that I'd mentioned maybe twice in our conversations? No, it's not him. Just another dim reflection that I won't chase after.

The song ends and I dip my head in thanks for the applause. When I look up, he's slipping out the door.

"I gotta use the loo," I whisper to Bridie.

Her brow curdles. She's tired of being stuck between the rock of Christy and the hard place of me. "Good. Cool your heels in there until you can behave." Then she steps up to the mic with a bright smile. "Our next song is in honor of our Upright Man and lovely Lady Bird." She turns to Likely Lad. "Do you know Red is the Rose?"

He nods and plucks the first chords of the melody. He really does know his stuff. Too bad I couldn't care less.

As they strike up the tune, I sidle along the edge of the crowd, away from the bathroom and toward the front of the pub. I'm out the front door and half expect to see Lennon leaning against wall, his brown eyes waiting for me.

As the song predicted, they're not.

A gusting ocean breeze lifts my skirt and I grasp the satin material before it swirls above my thighs. The wind barely stirs the thick fog already dampening my hair and clothes. The street lights are bright enough to pierce the murk for a block in either direction, but all I see are Bleaters, ordinary folk, walking in and out of the restaurants and bars.

Then I feel it. I'm being watched. Lennon. He's somewhere nearby.

I turn this way and that, scanning every doorway. I suck in fog and breathe out mist. The chill settles on my skin through my skimpy dance costume. Then I look down and realize I'm standing on a small road marker carved into the sidewalk, three embedded arrows pointing toward the entrance, designating the Auld Sod as an All Haven, meaning anyone on the

Crossroads is welcome. All Havens are rare and well-known in any given city, so that could have been Lennon. Right? Right.

I bite my lip, chew on disappointment, and force a laugh. What a ninny I am. The strains of Likely Lad's reedy voice reach me.

> *Red is the rose that in yonder garden grows,*
> *And fair is the lily of the valley;*
> *Clear is the water that flows from the Boyne*
> *But my love is fairer than any.*

I hope he finds his red rose, but it's not me. I'm not anyone's fair lily or bonny lassie. That stuff and nonsense is for the sort of Strowler that walks the Glory Road. I'm Penny Sparrow and I walk the Wayward Way. Alone.

Penny

Turnabout is fair play, yeah? If Lennon is stalking me, then I should be able to stalk him back. Problem is, there's only one place I can do that and it's not without complications. I have orders to fill this morning, so I think about it while I work.

After graduating from high school, I started my own online business, Pinafores and More. I love pinafores because the simple aesthetic allows for a wide variety of designs. I'm finishing two today, one a basic smock style in a rich brown fabric with lace-trimmed pockets, the other a plaid punk confection with narrow straps and a flirty skirt. The "More" part of my business is accessories, mostly leggings that I artfully snip and sew on snaps or buttons. Those are popular and I'm running out of some of my favorite buttons…

I stop fingering through my button box and rub my chin. I've found my excuse to go to Chinatown.

After going to the post office to ship the pinafores, I take a bus that drops me at the corner of Grant and Pacific. I stroll along Grant Avenue, past tourists roaming in and out of souvenir shops or angling for selfies against a backdrop of red lanterns and Chinese architecture. Touts work the street corners, handing out restaurant menus or religious tracts with equal fervor. I walk on the sunny side, enjoying a rare summer day without fog or clouds. I didn't bother with a jumper, despite the cold breeze blowing up from the bay. Some of the sleeveless, goose-pimpled tourists look as if they wished they had though.

Strowlers never leave home without a sham to cover their game. Mine is called the Devil's Workshop because Strowlers' hands are never idle when venturing among Bleaters. We always have a destination and a task in case we're questioned by the *gardaí* or other authorities.

I head up the steps of Shanghai Bazaar, past the fierce stone guardian lions and through the marble pillared entrance. Inside is a three-story emporium chock-full of imported goods, everything from clothing to kitchenware to funeral supplies, none of which interests me. I head straight for the small but tasty sewing department on the second floor and its wall of drool-worthy buttons. I grab handfuls of my favorites, dumping them into my basket, before lingering over the new arrivals, which I grab a few of as well.

I go to my favorite cashier, Lin, who, as always, shakes her head and chuckles as she rings me up. This is another bit of shammery called the Familiar Face. Being Button Girl makes me a regular customer, noticeable, but not suspicious.

Task complete and shopping bag in hand, I head back to Pacific Avenue. I'm almost there when I halt in my tracks. Bugger, there's a bus at the stop. I dive into the nearest tourist trap and paw through a stack of cheap T-shirts. I can't help wrinkling my nose at the cheesy designs. I learned to silkscreen at school and could do much better than this shite if I had the equipment at home. I hold up a T-shirt as if examining it while staring out the window. Sure enough, another bus pulls up as soon the previous one drives away. I roll my eyes. Typical. There's never a bus when you need one and two in a row when you don't.

I fold the T-shirt and wait until the bus pulls away from the curb before dashing out the door. I watch with seeming frustration as the bus heads up Pacific Avenue and trudge after it as if trying to catch up, which I almost do at the next stop because it's halted long enough to load someone in a wheelchair. Is the Universe trying to tell me something? Probably. I feel a squeeze of temptation - or is it panic - to get in and go home, but I'm made of stubborn stuff. I continue on my merry way, slowing my pace as the street becomes progressively steeper and more residential. The bus is long gone by the time I reach the stop catty-corner from Joseph Alley, the location of the Two Dragon Clan *kongsi*.

There's no one else waiting and I stand out like a sore thumb in clothing of my own design, a V-neck purple pinafore, black leggings with silver side buttons, Doc Martin boots, and a patchwork boho bag. Maybe I should've worn all black, but I don't want to look like Desperate Stalker Girl, even if that's what I feel like right now. There aren't any stores to duck into and the nearby doorways are all barred. If I linger out here for too long, I'll definitely be noticed. I check the bus schedule on my phone. Ten minutes until the next one arrives. What are the chances Lennon will come strolling out of the alley by then? Slim to none? No. Just none.

I wrap my mind around the sad truth: that wasn't Lennon last night and I need to get on the bus and go home. Forlorn hope keeps me watching the alley up to the last minute, when the gate behind me opens and a gaggle of old ladies spills out and crowds around me, most of them clutching handcarts. I spot a bus coming uphill and suck in a sigh that tastes of relief and disappointment. I take a last look at the alley. Three men come striding out, all dressed in ragged military fatigues. One of them is Jeremiah Walks Long, son of the Beggar Chief.

What is he doing here? Why would he come to the Two Dragon Clan *kongsi* in person rather than make a phone call? Excitement wiggles through my stomach along with fear. I don't want him or his men to spot me. The bus rumbles to a stop. While the old gals take their time boarding, I pretend to search my bag and pockets for my bus pass. I look at the driver and shake my head. The door slams shut and the bus trundles away. Jeremiah and his men are heading downhill. I wait until they turn the corner and follow them.

Yes, this is a stupid thing to do, but I can't stop myself. Strowlers believe our heads distract and our hearts deceive, so we go with our gut, and mine insists that Jeremiah was at the *kongsi* because of Lennon. This has no basis in fact, but it's all I've got, so I go with it.

I keep about half a block's distance between us as I follow them down Mason Street toward the Cable Car Museum. There are enough tourists heading in the same direction that I can blend in. Jeremiah and his men stride along in the manner of Beggars who take pride in their poverty. It must confuse Bleaters, but Rufflers, the criminal element, know who they are and not to mess with them. My footsteps falter as Jeremiah's escort glances around before following him into a gap between two buildings. I keep walking, heart pounding, passing the alley without a glance. Then I stop and look over my shoulder. No Jeremiah with his slate-eyed scowl. I breathe a sigh of relief as I double back and lean against the wall while pretending to search for something in my purse. I listen over the persistent hum of the cable car rails, hoping to hear Jeremiah or one of his men say something, anything, about Lennon.

The rails thrum as a familiar clang fills the air. Bollocks. A cable car is coming. I'm having no luck with public transport today. And, of course, the operator chose this moment to lay on heavy with the bloody bell. I want to spit as the rickety old thing, heavy laden with tourists, goes rattling by.

I take a chance and peer around the corner. The alley is dark and damp, and wide enough for dumpsters, but not cars. The Beggars have almost reached the other end. I gnaw my lip. If I'm caught, I'll have no excuse that won't land me in hot water with the Beggar Chief and Uncle Christy. Should I leave, having come thus far? My gut won't allow it. Not until I hear them talk. I count to ten once, hesitate, and count again before I peek around the corner.

They're gone. I skitter through the alley, my bag bouncing against my thigh. I've almost reached the dumpsters when I realize I better slow down or risk bumping into the Beggars if they're lingering around the corner. But I also risk losing them if I don't leg it. Bollocks.

I notice a large red stop sign with white Chinese characters spray painted on a wall. I don't think it's official since it's splattered with colorful droplets and has a tag that looks like a four. It could mean I've stumbled into some Ruffler gang's territory. In which case, I'd much rather be caught by Jeremiah. I pick up my pace again.

"Penny." The voice comes from right behind me, like a shouted whisper.

I jump a foot in the air. When I land, I'm face-to-face with Lennon.

I feel like I've been shoved underwater. My heart starts pounding and I can't breathe. My legs turn to jelly and I lean against a wall so I don't sink onto the gritty pavement. How can it be him?

"What are you doing?" His voice is deeper than I remember. His lips have grown fuller and cheekbones more pronounced, but that haunted look still casts a shadow across his face, even when he's scowling.

I give a little gasp as I suck in enough air to fill my lungs so I can talk. "Were you following me?"

"No." He sounds defensive. "I was already here."

"What are you doing here?"

"What are *you* doing here?"

I make a scoffing sound, as if he has any better reason to be skulking here than I do.

"Were you following Jeremiah?"

"Yeah."

"Why?"

"Why not?"

Those dark brown eyes go blank. Then he blinks and they storm over. "What the hell, Penny?"

He has a hell of a nerve asking me what the hell. "Why should you care if I'm following Jeremiah?"

"It's dangerous."

"Maybe I like danger." I don't, but it sounds flash. I lean against the wall with my arms crossed. This is the perfect time for Lennon to admit a certain something.

He leans beside me and tips back his head so it rests against the bricks. He seems taller, but that's no surprise after two years. Gone is that blond tuft of bangs in his otherwise jet black hair. Jeans and a leather biker jacket replace the army fatigues and pea coat he'd gotten from the Beggar Clan. When I first met Lennon, we were both skint: homeless, broke and broken. I'd be amazed by his transformation if I didn't know better, but I do.

He gives me a once over, too. Does he like what he sees? Who cares if he does, right? I look down and rub my heel with my foot. Right.

"I missed you." Three simple words I'd waited two years to hear.

I missed you, too. The reply sticks in my throat. I can't let him off the hook so easily.

He shifts and presses his shoulder against the wall. I do the same so we're facing each other, only a few inches apart. Last time we were this close, we'd been kissing as if it were the end of the world. And it was. The end of our world together, until now. My heart starts pounding again. It takes all my will not to step back. Or forward. My arms stay folded tight.

"I thought you were going to London," he says.

"And I thought you were in some kind of danger and we'd never each other again, but here we are." The words come out in a fast, angry jumble. "By the way, how was Seattle?" I feel a snick of satisfaction as his mouth drops open.

"How do you know about Seattle?" he whispers.

Really? He's still not going to tell me? Okay, then, what the hell. I'll tell him. "I know who you are. You're Paul Lau, the Dragon Son."

Lennon

For the last two years, there's only one person I've wanted to see and now she's beside me, close enough to touch, looking at me like I'm an utter tool.

How much does my life suck? A whole hell of a lot, thanks so much for asking.

Penny has changed. She's a little taller and a little more, um, filled out. Yeah, that turned out nice. She still has the greenest eyes I've ever seen and a mouth like a rosebud, even when it's pursed up with disgust. Her reddish-brown hair frames her face like a fringe cap that, along with her pointed nose and chin, makes her look like a pissed-off fairy princess. Why does she have to be so mad at me? Oh, yeah, I lied to her. She and her family thought I was some random runaway, and I was, but I never told her what I was actually running from.

"Who told you?"

"Who do you think?" Even angry, her lilting voice sounds musical.

The list of suspects is pretty short. It only has one name. "John Walks Long."

"He told me to forget about you."

He would and she should, but I can't make myself say so. "You asked him?"

"Yeah, but he wouldn't tell me who you really are."

The Beggar Chief hadn't betrayed me. Good to know. I scratched the back of my neck. "Um, Kingfisher?"

"Kingfisher? Why would that blighter tell us shite?" Her eyes narrow. "Wait? Did he know who you are?"

"I don't know." I really don't. "What happened to him anyway?"

"He's long gone. Don't change the subject."

"I'm not." I am, though I do want to know what happened to that shitbag. "So, who told you?"

"Aaron."

That name. It sucks the oxygen out of the alley. My voice strains through my tightened throat. "My cousin, Aaron?"

"Yeah, him."

"You know him?"

"Obviously."

"How?"

"I should be the one asking the questions." She stands taller and stares down her nose at me, imperious as a real princess. Then she sighs and her eyes become pragmatic so she looks like my friend, the girl who understands life is fucking complicated. "We did go to London, but it was only for a week. Bill kept pleading with Bridie to come back to San Francisco and clear his name with the *gardaí*. He said if she did, he wouldn't divorce her until we became permanent residents. Plus, Kai's grandparents wanted us to live here and offered to help us financially."

"Why would they do that?"

"They want Kai to have a connection to the Two Dragon Clan. Problem is, Matthew was kicked out when he decided to walk the Wayward Way. The London branch of the clan doesn't want anything to do with Kai. So, his grandparents reached out to the head of the clan in San Francisco…"

Heat spreads across my neck.

"A guy named Tony Lau."

God. Damn it.

"When we got back to San Francisco, we went to the *kongsi* in Chinatown and met Tony and Aaron. Tony was…"

An arrogant prick? A self-righteous ass?

My gut twists.

My Big Brother.

"Decent enough. He said Kai couldn't learn the clan's secret skills since he's a Strowler, but he offered to teach him some of their basic martial skills. In exchange, Bridie started giving Aaron violin lessons. Kai and Aaron saw each other almost every day and became best mates." She pauses and her eyes become puzzled. "Aaron needed a friend because, you know, because of his mum."

Deep, bitter bile fills my throat. I have nothing but hatred for Auntie Sylvia, dead or alive.

Her head tilts. "You weren't at the funeral."

I manage to choke out, "You were?"

"Tony invited our family so Kai could be there for Aaron."

I wish I'd been there. One last chance to spit in the face of the woman who'd killed my mother.

"After the funeral, we were in the banquet hall and Aaron showed us the lineage of the Dragon Sons, and there was your photo at the very end. We were gobsmacked. I don't think Aaron noticed because he was broken up about his mum. He told us your name was Paul and that you went to live in Seattle with your aunt after your parents died. Then he walked away and I just stared at your photo, trying not to believe it was really you, that you had lied to me like that." Her green eyes turn jade cold.

I dig my elbow into the wall. Two years ago, I'd almost told

Penny everything, but I couldn't bring myself to do it. Now it's biting me in the ass.

Her voice goes flat. "Don't worry, we didn't peach on you to Tony."

Silence occupies the narrow space between us. I shift to make room. Should I apologize? Will that help? Make things worse? What can I say to bring back her smile, the one I've dreamed about for two years?

Penny huffs and her breath grazes my cheek. "We took you in, sheltered you, fed you and didn't ask for anything in return. Why weren't you square with us?"

I mumble, "I couldn't be."

"Why not?"

I clear my throat and speak up. "My clan. I didn't want them to blame your family for hiding me from them."

"We weren't hiding you from them. How could we if we didn't know who you are?"

"Exactly. There was nothing to accuse you of because you didn't know, and I wanted to keep it that way."

Penny leans back against the wall. "Last time I saw you, you said you were trounced, that you might not survive. Then I hear you're going to school in Seattle. What am I supposed to think?"

That I'm looking out for you, protecting you, because you're my only friend. That I wanted you to like me for myself and not freak out about the truth. My chest tightens. That I'm a selfish bastard who pretended to be normal because he wanted a girlfriend. I can't say any of that, so I shrug. "I'm still in trouble. It's been delayed."

"Delayed? Until when?"

"Until I'm an adult. I don't turn eighteen until October."

Penny's arms drop from her chest. The green fire fades from her eyes. Her hand rests against the wall, next to mine, almost as if she's reaching out to me. My fingers itch to inch forward. Instead, I start picking at a crack in the cement. Her voice lowers to a whisper, "Is it about your parents? Aaron told us the Shinobi killed your dad and that your mum died because she was sick. You told me your relatives murdered your parents for their money. Which is it?"

My jaw clenches. The clan has its convenient version of the truth, as if that can hide their crimes. I speak through gritted teeth, "My parents were murdered."

"By who?"

I shake my head.

"You don't know?"

"I do know. No one believes me."

She leans closer, her shoulder brushing mine. "I'll believe you."

My chest tightens. All this time, all I wanted was for someone to believe me. After years of loneliness, avoiding friendship, and trying to replace anger with wisdom, here she stands, the one person in the world I want to tell everything to. I open my mouth, but the words still won't come. They're crammed inside, clutched so tightly I can't release them. I duck my head and my voice comes out as a croak, "I can't talk about it yet. It's too hard."

She lays her hand on my forearm. Something like an electric shock jolts through me. I force myself not to flinch. My heart pounds. If only I could hold her hand, feel her soft, cool skin and those little calluses on the tips of her thumb and forefinger. After a light squeeze, she lets go. "When did you move back here?"

"About a month ago, but I haven't gone to the *kongsi* or seen Tony or Aaron."

"Do they know you're back?"

"Yeah, I guess." I shrug like I don't care.

"So, you haven't talked at all to Aaron?"

I shake my head.

Her eyes narrow. "Because I was thinking he might've told you we were performing at the Auld Sod last night."

Damn. I knew she'd spotted me, staring at her like a stalker. I shrug so my words come out more casual. "I wanted to know what happened to you and your family, but I didn't know who to ask. Then I remembered you'd said you guys performed at a club on Clement Street. So, I went over there and looked around until I saw the All Haven road marker at the Auld Sod. I went inside and asked about the Sparrows, and the guy at the bar said you'd be performing on Thursday night, and there you were."

"Why did you run off?"

I point to myself. "Hello. Only Asian in the whole place. I didn't stand out or anything. I figured it was a Strowler crowd and they wouldn't appreciate us talking."

"They wouldn't care if we talked."

Yeah. Right.

She must see the skepticism in my eyes since she brushes a lock of hair from her forehead and shrugs. "Or maybe they would, but who gives a toss? Anyway, you came to see me… us?"

"Yeah."

"But you weren't going to say anything?"

My chest tightens as I remember how nervous I was going into the pub, late, wearing sunglasses, trying to be inconspicuous, and glad there was a crowd so I could try to blend in. My heart soared when I saw Penny and her family on stage. It felt like there was a magnet drawing me and I started moving toward the front of the stage until something stopped me. I almost don't want to say anything now, because then I'll have to face reality, that I've lost her. "Well, I saw that guy up on stage with you and I kinda thought, you know…"

Her eyes widen and she snorts. "Banjo boy? No way. He's just some guy Bridie let sit in with us."

I smile wide. I can't help it. "So, any guy?

"Nope." She smiles, too. Then her eyes go guarded again. "What about you?"

"No guys."

She grins.

"Or girls."

"No girls for me, either." She leans closer, and I do, too, almost so we're touching, but I don't want to be creepy. Her joyful smirk makes my heart leap. "We're such losers."

"Tell me about it."

She takes a breath and draws back again. "How about you tell me why you're lurking in a dark alley?"

Talk about a loaded question. Not one I'm ready to unpack. "Why were you following Jeremiah?"

We glare at each other, stalemated, waiting to see who will break first. I should've packed a lunch.

A breeze gusts downward as something heavy drops from the roof and lands in the alley. There's no impact sound and the shadows hide what I know to be there: at least two of them. Who the hell is it? Doesn't matter. I pull away from the wall and thrust out my left arm, palm forward, and take a deep breath to focus the power of my *chi*.

"Lennon?" says Penny. "What are you doing?"

I can't break my concentration by answering. I want to tell her to run, but that might put her in the hands of whoever's come to play.

The empty space wavers and folds into solid shape as two men appear before us. Both are Asian, dressed in tight, black Lycra clothes that cover them from their necks to their wrists and ankles, as if they're cat burglars or Goth cyclists. The taller one has spiky hair and narrow, cold eyes, like a snake. The shorter one has long black hair bound in a braid. Despite his weatherworn complexion, I can't tell his age. He could be an old thirty, a young fifty, or anywhere in-between.

Then the shorter one says something in Japanese.

Shinobi. They haven't come to play. They've come to kill.

I open my mouth and breath out a word, "Kaah."

Power pulses from my palm, strong enough to stun but not kill. I want them alive if possible, so I can find out who sent them.

They disappear. The wave of power hits the wall. A hairline fracture shoots up the cement like a bolt of lightning.

Damn! I missed. Since it wasn't a killing blow, I still have plenty of power and I'm plenty willing to use it.

"Did you do that?" Penny sounds more shocked than scared.

"Yeah." I don't know what else to say. I can't waste time explaining. Did Head Elder hire Shinobi again to finish the job? Two things don't work with that scenario. Head Elder needs a puppet Dragon Son to maintain his power. He should wait until I have an heir. Also, the Shinobi shouldn't be gunning for me when I'm underage.

Maybe Head Elder decided he doesn't need a puppet after all. And if the Shinobi are risking dishonor by killing a kid, then they'll also kill the only witness: Penny. I can't risk keeping them alive. My next shot has to kill. I whisper, "Stay back. Don't move until I tell you."

"Okay." She takes a deep breath. "Are they Shinobi?"

"Yeah."

"Shite."

Yeah.

A stone cold male voice calls out from above, "We won't harm you. We only want to talk. On our honor."

"Why should I believe you?" I know it's risky questioning their honor, but they snuck up on us, so they don't get an honor pass.

"On our honor," the voice emphasizes each word. "We have a proposition that will interest you."

I bite my lip to keep from saying 'piss off.' They want something and I need to know what. "Ten feet away. Any closer, you're dead."

The Shinobi reappear at roughly that distance. I don't lower my arm. Their honor isn't a currency I have any confidence in and I want them to know it. I nod toward Penny. "Let her go. She's not part of this."

The shorter man tilts his head to the side, listening to the taller one speak in Japanese. They have a little chat. Then the taller, snake-eyed guy speaks in English, "She lives on the Crossroads. It's for her to decide whether to stay or leave."

Penny moves to my side. "How do you know that?"

His lips thin as if she's insulted him. "Knowledge is our business."

She sucks in her breath before replying. "I'm staying."

Irritation tightens my throat even as warmth spreads through my chest. I knew she wouldn't leave me to face danger alone, but these dudes make Kingfisher look like a middle school bully. Doesn't she get that?

The shorter man speaks while Snake Eyes translates, "Dragon Son, I am Hasaki, head of the Kasumi Clan. Accept my challenge."

What the hell? "I can't accept challenges until I'm eighteen. You know that. What do you really want?"

Hasaki's expression remains cold and calm. "I want to be the first to challenge you when you come of age."

Okay, so this Hasaki guy is playing some kind of game. "The Beggar Clan has the right of first challenge. You know that, too."

"I know that the Dragon Son decides which clan has that right. When you come of age, you give that place to the Kasumi Clan and I will have right of first challenge."

I snort. "Why would I do that?"

"In exchange, I will kill anyone you name." Hasaki's eyes narrow ever so slightly. "Anyone."

"Anyone?" I spit out the word. A warning chill runs up my spine, but I can't hold back my anger. "Like my father? Was he anyone?"

Hasaki's face goes blank until Snake Eyes translates. He looks down for a moment before he speaks through Snake Eyes. "Do you blame the weapon or the one who fired the weapon?"

I grit my teeth. I blame both, but saying so won't get me anywhere. "The weapon can lead to the killer."

"Shinobi are not such weapons."

I smirk. I have something they want. Now I can watch them squirm. "Tell me who paid the Shinobi to kill my father and I'll give you the right of first challenge."

Hasaki's expression still doesn't change, but I feel some satisfaction when his hands ball into fists as he listens to Snake Eyes. "I can't tell you, not without dishonor. Those who hire us also hire our silence."

I shrug. "Then you have nothing I want."

"We will find another way." The Shinobi step back into the shadows and disappear.

Shit. I drop my arm and slump against the wall, power roiling through my body. A wave of dizziness drops a gray haze over my eyes. I take a deep breath, trying to balance my surging *chi* against the anger that's poisoned its flow. Dad had warned me against letting emotion get the better of me in a fight. Dad… if only he were alive.

"Are you okay?" Penny's voice sounds distant, as if she were calling to me from the other end of the alley.

Using my index fingers, I press the two pressure points at the back of my head. The haze dissolves. Everything comes back into focus, including her concerned expression.

"Lennon?"

"I'm okay." I sigh. "You should have run."

She shrugs. "I should do a lot of things, but I don't."

Damn it. Why does she have to be so awesome? Before I can think of a reply, she points at the crack in the wall. "What was that thing you did with your hand?"

"The Dragon Shout. It's..." I don't want to say, because I don't want to be Paul Lau to her. I want to be Lennon. Like that ship hasn't already sailed. "It's a weapon of the Dragon Son."

"So, only you can do that?"

"Yeah."

Her eyes go big. "Wow. That is so cool."

I rub the back of my neck. Yeah, it is, but it wouldn't be cool to say so out loud.

"Why do you call it a shout? It was more like a whisper."

"Um, dragons are kind of contrary that way."

She breathes out a laugh as if I'd told a joke, but that's how dragons are. At least the one I know. "You should go. The Shinobi, the Beggar Clan, everybody, they'll leave you alone if you tell me to piss off."

Penny leans in close enough that I can smell her hair and her scent. I never forgot how good she smells, sweet but not flowery, sort of like if you mixed vanilla and honey. My head spins. "What did I just say about doing things I should? I don't."

"Yeah, me neither." It's crazy how much I want to laugh. Instead, I clear my throat. "Guess we have that in common."

The corner of her mouth dimples. "Guess so."

My heartbeat marches double time. I know I should take her someplace safe and walk away, but I need a few more minutes with her. A little more time to feel like a normal person and not some snotty little shit everyone wants to kill. Besides, we have unfinished business. "I'll give you a ride home if you tell me why you were following Jeremiah."

She tilts her head. "You have a car?"

"No, but I can still give you a ride."

Her eyes widen and she clamps her hand over her mouth. It takes me a moment to realize what I said. My cheeks burn while Penny's giggles escape from between her fingers. My chest loosens and laughter bubbles up and out. It's been so long since I've laughed, it sounds dry and rusty.

Her hand moves from her mouth to her cheek. "How can I possibly say no to that?"

"I was counting on being irresistible."

She laughs again. I'm being funny. It's been so long, it feels weird and kind of scary. I want to run away, but it would be a dick move to leave Penny alone in the alley with the Shinobi.

She slides her arm through mine. "Why don't you show me your ride, big boy?"

A warm feeling spreads through my chest and it takes a moment for me to realize it's happiness. When was the last time I felt happy? Oh, yeah. With Penny. Doing what we shouldn't do.

Penny

"Told you I don't have a car." His chest puffs out with his words. I bite my lip to hide my smile. In a lot of ways, he's still such a kid.

I step off the curb and slowly circle the black and silver scooter, brand new and flash as can be. I run my fingertips over the chrome logo. "Vespa. Cool."

"It's an early birthday present from Auntie Cat."

"The one from Seattle?"

"Yeah, except she's from here, like me. We moved together to Seattle and back here again. She's been my guardian since," He exhales and his chest deflates. "Since my parents died."

"You like her?"

"Yeah, she's great."

If she's so great, why did he run away from her two years ago? There's so much he's not saying that must involve Tony and Aaron. Maybe it all has to do with their mother. I met her the day my family went to the *kongsi* for the first time. She smelled of roses and clutched her pearls as she stared at us like we were pickpockets or rubbish collectors, or both. I can totally see her diving headfirst into an inheritance battle.

Even if Lennon's not talking to his cousins, I'm surprised Aaron didn't tell Kai that the Dragon Son had returned to San Francisco. Maybe he doesn't want to talk about it, either. I look at Lennon's tight lips. He's not about to crack them open, so I go back to the matter at hand. "My parents had Vespas. That's how we got around. Kept them on a trailer hitched to the caravan."

He perks up at my words. "What kind?"

"The kind you find in scrapyards. Gerry was a good mechanic. He'd buy old scooters, fix them up and sell them. The ones we had were the best of the lot."

"Gerry sounds like he was really cool."

"He was," I say softly. Maybe that's why Lennon is avoiding all talk of parents. It can only bring us down. "So, about that ride," I rap my knuckles against the black helmet attached to the seat. "Don't we both need one of these?"

"Not a problem." He unlocks the container behind the seat and pulls out a powder blue, bubble-shaped helmet with a silver Vespa logo.

The tips of my ears burn. Did he lie about not having a girl-friend? Or worse? People on the Crossroads tend to marry young... The burn spreads to my face and chest, like my nerves are on fire. My arms fold tight. "Who does that belong to?"

Lennon gives me a puzzled look. "Um, Auntie Cat. It's her favorite color."

"Oh." Dear. Wow. What the hell was that? Jealousy? I'm not some bint who gets jealous over nothing. Am I? I definitely don't want Lennon to think so. I cough to clear the silence. "So, you give her rides?"

He snorts. "You don't give Auntie Cat rides. She borrows it to run errands when she doesn't want to take her car."

"It's a really cool helmet."

"It doesn't have a face shield."

"Face shields are for wussies."

"That's what Auntie Cat says." He hands it to me. "Let's see how it looks on you."

I tug the helmet on and try adjusting the strap as it swivels around my head. "It's kinda loose."

"Auntie Cat's got a big head."

I snicker. "Nice."

"She does." He reaches for the clasp. "Here, let me."

As he adjusts the strap, his fingers brush my neck. My skin tingles. Our eyes meet. Something passes between us, something sharp and taut. Then he looks down. I move away. "That's better."

"Good." He almost drops his sunglasses before fumbling them onto his face. The lenses are round, making him once again look like Lennon. I feel a sharp pain in my chest. I miss that boy. I want him back. "So, do I call you Paul now?"

"No. I'm Lennon."

I smile because I'll burst if I don't. "Okay then, Lennon, so, when is your birthday?"

"October twenty-seventh. Why?"

"Just wondering." Wondering how long I have my friend until he officially becomes the Dragon Son and head of the Crossroads. About two months. Not long at all. If I was smart, I'd walk away rather than take a ride with a boy who will break my heart again, but something about him makes me dumb. "You know, when I should get you a card."

He grins. "When's your birthday?"

"June seventeenth."

"Sorry I didn't get you card."

"That's okay. Next year." I grin, too, though the likelihood of that happening seems as remote as the moon.

He puts on his helmet and straddles the scooter before asking, "Where do you live?"

"NOPA, on the corner of Baker and Grove. Hope you don't mind driving that far."

"I'm going that way anyway. I live on Irving."

I climb on and wriggle back, trying to keep some space between us. He turns the ignition as I wrap my arms loosely around his waist. The engine snarls beneath us, way more powerful than Gerry's makeshift scooters. We pull out onto the road and head up Sacramento Street.

Chinatown is one of the hillier neighborhoods in the city and this is one of the steeper streets. Momentum pushes Lennon into my embrace. I start to slide and I'm forced to tighten my grip as I press against the length of his body. He'd been skinny before. Now, he has a lean strength that feels so good. I rest my chin on his shoulder and breathe in his scent of leather jacket with faint hints of paint and something else. Maybe glue? We turn a sharp corner, tilting toward the curb. As we straighten up, Lennon's hand grips my thigh to keep me steady. My heart jumps into my throat. This thing between us, I don't even have a word for it. 'Friends' doesn't cover it. He can't be my boyfriend, not if he's the Dragon Son, so where does that leave us?

My parents, Bridie and Gerry, had been best mates before they married. Unrelated Strowlers of the opposite sex are rarely friends, so that should have been her first clue. Gerry confessed he was gay shortly after I was born. Homosexuality on the Crossroads is mostly acceptable on the Wayward Way, but few on the Glory Road tolerate it. Strowlers are among the worst because we're basically stuck in the nineteenth century regarding sexual politics and most other things as well. I'm proud of Bridie that, once she set foot on the Wayward Way, she shook off that kind of moralizing. She and Gerry remained friends and stayed together for appearance sake and to raise me.

Then Matthew came into the picture. He and Bridie fell in

reckless love and she fell pregnant. By then, Matthew and Gerry were best mates and Gerry decided to stay and weather the storm following Kai's birth. It became common cackle on the Crossroads that Bridie had two husbands, and they played it up in grand style, enjoying the notoriety.

Is that what I'd have with Lennon? Notoriety? The Strowler lass who ran away with the Dragon Son. Do I want that?

Maybe.

The scooter idles at the top of the hill as Lennon waits for the light to change. Then he revs the engine again and heads through the intersection. We plunge downhill, rows of houses blurring past us. I don't want to think anymore. For these few moments, I want to ride through San Francisco on the back of a scooter with this boy and these feelings.

Lennon swerves in and out of traffic as we head down Divisadero before turning onto Grove, and drive past the huge, renovated Victorian houses painted bright colors and decorated with fancy trim. NOPA used to be a posh neighborhood full of toff stores and cafes that sold craft beer and slices of toast that cost more than a full meal. At least, that's what our neighbors tell us. Most of those places are gone now. Families and pensioners replaced the techies who moved out when the jobs evaporated.

We're skint most of the time, but it's a rum life compared to when Bridie was married to Bill. After we returned to the States, I was able to enroll in the San Francisco High School of Art and Design, where I learned enough to start my own business. Bridie got a job managing an apartment complex and adjoining launderette. For that, she's paid a bit of gelt, along with a free apartment, where we live and she teaches music...

Music.

Even as I think that word, Lennon is steering into a space between two parked cars in front of our building and I hear the acoustic version of 'Levon' by Elton John wafting down from the top of the stoop.

It's Thursday afternoon, about half past three, which means lessons are over, and those two will be jamming outside. The guitar strumming simply stops, but the violin screeches to a halt. Kai and Aaron stand and stare down at us with wide eyes and dropped jaws.

Lennon's body stiffens. His knuckles whiten around the scooter's grips. I try to think of something to say. All that comes out is, "Bollocks."

Bollocks. That's a good word. I should use it more, especially in situations like this. My stomach flops around my lunch and I feel like I'm going to lose it.

Kai comes slowly down the stairs. He looks older, less like a child, more like a teen in his frayed jeans, plaid flannel shirt, and purple beanie tugged loosely over his mop of wavy, dark brown hair. "Lennon?"

Aaron eases his violin into its case before sauntering down, his hands shoved in the pockets of his baggy jeans. He's wearing an oversized black t-shirt with the word "Misfits" stamped over the forehead of a skull. I never would've gotten away with a shirt like that when I was fourteen. Something's changed. Tony? Yeah, right. Before the shit hit the fan, Aaron had been my Little Brother. I schooled him in video games and comic books, and if said shit hadn't hit said fan, I would've taken part in Aaron's martial training, the way Tony had with me. An ache spreads across my chest. I want to say I missed him and I've never blamed him. Aaron won't accept that, like he can't accept that his parents are murderers. Even now, he stares down at me like a high school version of Tony, same square chin, high forehead and cold disdain in his deep-set eyes.

Penny squeezes my shoulders as she climbs off the scooter. Chills run down my spine. Is that a signal or is she trying to reassure me? Probably both. She tugs off Auntie Cat's helmet and gives an awkward cough. "So, funny thing. We ran into each other in Chinatown."

Aaron's sneer is directed at me. "What were you doing there? I thought you were too good for us, Lennon." He says my chosen name like an insult.

I climb off the Vespa and take off my sunglasses. I nod at Kai. He nods back with wary eyes. I can't think of anything to say to Aaron other than, "Hi."

"Hi? That's all you've got to say? Did you hear about my mom?"

"Yeah." I swallow my bile. I can't say I'm sorry Auntie Sylvia died a slow and painful death from cancer. I'm glad. She deserved that and worse. I'm only sorry that she faced karma and not justice for her crimes. "That must have been hard for you."

"Yeah. Yeah, it was." Aaron looks down and takes a deep breath. It doesn't relieve the anger in his voice. "You can't bother to come see your own family, but you can take Penny out on a date."

"Date?" Where the hell did he get that idea?

"Date?" Penny echoes. Her eyes narrow in a puzzled squint. "Wait a minute. How do you know to call him Lennon?"

Aaron's face goes blank. Then he stammers, "Um, yeah, um, Tony. He told me."

I scoff. "No, he didn't." Tony considers my chosen name a disgrace, taken when I lived as a runaway teen prostitute.

Penny jabs an accusing finger at her brother. "You peached."

The two boys exchange guilty glances. Then Kai gives a shrug. "Um, yeah, so I told Aaron about how Lennon lived with us and stuff."

Well. Shit.

"Can't you keep your fat gob shut?" demands Penny.

"Yeah. But, but…" Kai sputters.

"But what?"

Aaron jumps in. "He started asking me questions about Paul – excuse me – Lennon, and I asked why he was so interested."

"I didn't wanna lie," continues Kai. "I mean, Aaron's my friend and Lennon's his cousin."

"Does Tony know?" I ask.

Aaron shakes his head. "I didn't tell him. I promised Kai I wouldn't tell anyone."

"I don't want the clan knowing that the Sparrows helped me."

"I said I didn't tell anyone."

Penny's hands go to her hips. "Did you tell Kai that Lennon was back in the city?"

Both boys' faces go blank. With obvious effort, they don't look at each other.

"Really? What the hell, Kai?"

He licks his lips, but before he can defend himself, Aaron yanks his phone from his pocket. His eyes bulge as he stares at the screen. "It's a message from Tony. He's on his way to pick me up."

They all stare at me. I know my expression hasn't changed. For two years, I've forced myself not to think about Big Brother or talk to him, or care about his life. "I should go."

At the top of the stairs, the front door swings open and a woman with curly red hair steps out. She's wearing a striped minidress over black leggings and looks more like Penny's sister than her mother. She waves a dark blue hoodie and calls out, "Aaron, you forgot something." Her voice trails off. She blinks several times. "Lennon?"

My throat aches at the sight of her. For a short while, Bridie Sparrow was like a mother to me, giving me food and shelter without conditions, and refusing to accept money even when she was totally broke. I almost want to smile, except for one thing. She's not smiling at me.

"Well, Lennon. My goodness. How did you find us?" She sounds breathless and keeps glancing at Kai.

"We ran into each other." Penny frowns at her mother.

"Oh. So, just a coincidence?"

"Yeah. Why wouldn't it be?" She looks from her mother to her brother. They both look away. She gasps. "You knew."

Bridie's lips flop like a fish out of water before she manages, "Um… knew?"

"Cut it out, Mum. You knew Lennon was back in SF. Don't lie."

"I have no intention of lying," Bridie lifts her chin. "Your brother mentioned that he'd heard Lennon was back."

Penny's glare is so fiery, I'm surprised her family and Aaron don't combust. "Why didn't you tell me? I can't believe you. What's going on?"

"Nothing. We… we hadn't gotten around to telling you and, well… it's complicated…" Her voice fades into the background.

When I first returned to the city, I wished the Sparrows were still here. I imagined Bridie would invite me in for dinner and we'd pick up where we left off. Wishes are for people who have a life and a future. No one wants to be around a walking dead man. I speak, cold as a corpse, "It's me, that's what's going on. They want you to stay away from me and they're right. I'm outta here."

Penny's eyes go wide with protest, but before she can speak, her mother hurries down the stairs. "Please, Lennon, don't go. I can explain. In fact, why don't you stay for dinner tonight? I'm making a bubble and squeak. Remember how much you liked that?"

I do remember. Bridie made super yummy mom food. Not like my mom had, but still full of homey goodness. I'm not a charity case anymore. This is even worse, since she's offering out of guilt. I always thought if there was one place I'd be welcome, it'd be with the Sparrows. I was wrong. I shove on my sunglasses. "I gotta go."

"Lennon, please. It's not what you think."

"You don't owe me anything, okay?" That comes out harsh, but it makes Bridie stop with the phony remorse as her pleading eyes become startled. "You don't want anything to do with me because I'll bring you trouble with the Two Dragon Clan and everyone else who wants a piece of me. I get it. I'm gone."

I push past Kai and Aaron, and climb on my Vespa, tugging on my helmet hard enough to bend my ears. It hurts and I don't give a fuck.

Penny hurries over. Her cheeks are red and eyes shining. She looks so beautiful. The girl of my dreams. She chokes around her words, "I am so sorry."

"It's okay," I whisper. I take a deep breath. There's so much I want to say, but what's the point?

She holds out Auntie Cat's helmet. As I take it, she slips something in my hand, a business card, and she mouths, "Message me."

I should say no, but I look at her mother and brother, and my cousin. Why should they get what they want? I give the slightest nod before turning around to put away the helmet. Penny steps back and I turn on my scooter. As I pull out to the street, the look we exchange makes my chest tighten. She's not like everyone else. She doesn't care that my life is going to hell.

She'll be my friend no matter what. Which is why I should do what her family wants and stay away from her.

As I head down Baker Street, there's a guy approaching in the opposite direction on a Ducati Monster with all the trimmings. Damn sick. I'd wanted a Ducati so damn bad, but Auntie Cat vetoed that idea. The guy is dressed all in black, from his tight leather jacket to his biker gloves and boots. There's something familiar about him, though I can't see his face through his tinted helmet shield. As we pass each other, I feel it. It jumps off him and onto my skin. It's Tony.

When did Tony get a Ducati?

Talk about stupid first thoughts. My next thoughts are shit, shit and shit. The first stoplight I come to is green and I gun through it, but the next light goes red. I come to a stop and force myself not to turn around. I more than half expect to hear the rumble of a motorcycle engine come up beside me, but I'm surrounded only by cars.

I stay on Baker until I reach Buena Vista Park. My legs shake as I climb off my scooter. I pull off my helmet and stare down the street. Nothing. No Tony. I can't believe he didn't recognize me. I don't believe I'm that lucky. Will he grill Aaron and the Sparrows about me? Should I go back? Or will that make things worse?

I kick a clod of dirt across the grass. Why is my life so fucking complicated? I can't have friends. I can't have family. All I have is revenge and it tastes like hot dust.

I was in Chinatown checking out my latest piece. It's become a game of strategy between me and Tony. I throw up fierce art that exposes the truth and he sends his goons to scrub away the evidence, usually within hours. I chose a less obvious location this time and wanted to see if he'd noticed yet. That's what I was doing in that alley when Jeremiah and his goons came strolling by, with Penny following them. Why the hell

was she doing that? I reach into my pocket and pull out her
card.

Pinafores and More
Pinafore your lifestyle: trad, boho, goth, punk.
Adult and child sizes.
Penny Sparrow, Owner

She has her own business. I smile because I can't help it. If
anyone can make her own way in the world, it's Penny. She
doesn't need me back in her life. I should toss the card away,
but instead I press it to my chest, to my heart, and stifle a
weird impulse to sniff it.

My phone buzzes. Penny! No, it can't be her because, like
an idiot, I didn't give her my number. I pull out my phone and
stare at the screen. It's a message from Auntie Cat.

> Where are you? Come home. There's been
> another break-in.

Penny

I am so mad my cheeks are literally burning. I stomp up to Bridie so I'm in her face. "I can't believe you." My words come out husky with emotion. That won't work. I swallow hard to stop my voice from shaking. "How could you do that to Lennon, huh?"

Bridie folds her arms. "I didn't do anything to Lennon."

"Exactly. You treated him like a stranger, after all he did for us. For you."

Her gaze drops. "I-I did no such thing. I invited him in for dinner."

"Because you felt guilty for treating him like a bad bargain."

"That's not true."

"Oh no? Then why didn't you tell me Lennon was back in SF?"

"Dude, Tony," Aaron calls out.

Down the street, I can see his big brother approaching on his motorcycle. Bugger. I am not going to stand here and simper as if nothing's wrong. If the others want to, that's on them. I tromp up the stairs and into the building.

The musty smell of our apartment complex hits me in the face. I roll my eyes, not at all in the mood for fusty Mr. Cleary, the tenant who always complains about the cold breeze from the hall windows. I climb the threadbare staircase and jack open the windows on each landing, loud enough to make the glass rattle. He'll probably close them again. We need to find a way to lock them into place.

The complex is three-stories high and has forty apartments of all shapes and sizes, from studios to two bedrooms. From the odd placement of walls and doors, you can tell it used to have half that many units. During the tech boom, apartments were in low supply and places like this were renovated to squeeze in more people. The owners only do the bare minimum of maintenance, which is why they hired someone as unqualified as Bridie to manage the place. Well, it did help that she turned on the Charm during her interview.

Our apartment is in a back corner of the third floor. Bridie left the front door ajar, so I push it open and don't bother closing it. She and Kai will be up here as soon as they're done glad-handing Tony. I stride down the long, narrow hall, passing the front parlor, dining room, kitchen and loo. There are two bedrooms at the end of the hall, but neither is mine. I enter the master bedroom, Bridie's room, and walk through it to get to the only bathroom in the apartment. I mean, proper bathroom, with a sink, shower, tub, and toilet. The loo in the hall has only a toilet. Yeah, it's inconvenient and probably one of the reasons this place was given to the property manager.

I walk through the bathroom and open a door leading to the other reason, a large bonus room that can't be called a bedroom because it doesn't have a closet or heating vents. When we moved in, Bridie offered to take it, but I wanted it, bad, because, duh, privacy. The bathroom provides a sound buffer and I can sew late into the night without bothering her or Kai. A space heater keeps me warm and there are windows providing plenty of light and air.

I slam my door shut and lean against it with folded arms. Part of me wants to flop on my bed and have a proper tantrum with flailing arms and legs, but since it's an air mattress, that would be a bad idea. I could channel my anger into the energy necessary to complete a backlog of projects that need to be sewn and shipped out, but I'm so pissed off, I'd probably bung it all up. Instead, I dump my bag on the floor, cross my room and yank open the window that leads to the fire escape. It has a small deck sturdy enough for a row of tomato planters. The leafy vines have twined around their tall wire cages thick enough to provide me at least the illusion of privacy. I plop into the lone chair, refold my arms and fume. The deck faces west and I can see the ocean through a web of power lines. The cold, clean air eases the pounding in my temples, which is good. I need to think, not fret, but it's hard when I'm feeling so deceived by my own family. They didn't tell me about Lennon for a whole month. That thought alone makes me want to scream, so when Bridie pokes her head through the window after having barged into my room without my permission, I'm ready for a shouting match.

I open my mouth, but before something bitter pours out, she warns, "Tony Lau is in the living room. He wants to talk to you."

Bollocks. "Why does he want to talk to me?" I whisper. "Is it about Lennon?"

"I don't know. Please, I know you're upset, but tread carefully. He's not one to be trifled with."

I don't want to trifle with Tony Lau, but I should see him on the off-chance he'll patter about Lennon. It's not like I have a choice. When the Upright Man of the local Two Dragon Clan summons you, refusal is not an option. I follow Bridie to the front parlor. Kai and Aaron are seated on folding chair while

Tony sits on the couch, glancing around with unblinking eyes, as if expecting to spot something incriminating hiding in a corner. He was here before to talk to Bridie about Aaron's violin lessons and he'd been cold and stiff, but had made an attempt to be… I don't know. Pleasant? No. He doesn't do pleasant. Normal, maybe, but he doesn't do that, either. Human? Yeah, that works.

I sit beside Kai, letting Bridie take the bullet and join Tony on the couch. The parlor is more like a rehearsal studio with music and instrument stands, and shelves piled with sheet music, but no coffee table. We're forced to sit in a circle as if we're about to critique each other's poetry. The mental image of Tony reciting a poem makes me bite my lip to keep from smiling. Too bad Lennon isn't here. He would've found it funny, too. Or would he? Seeing Aaron had been difficult for him. Would seeing Tony have pushed him over the edge? Had they been close once?

Bridie leans forward so her clasped hands rest on her knees. "I'm afraid I can't talk for long. My next student will be here soon."

Tony's head turns toward her, though the rest of his body doesn't move. "You have many students?"

"All I can get. I don't get paid much for managing the apartment. Every penny counts. I'm sure you understand."

His frown indicates he doesn't have a clue. He turns to me and I realize I'm glaring at him, so I go poker-faced. This doesn't take him off the scent. "Why were you in Chinatown today?"

Uh-oh. "How do you know I was there?"

"Answer the question, please."

"I went to Shanghai Bazaar to buy some buttons."

"Buttons."

"Yeah. I go there all the time. They have a great selection."

"What did you do after you bought these buttons?"

"I missed my bus, so I started walking."

"Walking home?" He cocks a skeptical eyebrow.

My chest lifts with my rapid breath. I inhale through my nose to slow it down. "No. It's a nice day and I didn't feel like standing around, so I thought I'd walk through Chinatown to Market Street and catch a bus there."

"Were you there to meet my cousin, Paul?"

For a moment, I go blank. I don't have a clue what to say except, "No."

"You were seen with him. You got on his scooter and drove away, presumably here. I don't believe it's your habit to accept rides with strangers, so you must know him."

How do I answer? 'Paul, who?' would sound sketchy as hell. I'm done being fake. I want to be real, but I don't know how without betraying Lennon.

"Paul?" Bridie says, her voice an octave too high. "You mean, Lennon?" Tony's head swerves to look at her. She manages not to look atwitter. "We were so surprised when Lennon dropped Penny off just now."

"His name is Paul."

"Of course. Paul." Her voice comes easier. She relaxes back in her chair. "I didn't realize he'd returned to San Francisco. My goodness, but he's grown. I barely recognized him."

I barely breathe. She's turning on the Charm. That's one way to deal with Tony Lau, but it's a dangerous game.

Tony's eyes narrow. "Mrs. Sparrow, why have you never told me you knew Paul?"

"I didn't know him as Paul. I knew him as a homeless boy named Lennon."

"When did you meet him?"

"Two years ago. We took him in when we were living at the local Strowler Nest."

"You took in a boy you didn't know, just like that?"

"Of course not. We'd met him before. He'd helped Penny when she was being bullied."

"Raped." I state flatly. "Lennon saved me from being raped in Golden Gate Park."

Kai shifts and Aaron gawps. Bridie nudges me with her knee. Any kind of sexual talk, even assault, is taboo among mixed company on the Crossroads, but I don't care. Tony needs to know.

Something flickers in his eyes. An emotion. Maybe empathy? Then his gaze freezes over again. "You felt an obligation and took him in."

Bridie lifts her chin. "I saw a homeless boy who'd rescued my daughter. Obviously, he was in a bad way or he wouldn't be homeless, so of course I took him in."

"And you didn't know his true identity?"

"How would I know?"

"Kai's father was a member of the Two Dragon Clan."

My brother shrugs. "Yeah, but they kicked him out."

"As you know, Matthew walked the Wayward Way," Bridie adds. "He spoke very little about your clan after he joined us."

Tony seems to consider their words before he speaks again, "When did you realize Paul is the Dragon Son?"

"At your mother's funeral, we saw a photo in the banquet hall that looked like him, though we weren't sure."

"Why didn't you say anything?"

"It was hardly the right time. Besides, we hadn't seen him in almost two years and he looked very different in the photo. It was hard to believe our Lennon could be the Dragon Son." Bridie's eyes now have a sympathetic glow and her voice has taken on a subtly persuasive tone.

Doubt shadows Tony's face, but quickly disappears. "Paul. His name is Paul, not Lennon."

A teasing smile lights up her face. "Oh, teenagers, you know how they are." Her voice soothes and coaxes. "If he wants to call himself Lennon, let him. He'll get over it soon enough."

Tony settles back in the chair, his face blank. Then he blinks. His eyes turn to flint. "I've heard that Strowlers have their own skills, tricks to persuade their marks."

Uh-oh.

Bridie waves a hand. "People say all kinds of silly things about us."

"Not that you would use those skills on me."

"Assuming I had such skills, of course not." Her expression sobers into Concerned Mom. "I'm sorry about the misunderstanding with Lennon... Paul."

"Misunderstanding?" Tony draws out each syllable. "I need to know everything that happened while Paul was staying with you."

"I'm sorry, but I'm not comfortable discussing your cousin when he's not here. You should speak to him yourself. Tell him he has my permission to say anything he wants about his time with us."

He turns his coal black gaze to me. "Did you arrange to meet with Paul today?"

I shake my head. "This was the first time I've seen him in two years. I was totally surprised. He was, too."

"Why was he in Chinatown?"

"I don't know. He didn't tell me."

"What did you talk about?"

Do I tell him about the Shinobi? I don't know. I swallow my rising panic as I shrug. "Stuff. Mostly about how angry I was because he didn't tell me who he really is."

His expression doesn't change and neither does he speak. I wonder if he realizes I'm employing another Strowler "trick" called Truth Be Told. We tell the truth as far as it will serve us and no farther, with our eyes forward, not wandering with fallacy.

Tony stands. The rest of us flinch. He turns to his brother and jerks his head. Aaron jumps to his feet. "You may think you're helping my cousin with your silence, but you're not. Paul is a very troubled boy. His parents' deaths…" He pauses and for a moment looks uncertain. Then he clears his throat. "He took it hard. He hasn't been the same since. When Paul turns eighteen, he will become the leader of our clan and the Crossroads. I want to help him get over his grief and prepare himself. I don't need outsiders involved. For your own good, stay away from him." His icy gaze lingers on me before he turns and strides out of the room, Aaron on his heels. I expect him to slam the front door, but he closes it with a soft click.

I press my hand to my chest and massage my pounding heart. Kai sinks back in his chair and groans.

Bridie gusts out a shaky breath. "He's an uppish sort, that one."

Arrogant, yes. And nobody's fool. We're on his radar now, but not because of me. "This could've been avoided if you lot had been square with me."

"Ha. I know you too well, madam. If I'd told you Lennon was back, you would've run straight to the *kongsi* and landed us in the thick of it."

"No, we're in the thick of it now because you didn't tell me."

"Well, now you know, and now you'll keep your distance from Lennon." She overemphasizes each 'now.'

"No. Now," I overemphasize. "I'm an adult and I'll choose my own company."

"What about Christy?"

And there it is, what this is all about. Bloody Uncle Christy. "Who cares what he thinks?"

"He's the Upright Man. We're members of his family and we can't cause any trouble or disgrace."

Kai and I gawp at each other, our mouths literally hanging

open. Is she kidding? That ship sailed a long time ago, before we were born.

She huffs. "Just because I romped when I was young doesn't mean you two can."

I stride over to the mantle above the fireplace and grab a Polaroid photo, framed to keep it from damage. Gerry stares at me with a cocky grin and devilish gleam in his eyes while Matthew gazes off into space with a faraway look like a wandering minstrel. The Trickster and the Dreamer. My fathers and her husbands. I thrust the frame out at Bridie. "What would they want me to do?"

She hisses through her teeth. "That's not fair."

Like I'm interested in being fair. "What would they say? How would they want you to treat Lennon?"

The stern resolve in her face crumples as she takes the frame from me. "You already know."

"Of course I do. That's why I'm asking you. Are you on the Glory Road now or still on the Wayward Way?"

"If I was on the Glory Road, we'd be living in the Nest, not out here on our own." She stares at her husbands with their arms around each other. So alike and so different, like two sides of the same coin. Then she gives a wistful sigh as she hands it back to me. "They'd tell you to do whatever you damn well please. They wanted bold children, not tame ones."

"Well, then, bugger Uncle Christy, right?"

"Wrong. He's still my brother and your uncle. There's no reason to antagonize him. See Lennon if you must, but a word of caution. No romance. It can't work. Nothing can come of it but pain for you both." She speaks with the Voice of Experience, which makes my eyes roll. I know she wouldn't trade a single moment she had with Gerry and Matthew, including all the disgrace. The doorbell rings. "That'll be Bailey Anne. Son, buzz her in."

I head down the hall, not at all in the mood for Bailey

Anne's squeaky voice or the scratchy notes she torments out of her violin. When I get to my room, I lock the door, lean against it, and stare at the photo of my fathers. Maybe I shouldn't be so harsh with Bridie and Kai for keeping their secret, since I have one, too; one I've kept since coming of age. As soon as I've collected enough gelt from my business, I'm off to London to find out what happened to Gerry and Matthew.

I don't believe the official story, that they were killed during a botched robbery. They weren't thieves; not exactly. They specialized in retrieving stolen goods, a dicey business to be sure, and not one they took lightly. They never blundered and weren't fools going where angels feared to tread. I don't know who killed them or what was stolen. Bridie claims she doesn't know, either. Maybe she can live with that, but I can't. I won't rest until I have answers.

I pull my phone from my boho bag. No messages. I gnaw my lip. Did I fight for nothing? Maybe, between the Shinobi, Tony and my family, Lennon has decided to stay away... No. If Lennon came all the way to the Auld Sod for a glimpse of me, there's no way he won't call me. If he hasn't yet, it must be for a good reason, right? I close my eyes and take a deep breath.

Right.

Lennon

Auntie Cat's place has been trashed. The whole building from the first floor where she teaches Tai Chi to the loft that she uses for storage is a big fat fucking mess. Everything we own has been dumped onto the floor: clothes, food, dishes, books, all her jewelry and makeup.

Every. Fucking. Thing.

And that's not the worst of it. Our mattresses, the couch, and the armchairs have all been slashed open and the stuffing ripped out.

Same thing happened in Seattle a few months after we moved there, only it wasn't as bad. We were staying in a small furnished apartment and the perps had spared the furniture and the dishes. I say perps instead of thieves because nothing was stolen, then or now. My heart burns a hole in my chest as Auntie Cat stares at the slashed exercise mats in her studio. I can't think of a word bad enough to call Head Elder.

She sighs and shakes her head. She's my dad's younger sister and looks kind of like him with her high forehead and deep-set eyes. She has a round chin instead of a square one and a small nose, which usually make her look younger than she is.

Not right now. Her face is creased with the anger she's trying to hide from me. I wish she'd let it out. I wouldn't blame her one bit if she blamed me, but she won't. Two years ago, I turned her life upside down and she hasn't complained once, at least not to me.

"I better call my students and tell them class is cancelled for…" She huffs. "I don't know how long. And my old students were starting to come back, too."

The frustration in her voice stabs me. She'd left everything behind when we moved to Seattle, all for my sake. I can't stand the thought of her giving up anything again, even for a single day.

"No," my voice echoes off the mirrored walls. "Let's start down here first. I mean, there's not that much to do. We can get it ready for tomorrow's class."

"But the mats, look at them."

"They've only been slashed on one side. We can tape them and turn them over. No one will notice the difference." Hopefully. "That'll work until we order new ones."

The bitter sharpness in her eyes softens. "There should be enough mat tape, if we can find it in this mess. But upstairs," She throws up her hands. "Tape won't work on the mattresses."

"So, we'll sleep on the floor or whatever, but you have to open for business tomorrow. We can't let Head Elder think he got to us, right?"

"No. Definitely not. All right, then." She presses the heel of her hand to her forehead. "I could really use some coffee."

"Done." I head out the door before she can stop me. I walk because in San Francisco if you throw a rock you'll hit a cafe. She doesn't like the closest one, so I head for her favorite place on Ninth Street. There's a line out the door, like usual, and a couple of cops lounging at a table, enjoying their lattes, also the norm. I don't approach them for help. I can't. On the Crossroads, each clan governs itself, but there are a few rules we all live by and a big one is: no police. We don't go to court or rely on any country's laws. We have our own way of solving conflicts and dispensing justice.

Which is a big load of crap. My parents have been dead for two years and they still have no justice. In a couple of months, though, that's all going to change. I'm going to make justice happen.

I put a dollop of honey in Auntie Cat's black coffee to take the edge off the bitterness, the way she likes. Then I sprinkle cinnamon on top of my mocha. Penny taught me that trick. I finger the business card in my pocket. My stomach flutters. I want to message her, but I don't know what to say besides, "Hey." It'd be better to wait for when my head is clear and I'm not so damn mad.

When I get back to the studio, my aunt is looking at her phone with a puzzled frown. "Did you call Tony?" I ask, warily.

She sighs. "I thought about calling him, but I think it's better if he's not involved."

"Unless he is," I mutter.

"Tony wouldn't do something like this."

"He'd do anything Head Elder told him to do and you know it."

"No, I don't know that." She shoves the phone in her pocket and takes the cup from my hand. "Anyway, I was trying to call Roy, but he's not answering. I was talking to him when I got home and walked in on this mess."

"I wish he was here."

She chews her lip and doesn't reply, even though I know she feels the same. Uncle Roy was my dad's best friend. Growing up, I didn't see a whole lot of him because his family runs the Two Dragon Clan *kongsi* in Seattle. He'd come to SF for special occasions and to pal around with Dad. I always thought he was a cool dude.

After I returned home from running away, I didn't want anything to do with anyone in my family except Auntie Cat. I still needed to be trained and she couldn't do it all herself, so when she decided to move us to Seattle, I was okay with that. I wanted to get the hell out of San Francisco and away from everything that reminded me of my family. Uncle Roy was the only other clan member I could tolerate.

I'd heard over the years, through whispers and innuendos, that Auntie Cat and Uncle Roy had been an item before I was born. Something happened and they broke up, so to speak. Marriages are arranged in the Two Dragon Clan, though in modern times you have a lot more say over who you're arranged with. The only way to opt out is to stay single and that's what they did, which doesn't surprise me one bit. They're both stubborn as hell.

She takes a sip of coffee and a moment to relish that sweet caffeine. "Much better. Okay, I found the mat tape while you were out, so let's start with those."

"Sounds like a plan."

While we're laying the mats out, she stops and pulls out her phone. Her brow furrows as she reads the screen. "Oh, for crying out loud. I told him I can take care of this myself."

Did Roy call Tony? No, he wouldn't. Would he? "What's going on?"

She huffs out a sigh. "It's Roy. He's texting me from on board a plane. He's says we need backup, so he's coming down."

I bite my lip to keep from smiling. Of course, Roy called from the plane. If he'd called any sooner, she'd have told him not to come. He'd wanted to return to San Francisco with us, but she shut that right down, saying she could handle things on her own, and she can. Totally. But even I've got to admit some backup wouldn't hurt right now.

"He was coming next month, anyway, to help me train. What's the difference between now and then?"

Her eyes evade mine. "He's a busy man. I don't want to take up too much of his time."

Right. I almost gnaw off my lip so I don't say that aloud.

I was stupidly optimistic about there not being much to do in the studio. It takes hours to tape the mats, sort the different Tai Chi books, fold the uniforms, and restock everything on the shelves. Those goons even ripped apart the toilet paper and towels. Reluctantly, I agree with Auntie Cat. Tony wouldn't stoop to this kind of bullshit. I almost want to call him over so he can see what his precious Head Elder is capable of.

My shoulders tense when the doorbell rings. I hurry out of the stockroom in time to see Auntie Cat open the door for Uncle Roy. It's kind of cute, how her cheeks turn red and she glances down before looking up at him with a glare. "Why are you here? I told you I've got everything under control."

Uncle Roy towers over both of us. He's a couple of inches over six feet and has this cowlick above his forehead making him seem taller. He's got a deep voice, intense eyes and a beak that belongs on an eagle. All of that softens whenever he's around Auntie Cat. He rolls in his suitcase and sighs. "I just got off the plane, Cat. Let's not argue, okay?"

"Fine," she grumbles, as she closes the door.

Then they face each other and I can feel that tension, like they want to hug or kiss, but can't. While we lived in Seattle, something sparked, or rather re-sparked, though they tried to hide it. I don't know why they bother. I've caught them kissing once. It was embarrassing as hell, but it also made me happy. Auntie Cat gave up everything to take care of me and I've felt super shitty about it. If she's finding happiness with Uncle Roy, I want her to go for it without thinking I'm going to judge.

"Hey, Uncle Roy. Thanks for coming," I say and almost snicker as they jump apart.

"Lennon." He holds out his hand and we shake. He glances around. "Was there any damage down here?"

Auntie Cat answers, "Yes, but we've already cleaned up most of it. Upstairs is another story."

Roy is like Tony when it comes to suppressing emotion, but even he gasps as he looks over the destruction of our home. "You can't stay here tonight." He glances at his watch. "It's almost eight. Have you had dinner?"

We both shake our heads.

He takes out his phone. "I'll find a hotel, one with a restaurant. We'll eat, get some rest, and start fresh in the morning."

Auntie Cat swipes at the sweaty grime on her forehead. She opens her mouth and closes it again as he looks at her like she's the most beautiful woman in the world. Her eyelids flutter. It's adorable, seeing older people all in love. I don't want to get in the way of that.

"I can crash in my studio," I announce.

"What?" The resolve returns to my aunt's face. "Lennon, no. You stay with us."

"No offense, but I want to be alone. I need to think."

"You're alone too much."

I shrug. "Besides, I want to make sure Head Elder didn't crap all over my studio, too."

Auntie Cat's consciousness nudges my brain. I open up so we can talk privately, using the Silent Speech.

Are you going out later?

Definitely. I glance at Roy. *Have you told him what I've been doing?*

No. I'll tell him after you leave.

He can't stop me.

He won't. I won't let him. She sighs aloud. *You know I've been treating you like an adult and letting you make your own decisions so you'll be prepared when you turn eighteen. You realize I'm also allowing you to make mistakes and face the consequence, don't you?*

It's not a mistake. You're not afraid of Head Elder now, are you?

She gives me a withering look, which I fully deserve. She blames Head Elder for the death of my father and has refused any contact with him since then. *I'm worried about how this will affect your relationship with your cousin.*

I shrug and bite back on saying I wouldn't be doing this if Tony wasn't such a tool. I say aloud, "I'll see you guys in the morning."

Roy's hand clamps down on my shoulder. I hope to hell he's not going to try and dad me. "Call your aunt when you get to your studio. Let us know if anyone broke in."

"I'll text you both."

We give each other a man nod and his hand slips away. I turn to my aunt. "I'll be back in the morning. Uncle Roy and I can clean while you teach, so don't even think of canceling your classes."

A reluctant smile indents her mouth. Before she can speak, I grab my jacket and head out the door. Before it shuts, I glance back. She and Roy are hugging. I hope they go to a hotel room and do what I don't want to think about them doing. They deserve some happiness for putting up with my shitty life.

I get on my Vespa and head east, toward the bay, and drive along the Embarcadero to Pier 36. San Francisco used to be a major port, until Oakland took over most of the container business, and the piers were converted for other uses. This particular one got turned into an art space called The Kinetic Collective. The building was once used to repair shipping equipment and still has huge chains and hooks hanging from the steel beams, giving the place a cool, industrial vibe. The front half has been converted into art studios while the back half contains kilns and a forge used for large industrial projects. Entrance requires both a card and a code, but that would only slow down Head Elder's goons.

When I get inside, I nod at some people lounging on the couches in the common area. They nod back. I feel their eyes follow me. I'm younger than everyone here and I know they wonder about me. I've resisted most attempts at socializing. They're better off knowing nothing about me.

My studio is in the middle of the second floor. It's double-sized, more than I need, but I took it because it was the only one available. I like being here more than anywhere else in the whole world. This is my spot, where I can be who I am without any expectation. I'm accepted as an artist and I can do what-ever the hell I want. It's my piece of heaven and any violation of this sacred space won't be forgiven. I key in the code, open the door and turn on the light.

I blink several times because the mess I'm expecting doesn't appear. Everything looks exactly as I left it. How can that be? The clan must know about this place. The sound of a chisel hitting stone echoes off the roof. That's my neighbor, a sculptor named Barry. The walls, though high enough for privacy, don't reach the cathedral-style ceiling, allowing for ventilation since we don't have windows. Maybe the goons were afraid of being heard. The building has twenty-four-hour access and people are here all the time, people who would call the cops if they saw or heard intruders. Or maybe Head Elder found another way to intrude.

I whip out my phone and tap on the icon for a nifty app called SpyNot, which detects broadcast signals and electro-magnetic fields. I find the first camera concealed by a shelf and angled so the lens is pointing at the cot. Nausea crawls up my throat. The thought of Head Elder watching me while I sleep makes me want to puke and then punch something, preferably his face.

A sweep of the studio uncovers another camera and two

microphones. Heat spreads across my chest, and up my neck to my face. I want to scream with rage, but instead, I crush the devices, one by one, under my heel. Into the last microphone, I say, "Fuck you, assholes." before grinding it into the floor.

I don't know what makes me angrier, that they bugged my sanctuary or that they thought I was too stupid to notice. Maybe I am. I swept the studio on a daily basis when I first moved in, but when nothing happened, I got lazy and stopped. Maybe I should thank them for the reminder to be more vigilant. And I know exactly how to do it.

Lennon

I spend the next few hours cutting out the stencils I'll need. For inspiration, I go to a website that displays old school Chinese propaganda posters. I like their blocky, cartoonish style and there's this one image of Chairman Mao I've had my eye on. While I work, I put on my headphones and listen to the Clash. When I was a kid, I liked typical stuff, some rock, some hip hop. After all the shit in my life came down, I started listening to punk rock almost exclusively. It fuels my rage, even when I'm weary to the bone and want to curl up in a ball and go to sleep. If I do that, I'll wind up thinking about everything, not only the vandalism, but also about Penny and how much I want to see her again.

When I finish, it's after midnight. I take off my headphones. The chiseling has stopped, but the light from Barry's studio reflects off the ceiling. I'm pretty sure he lives in his studio, even though we're not supposed to. The women who rented my space had lived here. The cot, mini-fridge, microwave oven, and folding chairs had been left behind after they broke up.

I pack the stencils, along with black, white and red spray

paint cans into the backpack and head out. It's after midnight and a cold wind is whipping off the bay. I keep a firm grip on the Vespa's handlebars for the steep drive up Broadway, where the nightclubs are still hopping. Music pours out of open doors while exiled smokers cluster on the sidewalk, huddling close together against disapproval and the wet chill of thick fog. The hubbub dies once I'm in Chinatown. Even touristy Grant Street is deserted. A handful of restaurants stay open until the early morning hours, but those are easy to avoid. I park in a dark alley where the sliding clack of mahjong tiles echoes off the walls, accompanied by the singsong cadence of Cantonese opera.

I glance around, checking for lurking *Xia* or tourists who like to prowl the "exotic" Chinatown alleys after midnight. I'm not sure what they expect to see, except overflowing dumpsters and laundry hanging from fire escape railings. What I can't let them see is me practicing the Two Dragon Clan's secret arts. All Crossroads clans have their own sets of martial skills. The Two Dragon Clan have hard skills for fighting and soft skills, which are the more powerful, involving internal energy. Combining powerful chi with physical strength and endurance allows us to fly short distances, run faster than normal, and move without being seen or heard.

I take one breath to clear my mind and another to even the flow of my *chi*. Then I squat and, using the Flying Skill, launch myself off the ground and up to the roof of the building, landing in a catlike crouch. Using Swift Steps, I run and leap across a series of rooftops until I reach my destination. It's the top of a parking garage that closes at midnight. It has a brick wall facing Joseph Alley. Anyone looking out from the third floor of the *kongsi* will be able to see the wall in daylight. It's a risky spot, so I've been saving it for a special occasion.

I pause for a few moments to catch my breath and recharge. These skills might be soft, but their use expends more energy than the hard skills. I pull a water bottle out of my pack and take a few sips. Head cleared, I get to work.

Stencil graffiti might be guerrilla art, but it isn't an impulsive act. It takes planning and preparation. I studied the techniques of artists like Banksy and Shepard Fairey before I decided to try my hand. Turns out I'm a natural. The trick is being pissed off, but not blind mad. Anger fuels creativity. A cool head and steady hand makes the art happen. I first spray paint a white background. Then, using black paint and overlaying the stencils, I create an image of Head Elder as Chairman Mao with his arm stretched out over a graveyard rather than of a hoard of Little Red Book bearing students. Then I create a red splatter effect over the entire image. Beneath that, I spray paint in red Chinese characters: *Murder your daughter to achieve victory.*

I finish with my tag, which looks like a four with a tail. Actually, it's my initials, LL. That might seem kind of basic, but it's my way of saying I'm Lennon Lau, not Paul Lau. Also, in Chinese numerology, the number four is super unlucky because it sounds like the word 'death,' which is what my graffiti is all about. Over the sound of distant traffic, I hear a soft thump. I spin around, hoping to see the Shinobi or anyone other than who I know it must be.

Tony rises from his crouch. It's weird, because the first thing I want to do is ask how he likes the Ducati. The second is to stare at him because I want to see how he's changed. At first, it's hard to tell since he's dressed all in black, like a Shinobi. Then he steps from the shadows into a shard of light and I gasp. He looks so much like my father; my heart starts pounding. I mean, he's always looked like Dad, way more than me. It's no surprise, since our fathers are twin brothers, fraternal, not identical, but still. The passing years have sharpened the planes of Tony's face, making him look like he's the identical twin brother. The big difference is the eyes. Dad always had this spark of fire in his expression, while Tony's gaze can freeze a statue. Given the right moment and the right circumstances, I could make him smile and even laugh.

I tell myself I don't hate him and I don't blame him for not believing me, his sworn brother, over the evil bastards who did this to our family. After all, the evil bastards in question are our family.

"Why are you doing this?" His voice holds no emotion, though he must be deeply pissed.

I shrug away the emotion clogging my throat. "Shits and giggles."

"You think this is funny?"

"Oh, yeah. It's hilarious." I nod toward my artwork. "He kills my parents and nothing happens. It's a fucking joke."

"Paul…"

"Lennon. Call me Lennon or don't talk to me."

His lips press in a thin line. "I can't talk to you, not like this. You won't listen."

I shrug and start packing my gear. Even though I act like I don't give a fuck, truth is, my throat aches from wanting to ask how he is. To tell him I'm sorry I haven't been there for him, because I know things have been tough. I shoulder my bag, but my feet won't let me move, because I don't hate him, even though he might hate me.

I clear my throat. "Auntie Cat told me you got married."

A sigh hisses through his teeth. "Yeah." We stare at each other until I figure that's all he's going to say. I start to move away and he speaks. "May. She's from the Chisel Knife compound. Her parents are doctors and so is she."

"Yeah, the Kwans. Auntie told me. Nice people." I mean it. The male Dr. Kwan is descended from a long line of Chinese medicine doctors who have treated the various ailments of our clan. His mother is Fourth Elder, one of the leaders of our clan, who was a big supporter of my father. I remember May and

I'm almost certain she's older than Tony, but I know better than to mention that. If it's true, she got married late. Most members of our clan are married by Tony's age, twenty-two.

"We got married before Mother died, so May could help me take care of her." He pauses. "Even though Mother didn't want her to."

No. Shit. Auntie Sylvia didn't like sharing Tony with anyone. I shudder at the thought of how she must've treated May. Auntie Sylvia never lifted a finger around the house and had no appreciation for the hard work of other people. She went through a string of maids who quit rather than deal with her abuse.

I want to say 'and you're still married?' but I restrain myself. "She sounds great."

"She is. Better than I deserve." He takes a hesitant breath. "I want to ask you and Auntie Cat to come over for dinner so you can meet her."

"No." The word comes out harsh. I say more softly, "Sorry." It's weird, but I want to keep talking to him. I want to know more. "So, you let Aaron keep taking violin lessons."

"Music teaches discipline and consistency. He needs that."

Much as I want to mouth off, I don't, because there's something about the way he speaks, as if he's convincing himself that's the real reason and not because he wants to make Aaron happy. "All art is a discipline if you're serious about it."

He looks at the wall. "Art. Is that what you call defacing property?"

"You don't know anything about graffiti. Have you even heard of Keith Haring or Basquiat?"

"Yes. You're not as good as them."

I almost smile. Damn it. Tony is the most unintentionally funny person I know. "Not yet. Give me time."

"You're running out of time." He turns to me, his eyes like coal. "This is foolish. It serves no purpose. You must stop.

There's not much time left. You must come home so I can train you."

"Uncle Roy is here. He can train me."

Surprise makes him pause. "When did he get here?"

"Today. Auntie Cat called him after our place was trashed. All our shit thrown all over the place. All the furniture ripped to shreds. But nothing stolen. How about that? Who would do something like that? Any clues?" Tony clams up, but I'm just getting started. "So, then I go to my art studio and guess what? It's been bugged. Yeah. Audio and video. I suspect a pedophile. What do you think?" I search his face, but it remains a blank slate, so I jerk my thumb at the graffiti. "You can remove that, but it won't remove his crimes or your part in them."

"My part?"

I raise my arms, like what-the-hell? "Didn't you see my last graffiti, Complacency Equals Complicity?" He doesn't blink. "The one with the monkeys." It portrayed the see-no, hear-no, and talk-no-evil monkeys perched on a pair of gravestones engraved with my parents' names. "It was meant for you and everyone else in the clan who bends over and does his evil shit for him."

His face freezes over and I'm sure he wants to hit me. I wait for a few moments, to give him his chance, because I'd like an excuse to hit him, too. Then I think of the two of us fighting up here. Stupid, pointless, macho bullshit. That's what Penny would say. I almost smile. Instead I sigh. It's cold and I'm tired.

"I gotta go." I step up to the ledge, turning my back to him.

"We swore an oath, in the presence of your father and our ancestors, that we would be brothers and take each other's side against all adversaries."

Guilt punches a hole in my stomach. If Dad could see us now, he'd be so disappointed. More than that, he'd knock our heads together and make us cooperate. But Dad is gone and

Tony knows it, and he knows who's responsible, even if he doesn't want to admit it.

He comes up beside me. "I didn't break that oath."

"Neither did I." I leap off the ledge, into the fog, away from Chinatown and Tony, and obligation and regret.

Penny

It's been two days since I saw Lennon and he hasn't called or messaged. Every buzz of my phone starts my heart pounding, all for nothing. I don't know who I'm more vexed with. Bridie is high on my shit list. Tony, too. And Kai and Aaron for being such prats. Most of all, though, I'm vexed with Lennon. Does he care so little about me? Or does he care so much that he's cut me off for my own sake or some such shite? Both thoughts make me fume.

Last night, my family performed at Alternative Ulster in the Castro. A Bleater pub in a Gay neighborhood meant we were relieved of Uncle Christy's lofty presence, though Likely Lad surprised us by showing up with a banjo on his knee. Bridie welcomed him to join us, which vexed me even more. I gritted my teeth, but carried on because I was wearing a new costume with rainbow trim, sewn for this occasion. I ignored those twinkling blue eyes and danced like I hadn't a care in the world. Like I wasn't scanning every corner of the pub for a pair of brown eyes.

Today, I'm done. I spend the morning concentrating on what's important, my business. Using a pattern, I cut a diagonal row of diamond shapes up to the knees on a pair of leggings. Then, I sew on functional buttons with little straps between each diamond. Sounds easy, but it's labor intensive and I'm knackered after six pairs. I take photos and load those onto my online store, along with a description and price. Despite my business being named Pinafores and More, leggings are my bestsellers, probably because they're less expensive. These should sell in a couple of days, which will be great. I can use the money.

That done, I toss my phone on the bed and head for the kitchen to heat up some leftover shepherd's pie for lunch. Bridie walks in, and I give her side-eye before turning a cold shoulder and taking my food to my room. It's a nice enough day that I decide to eat on my balcony. I almost make it out there before zig-zagging back and snatching my phone. I turn it on while I eat, pretending I'm only going to check my email. I suck in my breath as it vibrates and a message appears on the screen. I roll my eyes when I realize it's from Bridie. It contains no words, only a heart and a blushing smiley face. This is how she wiggles her way through life, but it works because I send the same back to her. As I glumly thumb through my mail, another message appears on the screen.

> Hey. It's Lennon.

Those three words makes my heart pound so hard, I can't hear anything else. I take a deep breath and text back.

> Hey.

> Can I see you today?

He wants to see me. I'm going to see him. No, wait. He left me dangling for two days. Should he be rewarded for that? Air hisses through my clenched teeth. I don't know. See, this is what comes of having never had a boyfriend. I don't have a clue what to do. I think I'm supposed to play some kind of shite game, but who has time for that? I want to see Lennon so he can tell me to my face what the problem is.

Ok. When?

When is good for you?

Now would be good, but I can't say that, right? Then, almost as if he was reading my mind…

I can come now, if that works.

Ok.

I'll be there in about twenty minutes. Meet me downstairs.

Ok.

Twenty minutes. Enough time to take a shower, smear on some makeup and change out of my sweats and into a pair of jeans and my Funky Chunky Jumper. No, that's not a brand name, though maybe it should be. I took a knitting class my last semester in high school and this jumper was my final project. I got a bit of yarn from everyone in class and the result was this bulky pullover with mismatched stripes and too-long sleeves. The teacher gave me a B for effort. I don't care because I love it, even though each wash seems to stretch it further so that it now covers my thighs.

I creep down the hall, but Bridie's voice stops me before I reach the door. "Where are you off to?"

To lie or not to lie, that is the question. I'm done with being fake, but I've come to learn the truth has its own complications. I turn and see Bridie's face. She knows, so I might as well say it.

"I'm going to meet Lennon." I hold my breath.

Her mouth puckers like she's sucked a lemon. Then she looks me up and down, and I can tell Funky Chunky Jumper has worked its magic. "All right, but don't do anything foolish." By which she means, *don't do what I did when I was your age*. No worries there.

Lennon is sitting on the stoop, staring at the street with that broody, owlish face. I give a breathless, "Hi," even though I'm not out of breath.

"Hi." He stands and his smile banishes the gloom from his face. "You look great."

He's being nice, because this jumper makes me look like a funky chunky lump. "Thanks. I knit this myself."

"I kinda figured. Looks totally you."

I guess that's a compliment? "What took you so long to message me?"

"My aunt's house got trashed. I mean, everything dumped on the ground and broken and torn apart."

My mouth drops open. That's not the excuse I expected. "Were you robbed?"

He shakes his head.

"Do you know who did it?"

"Yeah. Head Elder. I mean, not personally, but on his orders. He bugged my studio, too."

"Studio? I thought you lived with your aunt?"

"I have an art studio."

Of course he does. He shows up looking flash in a leather jacket and biker boots, and he's not even eighteen yet and he's got his own studio. He's got money to burn while my family counts pennies. He might call himself Lennon, but he's not that homeless boy anymore and I need to remember that. "What do you mean, bugged? You mean, with hidden cameras?"

"Yeah." He shrugs. "I totally don't blame you if you don't want to hang out anymore."

"No, I do." I really do. More than ever. Why is that? Excitement at danger? Wanting to support my friend? Maybe both? "Where should we go?"

"We can go to my studio."

"The buggy one?"

"No. I mean, yeah. The bugs are gone, so it's safe."

"Is it?"

"No, not really."

"Okay, then. Let's go."

He shakes his head and breathes out a laugh.

"What?"

"Nothing. Just… I missed you."

I bite my lip so I don't say I missed him, too. I put on the blue helmet, strapping it to the last notch. His aunt must be a genius to have such a big brain. Speaking of family… "Um, I have to be back by five."

He twists to face me with a rueful smile. "That's an early curfew. Bridie really doesn't trust me."

"It's not that. We're going out for dinner." Like we do every Friday night. I need to tell Lennon about Uncle Christy.

As soon as I climb onto the Vespa, my heart starts pounding against his back. He shifts within the circle of my arms and I close my eyes against the sparks that shoot through me.

Don't do anything foolish.

I suck in my breath as the scooter pulls into traffic and lift my head to allow the air to cool my cheeks. I have feelings for him, feelings that won't go away. All I can do is contain them so I won't do anything foolish.

We cross the city all the way to the bay, and drive along the Embarcadero until Lennon pulls up in front of a huge concrete warehouse with an Art Deco facade. The sign outside reads,

The Kinetic Collective. The inside reminds me of a beehive because it is literally humming with activity. Orange and gold sparks fly at the far end of building, where a group of people are using welding equipment on a huge metallic head coiled with a colorful array of fearsome snakes.

"They're a group of makers called Junkyard Metallurgy. They're taking that to Burning Man," Lennon explains over the noise.

"Cool," I shout back, though cool barely covers it. Everything about this place is brilliant. We pass open doors where artists paint, sculpt, solder, and weave. "It's making me miss school."

"School?" says Lennon, as he leads the way up a circular metal staircase. "I thought you hated Parkside."

"I do." I shudder. Parkside Academy, where my stepfather had enrolled me, had been hell on Earth. "After we got back from London, I was accepted into the High School of Art and Design."

"What?" He stops and turns. "Really? I wanted to go there, but my parents wouldn't let me. They said it's not an appropriate school for someone on the Crossroads."

"That's funny because Aaron's going there this fall. He and Kai got accepted into the music program."

"Tony let Aaron go to art school?" Lennon frowns and rubs his chin. I can't tell if he's puzzled or angry, or both.

"Why is that a big deal?"

"It's not." He sounds defensive. He must know it, too, because then he shrugs like it's no big deal. "Our clan doesn't support artistic-ness, so I don't get why Tony would let him go there."

"I think it was May. Tony's wife. She's super nice."

"Oh, her," he mumbles, as he turns away.

We clank the rest of the way up without speaking. As we

head down the hall, he ducks his head and says, "I guess you think it's weird that I don't talk to my family."

My shoulders lift in a tight shrug. "Gerry's family disowned him and most of Bridie's family treat us like we're outcasts, so no, not at all."

Lennon opens his studio door, releasing a strong odor of paint mingled with a fainter scent of aerosol. Stepping inside, I see the source, a rickety bookshelf overflowing with spray paint cans. I wander over to a worktable with a cutting board and a pile of stencils, most of them Chinese characters. I turn and see him staring at his phone. After a few moments, he declares, "Okay, we're clean."

"Of bugs?"

"Yeah."

"You do that every time you come in here? That sucks."

"Yeah."

The overhead light reflects off his glasses, making him look even more owlish. My quiet Owl Boy. Maybe he hasn't changed so much. He closes the door and takes off his glasses. No longer an owl. I want to ask him to put them back on. It's easier talking to an owl than with a boy I want to kiss. "I thought you didn't live here."

"I don't."

"What's all that?" I nod at a cot piled with pillows, blankets and clothes.

He shrugs. "This was the only space available and I'm subleasing it. A couple lived here, and when they broke up, they left a bunch of their stuff behind. Sometimes, I spend the night here when I'm out late."

Out late. What does that mean? Somehow, I don't think he's clubbing.

He nods toward a couple of folding chairs next to the bed. I snuggle into one, wrapping my arms around my legs, thankful once again for Funky Chunky Jumper.

"Sorry. It gets kind of cold in here. I should get a space heater."

"Don't you get cold?"

"I'm used to it." He hands me a blanket off the cot.

I wrap it around me. It smells like him, musky with hints of aerosol and paint. My head swims and I swallow away the feelings. He sits beside me and leans forward, resting his fore-arms on his knees. At first, I think he's actually going to say something, but no. He's gone owl again. I glance up at the large painting of a dragon above the bed. "Did you do that?"

He nods.

"It's brilliant." The details, with the coiling body and vibrant blue and green scales, had to be a lot of work. And a lot of stencils. "Is this what you've been doing since you got back?"

"Pretty much."

"Bullshit."

The owl blinks.

"I went to art school, remember? I know what stencils and spray paint are for." I snap my fingers. "That stop sign with the Chinese characters. Did you do that?"

His lips quirk with a smile. "Yeah."

"What'd it say?"

"The trees want to remain quiet, but the wind will not stop."

I shift and blink, wrapping my mind around that. "That's deep. Did you make that up or is it, like, a saying?"

"It's a saying. You know, a proverb."

"Are you supposed to be the wind?"

He fidgets. "Kinda. Not really. It's more like Truth is the wind."

I'm dying to ask what the truth is, but I don't want to spook him into silence. "Does Tony know about your graffiti?"

His gaze becomes guarded. "Yeah. Why?"

"After you left, he came inside to talk to us about you. He said you're troubled and need help."

Lennon's hands clench into fists. He mutters, "God damn it," under his breath before asking, "What else did he say?"

"Not much. He mostly demanded answers about how we knew you." I tell him about Tony's interrogation.

He looks surprised that Bridie stood up for him. "I thought she didn't like me anymore."

"It's nothing to do with liking you. She's afraid we're going to fall in love and run away together, and I'll get knocked up, and it'll cause a big stink."

He blinks. "That escalated quickly."

"I know, right?" I lean forward. "It pisses me off, too. She should trust me."

"Um, does she know you're following Jeremiah down dark alleys?"

The back of my neck heats up. "No. And I don't follow Jeremiah around. Just that once."

"Why?"

Ugh. Confession time. How do I say this so I don't sound like a desperate stalker girl? "I was waiting for a bus near the *kongsi* and I saw Jeremiah leave Joseph Alley." I pause, trying to think of a way to explain. "Bridie's been training me in Second Sight, the Strowler arts. We believe in gut instincts and my gut told me to follow him, so I did, and he led me to you."

Lennon's brow rises. "Do you believe in coincidence?"

I lift my chin. "Don't make fun of another clan's magic, Mr. Descended-from-dragons."

"I'm not. And it's only one dragon."

So not impressed. I lean forward as if sharing a secret. "You know, Strowlers are descended from a dragon, too."

His face goes blank. Then he blinks several times before saying, "Are you kidding?"

I can't hold back my smirk. "Did you think the Two Dragon

Clan were the only ones on the Crossroads to make that claim? Our story goes like this: Maeve, the queen of the fairies, had a daughter, Leannán Sidhe, whose game was to seduce and abandon artists and poets, who then waste away for the want of her. One day, she comes to a rocky shore where a fair-faced, dark-haired, altogether bonny young man is singing soulfully to the waves. Perfect, thinks she, and she sets about the seduction."

"Right there on the beach?"

"No, they got a hotel room. Anyway, afterward he thanks her, saying 'I couldn't return to my home until I had the love of a woman.' Then he turns into Master Stoorworm, the great dragon that lives in the Irish Sea, and dives into the waves."

Lennon squirms as if the story is actually bugging him. "That was cold."

"It gets worse, because she gets pregnant. Queen Maeve won't have such a monstrosity in her court, so she orders Leannán Sidhe to be rid of the child or she'll kill it. Leannán Sidhe returns to the mortal world and searches until she finds a traveling tinker and his wife with a newborn babe. While they sleep, she exchanges her child for theirs and places a spell on them and her babe's descendants, that they'll wander forever so Queen Maeve can never find them."

"They didn't notice their kid got switched with a dragon-fairy?"

I grin because I'd asked that same question when Bridie first told me that story. I give him her answer. "Leannán Sidhe looks human, so the baby did, too. What about your dragon baby daddy? Did anyone notice his kid wasn't normal?"

"That's different. Jade Dragon wasn't the baby daddy. He was the baby."

"Another switched-at-birth story?"

"Not exactly." He pauses and looks down, as if measuring his words and deciding what he'll dole out. "See, dragons are super curious by nature, and Jade Dragon wanted to know what it was like to live as a human. Dragons can shrink to the microscopic level, so he did, and he implanted himself in the body of a woman who'd just conceived. She gave birth to what seemed like a completely normal baby. In fact, Jade Dragon didn't know he was a dragon until he was fifteen. Something about going through puberty fired off something inside him and he realized his dragon nature. He lived as a human for eighty-eight years and during that time founded the Two Dragon Clan and devised our secret martial skills."

"Like that Dragon Shout thing you did?"

"Yeah, that. Anyway, all dragons have a pearl at their throat that contains the essence of their power. Jade Dragon broke off pieces of his pearl to give to us, to keep us powerful and protected."

"Wow." I've been listening with my chin resting in my hand, but now I settle back with a sigh. "Master Stoorworm sucks compared to Jade Dragon."

"Didn't Master Stoorworm leave you with any powers?"

"I guess. I mean, Strowlers believe we inherited Second Sight from Leannán Sidhe and guile from Master Stoorworm."

"When you say Second Sight, do you mean ESP?"

"Sorta. We manifest our fairy power through Fake, which is how we deceive, and Charm, how we persuade, plus curses, and fortune telling."

His eyebrows lift. "Fortune telling?"

"It's considered a female art and how Strowler women earn money." I hold out my hand and beckon with my fingers. After a moment's hesitation, he lays his hand on mine, palm up. "So, if you were a Bleater, I'd pretend to read the lines, but that's not how Strowler palmistry works. We believe the hand is the opening to the soul, since all deeds are carried out by our hands." I press my thumb to the center of his palm and, using my gut, sense through the roil of his emotions to the defining moment that sent him on his current path. I suck in my breath as I feel death, despair and the end of everything he knows. My poor Owl Boy. The loss of his parents weighs on him like a cement shroud. Where does that path lead? I press a little deeper. "You're searching for answers and when you find them, you'll discover you've been deceived..." Oh crap. He's not going to like this.

Lennon leans forward. "What?"

I gnaw my lip.

"Just tell me."

Oh, God, I hope he doesn't hate me. I take a deep breath. "Deceived by your parents."

He takes back his hand and tucks it under his arm. We sit in tense silence until he admits, "My parents were hiding something from me before they died. I need to find out what it was."

"Do you have any idea what it might be?"

He shakes his head. "But I'm sure it's the reason my grandfather had them killed."

My eyes widen. Is he finally going to tell me the truth of what happened to him? "Your grandfather killed your parents?"

"Yeah. Well, not personally. He got my aunt and uncle to do his dirty work." He speaks so calmly, I wonder if he's kidding, except who would kid about that?

"Your aunt and uncle... you mean, Tony and Aaron's parents?" He nods. "Killed your parents?"

"Yeah."

"For their money?"

"No. I made that up because I didn't want you to figure out who I really am."

He'd been forced to be fake, the way I'd been back then, so I can't get too mad, but I hope he realizes that if he's going to be the unstoppable wind, he's got to be truthful with me now. "So, why did they do it?"

"I don't know. That's what I need to find out."

"I'd see your aunt sometimes when I'd pick up Kai at the *kongsi*. She looked…" I picture Sylvia Lau's bone-thin body, the silk scarf wrapped around her bald scalp, her pain-hollowed eyes crusted with thick makeup, and the heavy scent of roses that barely covered the stench of her illness. "Frail. She didn't seem strong enough to kill anyone."

"She did. She killed my mother. I saw her do it."

My heart jumps to my throat and pounds painfully as the details spill out about his parents' deaths, how his aunt suffocated his mother and how his uncle stood by while the Shinobi killed his father. I press my hand to my chest to slow the pounding as I whisper, "Oh, my god," over and over.

"Head Elder. It's him. He has some big secret he was holding over all of them. I don't know what it is, but I'm going to find out."

"After you become the Dragon Son?"

Lennon blinks, as if he's forgotten I was sitting there. "On my birthday, I'm going to be challenged by the Beggar Clan, by Jeremiah standing in for his dad." He takes a deep breath. "And I'm going to throw the fight. Let John Walks Long win."

My brow furrows. "But, if he wins…"

"Yeah."

Yeah. The Two Dragon Clan will no longer be the head clan of the Crossroads, not only in SF, but the whole world. The Beggar Clan will take over control. All other clans will pay them tribute and abide by their division of territory, which means the Two Dragon Clan's power base will shrink considerably.

"How is becoming less powerful going to help you?"

"If the clan wants me to cooperate, if they want me to challenge Jeremiah and win back our position, they're going to have to give me what I want."

"Which is?"

"I want Head Elder and my uncle to confess they murdered my parents, and to face the justice of the clan. I'm willing to risk everything. If I die, the clan dies, because no one can take my place."

All my muscles are clenched. I take a breath and shift around to ease the tension. Lennon searches my face with dark, wary eyes. Do I believe him now? Yes, but that doesn't mean I think he should throw away his life for revenge. "I know you think you're irreplaceable, but don't bet on your death stopping them. People have a way of rewriting history."

"What do you mean?"

I take a hesitant breath because I'm not eager to share. Still, he cut himself open and bled. As his friend, I should do the same. "Gerry's family disowned both him and me, saying I couldn't possibly be his daughter since he was a poof, but that's not the worst of it." I take a hard breath. "They claimed Bridie was a witch and that she cast a spell to turn Gerry gay so she could sleep around." I almost laugh when Lennon's mouth pops open, except it's so not funny. "Your family could do the same. I mean, find a way to trash you so they can replace you."

He shrugs. "They already trash me. Replacing me isn't so easy." He chews his lip as if deciding whether or not to elaborate. He goes with not. "Your mom's family wasn't so bad, right?"

"They couldn't deny me and Kai were hers, if that's what you mean. Her parents took us in, but they weren't nice about it. Only Uncle Christy." I pause. "That reminds me." I tell him about Christy defeating Kingfisher and becoming the Upright Man. "You didn't know?"

"I haven't talked to anyone since I got back to the city, not even John Walks Long." His eyes meet mine with that dark brown sadness that catches my soul. "I thought about going to him and asking about you, but I knew he wouldn't tell me, so why bother? Maybe you should take his advice. If you hang out with me, it'll look like you're taking my side."

"I am taking your side. Look," I lean forward, stifling an impulse to take his hand. "I know how you feel. My family never got justice for Gerry and Matthew. Someday, I'm going back to London to find out why they were killed."

His sorrow shifts to concern. "By yourself?"

"I thought about waiting for Kai to come with, but the trail will be frozen cold by the time he's old enough. I can't wait much longer. It needs to be soon."

"I'll come with you."

My heart swells at how instantly he spoke. I haven't had a real friend since we separated. I made friends at school, but that's all they were, school friends, Bleaters who can't know about the Crossroads. What I needed was an ally and here he is. If only. I cock my head with a crooked grin. "Thanks, but I need to be inconspicuous. I can't do that with the Dragon Son along."

"No one can be more inconspicuous than me. How do you think I've been tagging all over the city? And..." His voice trails off. He thinks for a moment before giving a decisive nod. "And I'll teach you the stealth skills so you can be inconspicuous too."

"Wait. What? The Two Dragon Clan stealth skills?"

"Yeah, those."

"But it's forbidden to teach outsiders those skills, right? Won't you get in trouble if someone finds out?"

He snorts. "I'm already in trouble. Let me teach you and..." A wistful look crosses his face. "If I survive the coming shit storm, I'll go to London with you and we can do it together."

Lennon and I against the world. Heroes, like in that David

Bowie song, except nobody sees us as heroes. Rebels, more like. Which is another Bowie song. So be it. "Deal, but only if you let me help you against the shit storm."

Lennon sits back in his chair and stares at the wall in owlish silence. Ugh. When he goes all enigmatic like that, I want to shake him. Or kiss him. Or both. Then his head swivels toward me. "Confusion to the enemy."

Um. "Okay?"

"Haven't you read The Art of War?"

Um. "No?"

"Okay, so this guy, Sun Tzu, a couple thousand years ago, wrote this manual about war. He said the secret to successful warfare lies in confusing the enemy, so he can't figure out your real plans."

"So, how do we confuse our enemies?"

"By hanging out here. They're going to wonder what we're doing and make a big stink about it. Head Elder will think I'm being distracted by a girl and can be lulled into complacency. Your family will think you're hanging out with the wrong guy, same result."

Except mine won't be complacent. They'll be pissed. Still, if it means being with Lennon… I glance around. "Actually, I'd love it if you'd teach me how to spray paint with stencils. I could create a whole new line of clothing with graffiti art."

"That's brilliant." He shoots out of his chair and starts pacing. "Let's totally do that. If anyone asks what we're doing here, that's what we'll say."

I stand, too. "Strowlers have a similar strategy. It's called the Devil's Workshop. Our hands are never idle. We always have somewhere to go or something to do, so if anyone asks what we're up to, we have an answer, regardless of what we're actually up to."

Lennon smiles and my heart breaks wide open. I'd do

anything to be with him, to help him, even if it means vexing every Strowler living, including my own family.

"This is going to be amazing." He puts his arms around me, lifts and we spin together, knocking into the chairs. I put my arms around his neck to steady myself and laugh, because it is going to be amazing, and dangerous, and I don't care, not when Lennon is holding me this close.

He sets me down and I slide off him, my arms still around his neck. We look at each other. He's breathless and in his eyes, I can see it, he wants to kiss me. I want to kiss him. For a single, sharp moment, it feels like it's going to happen and change everything. Then his hands slide away and I step away. We both take deep breaths.

"So, when do we start?" I ask.

"How about right now? I know a place that sells all kinds of spray paint, including for fabric."

As we leave the studio, I think about what to work on first. Leggings. If I can create some cool stencil designs with an urban edge, those will fly off the shelf. I'm so excited, I forget the forbidden element, until we reach the door to the building. How long it will take before anyone notices what we're up to?

We step outside and discover it took no time at all.

Good things can't last. I learned that the hard way and now I expect to be crapped on a daily basis. So, I'm not surprised to see the Beggar Chief's son standing beside my Vespa. Jeremiah doesn't look any different than the last time I saw him. He's still wearing ragged military fatigues, and has dark stubble and a shaved head, like he's motherfucking Travis Bickle from *Taxi Driver*. He's got hard, battle-scarred eyes and actual battle scars. Half his body from the neck down is covered with burn marks from a car bomb in Kabul. The other half is inked with tattoos.

"Chief wants to see you," he announces in that gravelly, smoke-damaged voice of his.

Well, hello to you, too. "Okay. Let me take Penny home first."

"He wants to see both of you."

Penny manages to look puzzled. "Why does the Chief want to see me?"

Jeremiah jerks his chin at me. "Why do you think?"

"Because of Lennon?"

"Don't act dense, Penny. You know who he is."

Her hands go to her hips. "I'm not acting dense, Jeremiah. Of course, I know who Lennon is. That doesn't explain why the Chief wants to see me."

Whoa, she's good. I haven't even warmed up to getting that snotty yet.

Jeremiah tries to burn her with a glare. "You refuse to see him?"

"Of course not. You're the one being touchy because I asked a question." She turns to me with raised eyebrows. "Seems His Nibs wants to see us. Shall we?"

I shrug, like, whatever. "Tell the Chief we're on our way."

While we get on my scooter, Jeremiah talks into his phone like it's a walkie-talkie. Penny wraps her arms around me in a defiant sort of way that makes it hard not to smile. This is damn serious and shouldn't be fun, but it is. I shouldn't be so glad that Penny is here with me, in danger, but I can't help it. My shitty life is somewhat less shitty and how can I not be happy about that?

I head for the part of the bayshore that used to be a military shipyard. During the tech boom, toxic waste kept this area from being gentrified and developed into upscale housing. We pass rows of warehouses and a huge cement factory until we get to a chain link fence topped with barbed wire. Leaning against the open gate is a mud-spattered plywood board spray-painted with an open-bottom rectangle covering three parallel dots, the road marker for a Beggar Clan Abode. My stomach tingles as we pass through the gate. I've been avoiding this moment since I got back. I don't want to see the Chief. I don't want to be reminded of what I owe him.

At the end of a gravel road, we reach a closed gate where two Beggars strain forward from their post like identical guard dogs. I recognize them immediately from their floppy blond hair and the acne that makes it possible to tell them apart. I'd hung out with Tyler and Cody during my time here. We're the same age, so they were assigned to be my buddies, and were friendly enough, but I was wary, convinced the Chief was having them spy on me.

Cody grins while his brother hoots and calls out, "Lennon, you bastard. What the fuck? You're the Dragon Son?"

I come to a stop. "Just Lennon. Forget the Dragon Son bullshit."

"Okay, then." He turns to Penny and his face reddens to the color of his zits. "Hey, Penny."

"Hey, Tyler." She nods at his brother. "Cody."

Cody shuffles his feet while he nods. A sharp burn spreads across my chest. They know and like her. How can they not when she's so amazing? Thing is, they can't act on those feelings, any more than I can. That should make me feel better, but it doesn't.

"Jeremiah said to let you guys through." Tyler's eyes zigzag between us. He's obviously dying to know what's going on.

We pass through the gate and head for the huge weather-worn warehouse moldering at the end of the pier. I park at the entrance and as we climb off, Penny says, "My family still performs at the Beggars' Banquet."

"Are you sure you want to go through with this? Because, you know, consequences."

Her chin lifts. "If I'm not welcome back because I'm your friend, I'd rather know now, because that's not going to change."

The burn eases out of my chest, replaced by a warm glow. That obstinate look in her green eyes fills me with the confidence I need to face the Chief.

Past the chipped paint and rust lies the clean, well-insulated hive that is the Beggar Abode, the housing complex and training grounds for the clan. Single people live in dorms, couples in single rooms and families in doubles. There are few personal possessions and most things are shared, including clothes. Money is only handed out when needed for clan purposes. Given all that, there's no shortage of eager recruits, mostly among former military and ex-professional fighters. While living here, I'd been considered a runaway orphan rescued by the Chief and being groomed for membership, which was basically true. Before I'd left, he asked me to defect, which would've made the Beggar Clan, and him, the head of the Crossroads. I refused and he let me go anyway, when he could've done any number of things, including kill me. To say I owe him doesn't do justice to how much I'm in his debt.

We pass a fight cage where two women are practicing their MMA moves and head over to the empty boxing ring. It's surrounded by benches and a single, large armchair with worn and patched upholstery. Same chair as when I'd been here before and same occupant. John Walks Long, the Beggar Chief, rises as we approach him. He hasn't changed much, either. He still has wild, wiry gray hair and a beard that reaches his chest. He wears his long, multi-colored patched coat like a robe of state and holds his tall wooden staff like a scepter. Part of me wants to bow. Part of me wants to hug him and thank him again for all he did for me, except for one thing. He and I both know it came with a price. One that's come due.

"Lennon, son." His voice has a deep, gentle rumble, despite his steel gray eyes. "Walk in peace."

I nod my head. "Walk in peace, Beggar Chief."

He turns to Penny. "Child, why are you with this boy when I told you to forget him?"

She lifts her chin. "With all respect, Beggar Chief, I'm no longer a child. I'm eighteen and I choose my friends. And, also, with respect." She raises her voice. He raises a bushy brow. "Why didn't you tell me who Lennon really is?"

"Because knowing would do you no good. You cannot continue your friendship with him."

"Why not? Because we're in different clans? You're friends with my mother. How's that different?"

"My friendship with your mother ruined her marriage."

"No, what ruined her marriage was that Bill was a berk and a Bleater, and she never should've married him. That had nothing to do with you." She pauses before quickly adding, "Sir."

"You're not a fool, Penny Sparrow. You know full well the implications of your friendship with the Dragon Son."

Penny gnaws her lip. The defiance sparking in her eyes speaks more than words and I love her for it.

I love her.

I'm totally crazy in love with Penny.

My head spins. I want to laugh because this is totally the wrong place to realize something huge like that.

The Beggar Chief's steel eyes narrow in on me. "You find this amusing?"

I can't speak or even look at Penny, so I shrug.

"Lennon and I aren't doing anything wrong or even anything romantic," continues Penny. "If you must know, Lennon's letting me share his art studio so I can expand my business."

I watch the Chief's face as he listens to her explain about stencils and fashion design. The lines in his brow deepen into crevices. "You expect me to believe this nonsense?"

"Check my online store in a couple of weeks and you'll see."

He scoffs before he motions for a nearby guard to join us. "Escort Miss Sparrow to the light rail. Stay with her until she gets on the train." He beams disappointment down on Penny. "Walk in peace. Child."

Penny bobs her head. "Walk in peace. Sir." As she turns away from him, she winks at me, her lips curled up.

I can't wink or smile back because my heart is pounding

too hard. She walks with a confident stride, her head held high, and that crazy, artsy sweater making her look like the personification of the Wayward Way.

"She's quite a girl," remarks the Chief in such a way that I know he knows how I feel.

Heat flushes my face. I attempt to recover with a casual shrug. "She's cool."

"Maybe you don't know much about Strowlers, despite having lived among them. The more time you spend with her, the more of an outcast you make her among her own people. She'll be disgraced. No man will marry her."

My breath hitches in my throat, mainly because I realize I'm selfish bastard who doesn't want anyone else to marry her. I manage a lame comeback, "We're not doing anything wrong."

"Yet."

"You really think I'd do anything to hurt Penny?"

"I know you're a seventeen-year-old boy in the company of a pretty girl looking for an adventure. Time spent alone with each other is full of temptations you'd be wise to avoid."

Wow. The plan is working better than I thought. He thinks we're that stupid. I shrug defiantly. "You don't know us at all."

He motions me to sit on a folding chair before settling on his threadbare throne. "Your father and I once talked about you."

Really? He's going there?

"We happened to meet on the street and bought each other drinks in a nearby bar."

Okay, now it sounds like a joke: 'The Dragon Son and the Beggar Chief walk into a bar…' except I don't think I'm going to laugh at the punchline.

"We talked about our sons, as fathers will. Michael was proud of your academic achievements, but he worried about your martial endeavors. He said your skills were exceptional, but he feared you were merely trying to please him, that your heart wasn't in it."

It takes all my willpower not to squirm. I didn't think Dad knew or cared that I preferred school to martial training. Why would he reveal such a weakness to the leader of a rival clan?

"I, in turn, told him how Jeremiah defied me and left the clan to join the military. He returned to me scarred and broken. As he healed, he became a stronger, better man. I doubt there's a more powerful fighter on the Crossroads today."

Oh, is that what he's getting at? "So, you're saying Jeremiah's gonna kick my punk ass because he's all healed up while I'm still a broken toy?"

"Are you?"

"Guess you'll find out on my birthday. Or maybe you won't." I pause long enough for a hint of doubt to flicker in his eyes. "A guy named Hasaki dropped in on me."

His face freezes. Then he rumbles, "Ah. Hasaki. He paid me a visit, too."

"Then you know what he wants. I don't get why he's gunning to be first in line to challenge me."

"You've heard of the twenty-year rule."

Challenges on the Crossroads can only be fought between people who are within twenty years age of each other. If the age difference is more than that, then a surrogate is chosen. Jeremiah was agreed upon by both the Two Dragon Clan and the Beggar Clan. Not that anyone asked me, of course.

"Hasaki will turn thirty-nine two days after your birthday. That's a very narrow window of opportunity to challenge you."

"How do you know when his birthday is?"

"He challenged me last month. I asked his birthdate. As it turns out, the difference in our ages is twenty years, except for a gap of about six weeks."

"Did you accept his challenge?"

"I did. I agreed to fight him after your birthday. By that time, Jeremiah will be my surrogate."

None of this surprises me. Rival clan challenges have a strict set of rules, one of which is that the challenged party can set the date. The only exception is that once a year, on a given day, the Head of the Crossroads, meaning the Dragon Son, is required to accept the challenge of a rival Chief. Right of first challenge has always gone to the Beggar Clan, the second most powerful clan on the Crossroads. If they decline, then the next most powerful clan can make that challenge. I don't know where the Kasumi Clan stands in the Crossroads hierarchy, but probably far back. No wonder Hasaki is gunning to have first go at me.

The Chief's smile shows his yellow, uneven teeth. "Navigating the Crossroads is like playing chess, son. It's all about strategy."

It sure is. "Hasaki made me an interesting offer. He said if I gave him right of first challenge, he'd kill anyone I named."

The smile disappears. "Did you take him up on this offer?"

"It was tempting, but I made him a counter offer. I'll give him what he wants if he'll tell me who paid the Shinobi to kill my father."

"Did he accept that offer?"

"Nope, but it still stands."

His eyes harden. "This is how you thank us for taking you in?"

There it is. What I've been expecting since I walked in. "Are you saying it's payback time?"

His knuckles whiten around his staff. "You know you owe me nothing. To suggest otherwise is to question my honor."

On the Crossroads, children are exempt from debt for the kind of help he gave me when I ran away. Maybe if I was a nobody named Lennon, that would be true, but I'm the Dragon

Son and I don't get a kid-pass, even if the Beggar Chief insists, on his fucking honor, that I do.

"You're the one who brought it up."

The Chief stands. "I demand, on your honor, that you follow the protocol of the Crossroads. The Beggar Clan has the right of first challenge."

I stand, too. "I'm sorry. I really am. I respect you and the clan, and I'll always be grateful, but I don't care about anything, not even my life, as long as I get revenge." I've said too much. Damn it. Damn him and his kindness. "I gotta go."

"Lennon," John Walks Long calls after me. "Your parents wouldn't want that for you."

Talk about stating the obvious. Of course, they wouldn't. What parent would? It doesn't matter. It's all I've got. Shoulders stiff, I hurry through the Abode. No one tries stopping me, not even Jeremiah, who's standing at the front entrance. He tries giving me one of those *mano-a-mano* challenge stares, which is supposed to make him look manly, I guess, but since he's twice my age, makes him look creepy. I roll my eyes, like, give me a break, and keep walking.

I feel deflated as I drive away, like I did when I left the Sparrows'. The Beggar Abode was another place that I'd somehow thought of as home. That was stupid of me. Home is something I lost when my parents died and all my longing, and even revenge, will never bring that back.

Penny

I'm no sooner through the front door when Bridie leaps off the couch and down my throat. She's already dressed in flash duds, strappy heels, and curls brushed and sprayed into reluctant submission. I need to face the fact that the rebellious Bridie of London is truly gone. The thought makes my arms cross and my chin tilt upward.

"Do you know who just called?" she demands. I grit my teeth against an impulse to go back out the door. My shrug makes her voice snap. "John Walks Long. He said you and Lennon were bold as brass, and took no heed to his warning."

"That's not true. He talked to us and we listened and were totally respectful. I mean, we didn't agree with him, but…"

"No buts, madam. You don't give lip to the Beggar Chief. I knew this would happen, the moment you set off with Lennon."

"We didn't do anything wrong. Jeremiah waylaid us and ordered us to go see the Chief. Which we did because we have nothing to hide." Except we do. My stomach twists at the thought. I don't like shamming my family.

"And where did Jeremiah find you?"

"At Lennon's art studio." Her surprised blink gives me the mettle to go on. "He's got a studio at this artists' collective in an old warehouse on one of the piers. You should see this place, Mum, it's brilliant. All these cool people were there working on these cool projects. Anyway, Lennon took me there and showed me what he's working on."

Her eyes go misty with nostalgia. "Remember when Matthew used to take us to the shows at the Tate Modern?"

"And Gerry wouldn't go because he said it was a load of bollocks?"

A wisp of a smile plays around her lips before fading. "And Jeremiah knew to find you both there."

"Well, yeah." Everyone knows the Beggar Clan has spies standing or crouching, despised and disregarded, in doorways and alleys throughout the city. That network is part of what makes them so powerful. Information is their business, and their eyes and ears are everywhere. "Anyway, we talked to John Walks Long and told him we're just friends."

"And he believed that?"

I ignore that.

"Christy called right after John Walks Long. I was afraid it was about you, but it wasn't. He's been challenged."

My snotty attitude slides off me. "Again?"

She gives a tense nod. "The fight's in an hour and he wants us there, so hurry up and get ready."

I go to my room and yank off Funky Chunky Jumper. Strowler bouts are formal affairs and require rum riggings. I paw through the dresses on my rack and pull out a blue floral dress, which I pull on over orange tights and spangly ballet flats. Then I go to the bathroom and layer on more makeup. A Strowler woman's primary goal is to be ultra-feminine in all things. I love wearing pretty clothes, but I hate doing it because I'm supposed to appear pleasing and submissive.

My phone buzzes and I snatch it off my desk. My heart lifts at the sight of Lennon's name.

Hi. You get home ok?

Yeah. How about you?

I'm back at my studio.

How'd it go with the Chief.

He was up in my shit about the challenge.

It's ok. It's what I expected.

Don't let him get to you.

I won't.

There's a rap on my door and Bridie calls out, "We're leaving. Move your arse."

Gotta go. Uncle Christy's been challenged and we have to be there for the bout.

Wow. Ok. Challenged by who?

Dunno. Tell you later.

I shove the phone in my pocket and head out.

Kai is waiting with our mother by the front door. He's wearing his best jeans, a purple button-down shirt, and has a short, colorful scarf tied around his neck. That last bit always lifts my heart. American Strowlers don't wear neck scarves, but the European ones do. When Uncle Christy became Upright Man, he brought that tradition with him.

Bridie decides to drive through the city rather than risk rush hour traffic on the freeway, but we run into a construction zone that has traffic backed up for blocks. San Francisco is starting to recover from the technology bust and businesses are returning to the abandoned buildings. It's good news for Bleaters, I suppose, but barely impacts those on the Cross-roads. We have our own economy and aren't as attached to property and possessions. Territory is a whole other matter and the cause of most challenges.

The Nest is located on an industrial scrap of land beside the bay, on the southeastern border of the city. Strowlers always end up where the Bleaters don't want to be, which is fine. We take their hay and spin gold. Our car bumps along a gravel road until we reach the barbed-wire boundaries, where the guard waves us through the gate. Inside, rows of caravans are neatly parked under the lush trees of the Nest's mini-forest. Usually, on a nice evening like this, the common area would be packed with children running around the playground while their fathers cooked at the grills and their mothers prepared the rest of the meal on the picnic tables, but it's deserted. Everyone must already be at the challenge.

Uncle Christy and his family live in the only permanent dwelling on the lot, a prefab house once occupied by the former Upright Man, Kingfisher. The fighting dogs and their chain link prison are gone, replaced by a white picket fence and a vegetable garden. Under a tree sits a small stool set with a glass of milk and a bowl of fruit, Joanne's daily offering to the *Aos Sí*, the fairies, on behalf of the Nest.

Nests and caravans are the domain of Strowler women. Their upkeep, along with taking care of all the family needs, is a woman's Glory Road. A proper Strowler man leaves the caravan to support the family with manual labor, wagered fist fights and shamming Bleaters. Only the Upright Man stays in the Nest to ward off interlopers and protect his wife, the

Mother Bird, who rules the Nest. Kingfisher didn't have a Mother Bird and treated his mort, Doreen, like a trull. Someone like him would never have been allowed to be an Upright Man in Ireland or the U.K. Here in the U.S., though, things are less organized. Nests are few and far apart and men like Kingfisher can bollock up traditions without being challenged. That is, until someone like Uncle Christy comes along.

Bridie opens the front door without knocking. "Hello? Anyone here?"

Aunt Joanne leans out the kitchen. She's wearing a ruffled apron over a bright yellow spandex dress that dimples and folds around the parts of her body stretched and rolled from bearing six children. "You're late. Fight's started."

Bridie waves a hand. "I've had my fill of bouts. I'll stay and help you."

"That's fine, but Christy wants your kinchin there."

Kai and I are out the door and take off running through the Nest. Most of the lights are off in the caravans we pass and everything is eerily quiet until we reach the end of the road. After Christy became Upright Man, he installed a prefabricated warehouse and turned it into a gym. Light and noise pour out the large open door and jack up my nerves. The two men guarding the entrance step aside without a word. We hurry past the punching bags and weight equipment to the end of the building where a boxing ring is surrounded by bleachers. All the seats are taken and the noise is deafening, as if every man, woman and child in the Nest is present and shouting at the top of their lungs. We squirm past the men crowding the aisles until we reach the corner of the ring where Uncle Christy's youngest son is manning the bell.

"All right, Brendan," I shout.

"All right, Penny," he shouts back. He and Kai exchange nods.

"What's up?"

Brendan keeps his eye on his phone's timer as he answers, "The usual. That fat bugger claims he's Kingfisher's kin. Says he wants revenge. Da's handing him his arse in a bucket."

In the ring, two middle-aged men stripped down to their wife beaters circle each other, heads unprotected and knuckles bare. The harsh fluorescent lights gleam off Uncle Christy's thick torso, muscular arms and bright red hair. His freckled face shows no emotion and his breath is even. His opponent outweighs him by at least four stone and has turned an unhealthy color as he heaves and wheezes, trying to land a punch. Blood drips from a cut above his left eye. Christy weaves past a powerful but inexpert roundhouse and steps in to deliver an uppercut to the chin. The opponent staggers back. He starts to raise his guard, but Christy is on top of him, delivering a cross punch that connects with the other man's jaw. Blood spews from the opponent's mouth and flies in an arc before splattering onto the ring and anyone standing too close. His eyes roll up as he crumbles to the floor

The crowd roars and chants Christy's name as the referee calls the fight. Brendan, Kai and I jump up and down, pumping our fists in the air.

Christy walks the ropes, his arms lifted in the air. Then he signals for silence. "Anyone else?" Laughter circles the bleachers. He glances down at the men tending to the fat bugger. "Tell Kingfisher that Christy Sparrow says he's welcome back for a rematch anytime."

He goes to his corner and sits. Jack, his oldest son, fans him with a towel while Casey, the middle son, squirts water in his mouth, which Christy spits into a bucket at first before taking a drink. I wince at the sight of his torn and bloody hands, and my joy fades. This is his third fight in as many weeks. He's not going to be able to keep this up for much longer.

What's happening to Christy is called softening. Kingfisher has been sending lesser men to challenge Christy, wearing him out and giving his hands no time to heal. Bare-knuckle boxing is the Strowlers' martial art and all challenges are fought without protection. Strowlers don't follow the Crossroads rule that the challenged man can name the date of the fight. Challenges are fought the same day and fighters are allowed no more than one week between bouts. Kingfisher is waiting until Christy's hands are too damaged for further brawls, and then he'll challenge him.

The only defense Christy has would be to send his own allies to challenge Kingfisher. The problem is, we don't know where Kingfisher is and Christy hasn't been Upright Man long enough to establish the strong connections necessary to do his dirty work. Kingfisher must've promised his allies the moon to get them to challenge and be beaten by my uncle. What I don't get is why now. I have a sick feeling in my gut that it has something to do with my family.

Brendan leans over to me and gestures with his chin. "That longshanks, Conor, is o'er yonder."

Uh-oh. I scan the bleachers, past a large flock of Egrets, until I spot the Herons. Tallest among them is the Likely Lad. He's sucking down a bottle of beer while his kin laugh and shout among themselves. I roll my eyes. "So?"

"Seems his mum is Mother Bird of that big Heron Nest in Seattle," says Brendan.

"She can be the bloody Queen of England for all I care."

"You best care, lass. The Herons are a powerful family. Da needs their support against Kingfisher."

My stomach drops.

Christy's whistle pierces the air. "Oi, Conor, lad, you walk my niece back to ours, yeah?"

It's not an exaggeration to say literally everyone, even the fat bugger Christy pounded, watches while Conor clambers down from the bleachers and joins me next to the ring. I don't like that he towers over me. Gerry and Matthew were both under six feet tall, which I suppose dictates my taste in men.

Kai smirks before saying, "Let's go."

I'm an adult, four years older than him, but according to Strowler ways, a courting couple requires an escort related to the girl. Except Conor and I are not courting and this is a load of shite. It takes all my will not to stalk out of the building. I walk between the two boys, biting my tongue the whole way back to Uncle Christy's. They talk about the fight. For once, I'm grateful that, being female, I'm not required to take an interest.

Inside the house, I dive into the kitchen. "Uncle Christy won."

"Of course, he did," says my aunt. "Did Conor come with?"

"He's out there with Kai." Before she can tell me to go out and entertain him, I turn to Shannon, Jack's wife, who's balancing a fussy baby on one hip while attempting to toss the salad. "I'll do that. Looks like Lily's hungry."

"She's always hungry." Shannon sighs as she sits and pops out a boob. I can't help but shiver over the sight of her dark red, chafed, protruding nipple. She's about two years older than me.

Aunt Joanne and Bridie start talking about what goes into a proper spotted dick. That's not what it sounds like. It's a pudding made with dried currants and suet pastry dough. A lot of Americans can't stomach beef lard in a pudding, so Joanne decided to use butter instead, for Conor's sake. I gag.

Boisterous voices announce the rest of the family returns. Danielle, Casey's heavily pregnant wife, waddles into the kitchen along with Fiona, Christy and Joanne's twelve-year-old daughter. She has her father's red hair and her mother's blue eyes, and looks to be a beauty, though for now she's gangly and trips over her own feet. She and I are given beer and peanuts to hand out to the men, who are sprawled in the living room, as is their due. The huge TV is showing sport,

Manchester United versus Watford FC. As far as I know it only shows sport, since I've never seen anything else on it.

Kai scowls when I hand him a ginger beer. If Bridie wasn't here, Christy would allow him to drink the real thing. A Strowler boy is considered a man by age fourteen, though he must be established, with his own trailer and means of support, before he can marry. I place Uncle Christy's beer on the coffee table and chew back a wince at the blood seeping through his bandaged knuckles. Fiona hands Conor his drink. His wink turns her bright red and she scurries back to the kitchen.

My stomach drops again. Would Uncle Christy be offering up Fiona if she were a couple of years older? Sixteen is the ideal marriageable age for Strowler girls, but younger isn't unheard of. Lucky for her, twelve is too young by any standard. The families could arrange something for later, but they can't force Fiona to honor that arrangement once she turns sixteen. Can they?

At the dinner table, men and women sit separately, though I'm placed in the middle, next to Conor. I make a point of turning a shoulder to him and giving all my attention to Danielle, who's seated beside me, probably as an example for me to aspire to. I ask every gory detail about her pregnancy, including morning sickness. I don't have much appetite anyway. It seems to do the trick, because Conor makes no effort to join in our conversation.

Since he's sitting so close, I can't help but notice what he says and does. He seems a decent sort, not overloud or macho. He's easy on the eyes and I might find him attractive if my heart wasn't already spoken for.

Spoken for by a boy who can't return my love.

If Lennon didn't exist, would I be more tempted by Conor? A single person, man or woman, is an oddity among Strowlers, even those on the Wayward Way. Which means I'll be the odd one, because I can't imagine marrying anyone, not even Lennon.

The evening ends like Friday dinners usually do, Bridie begging off because we must return to our building to close the launderette. Who knew that place would be such a blessing? I exchange polite fare-thee-wells with Conor, wishing him luck on the road.

Christy escorts us to our car. He juts his chin at me. "The girl could do worse than Conor."

"He seems a nice lad," says Bridie in that vague, polite way that sets my teeth on edge.

"You know, it's different here in the States. The groom's family pays the dowry. They're eager for a good match and she'll fetch a fine price."

I moo.

They stop talking and stare at me. Kai snorts.

"I'm not a prize heifer and I'm not marrying him or any Likely Lad you throw my way so you might as well stop now."

I climb in the front seat and slam the door shut. Kai slides into the back and we fist bump.

Christy and Bridie move away from the car and keep talking in voices too low for us to hear, though their hand gestures become animated from time-to-time. My chest tightens as I remember moving into the Sparrow Nest near Dublin right after Gerry and Matthew died. Christy bought us a caravan and Joanne stocked it with kitchenware, bedding, and towels. They made sure we had enough to eat, and wouldn't let anyone talk shit when we were present. If Kingfisher manages to soften Christy up enough to win, their family will be forced to return to Ireland, disgraced.

They talk long enough that Kai settles back and starts playing a game on his phone. I double-check, but I've got no messages from Lennon. I think and re-think about sending one before turning my phone off.

Bridie climbs in the car and we drive away in silence. Once we're out of the Nest, I chew down my pride to say, "I'm sorry I was rude to Uncle Christy."

"You should say that to him."

"I know, I will, but I feel like he's bartering my body to save his skin."

"He doesn't expect you to court Conor or anyone you're not taken with." She heaves a sigh. "Christy told me why Kingfisher chose this time to soften him. It's because of Lennon. Kingfisher thinks Lennon is weak and wants to be the Upright Man so he can challenge him when he becomes the Dragon Son."

"What?" Kai drawls out.

"No way," I say. "He's gotta be at least thirty years older than Lennon."

"Mikey-Boy will be his proxy."

Kai and I exchange double takes before we burst out laughing.

Bridie's brow knits tight. "What's so funny?"

"Lennon will hand Mikey-Boy his arse in a basket. It'd almost be worth it to see that."

Our mother shakes her head. "You don't get it. Kingfisher doesn't care if Mikey-Boy beats Lennon or not. He's using the challenge as a rallying cry to get other Strowlers on his side. The worst sort of Strowlers, ones like him who beat their women and don't accept the authority of a Mother Bird, and use their father's surnames instead of their mother's. They want to turn the Nests in a male domain, where they'll run thieves' dens and dog fighting pits. Those are the men he's using to soften Christy. That's why Christy needs allies."

My mouth goes dry. The weight of my people's future suddenly rests on my shoulders and I sag into my seat. Shite.

Bridie pats my knee. "It's not for you to worry about. I told

Christy he should've told me sooner. Now I can help him figure something out."

She's plenty devious, but figuring something out isn't her strong point. Am I being selfish not to offer myself up? Give up Lennon and my quest for answers so I can save the day by marrying a boy I don't know. My gut twists. I can't do it. I won't. So, what am I going to do? I stare out the window, looking for answers that won't come.

Lennon

I gnaw my lip and bulge my eyes while applying blue spray paint over a white base. A yawn will make the stencil go crooked and I don't want that, not when it's a silhouette of my mom. It's part of a set of stencils depicting my parents facing each other with a broken heart between them, along with the Chinese characters for 'murdered.'

I've thrown up this piece all over the city, not just China-town. Right now, I'm in North Beach, using a bare patch of the back-alley wall of the Purple Turtle Youth Hostel. They encourage outlaw artwork to add to their cred as a party hostel, so I know it won't be scrubbed off any time soon. Not until Tony finds it.

I hadn't planned to go out tonight, but being with Penny made me think about my parents. Think about having a broken heart. I don't want anything bad to happen to her because of me. That's part of it, but I'm also thinking about myself, my broken heart. I want to be around her as long as I can, but it will never be enough, not when all we can have is friendship. Is it so wrong for me to want to have a girlfriend like a normal person? I know it's not the way things work in our clans, but why not? Why is everything written in stone for mindless obedience? And is that why my parents died, because they wouldn't mindlessly obey?

I finish the portrait and stare at it for a few moments. Usually, after I'm done, I feel elated or angry, or both. Tonight, I feel… I dunno. Depressed? I want to have with Penny the kind of relationship my parents had. At the same time, I wish they hadn't died and I wasn't having to deal with all this shit, but then I wouldn't have met her. Or maybe I would have. Kai's grandparents still would've sent him to the *kongsi*, which means there's a good chance I would've eventually met her. There's no way my parents would've approved of any kind of relationship with her, which means I would've had to defy them. I wish they were alive so they could be furious with me for loving Penny. How messed up is that?

I grab the black spray paint so I can finish with my tag when there's a soft thud behind me. I grit my teeth and don't turn around. I consider "accidentally" spraying Tony, except he'll be dressed in black so the impact will be lost. I start shaking the can, speaking over the rattle of the metal ball within. "What?"

"Why are you being such a dick?"

Not Tony. The metal ball rolls to a halt as I spin around to face Aaron. He's wearing jeans and a plaid shirt, and has his hands shoved in his pockets. The anger drains out of me, despite his scowl. "What are you doing here?"

"Tony sent me."

"Lucky you. Tell him to do his own dirty work."

"Yeah, sure, I'll go do that." He doesn't budge.

Okay, then. I turn around and spray my tag. Despite my pretense, I listen over the hiss of the can for any movement. When I finish, I turn and he's still standing there. In the dim light, his eyes are coal black against the pale anger of his face. "What?"

"So that's what you think, that we're murderers?"

I suck in my breath. "I don't think you're a murderer."

"But my mom and my dad, right? And Tony?"

I shake my head slowly. "Not Tony."

"You don't think this," his hands yank from his pockets to gesture at my artwork, "hurts us, too?"

I suck in a hard breath. I hadn't thought about that. All I've thought about is my hurt because I'm a selfish little shit. I lick my lips. "What does Tony want?"

"To talk like a person, except you won't do that. That's why I gotta do his 'dirty work'." He uses air quotes. "You know, I waited two fucking years for you to talk to me about everything, to tell me your side, but you won't do that. You're supposed to be my Big Brother, but you treat me like shit."

My mouth goes dry. Before my parents died, Aaron was my Little Brother. I helped him with his homework, gave him my comic books when I was done, and roughhoused some to toughen him up. He made me smile and feel important. I don't want to admit I miss that, miss him, but I do. I hate myself for the years I cut him off, him and Tony.

"So, do you want me to go someplace with you or something?"

His eyes become cautious. "Yeah. Home."

Talk about a loaded word. I want to shout, 'Not my home!', but all that would do is hurt Aaron even more and nothing I've done has ever been about that. I need to make it up to him so he'll know that. Beside, I've got to go back to the *kongsi* eventually and now is a good time. This late at night, no one will be around except the guards.

"Okay. I gotta pack my gear first."

Aaron's eyes widen before fluttering with startled blinks. "You're coming?"

"Yup." I carefully slide the stencils into a plastic sleeve

before placing them and the spray cans into my backpack. "My Vespa's around the corner."

He trots alongside me. "You giving me a lift?"

"Yeah."

"Cool."

I almost smile.

When we get to my bike, he looks like an eager puppy, until I hold out Auntie Cat's blue helmet. "Kidding? No fuckin' way I'm wearing that."

And there's no fucking way I'm getting pulled over by the cops with spray paint in my backpack. Rather than argue, I put on the offending helmet. I hand Aaron my helmet and, funny thing, it doesn't fit because, like Auntie Cat, he's got a big head. We switch without further hassle, aside from my smirk.

Aaron clambers on behind me and I realize how much bigger he's grown. Give him another couple of years and he'll be taller than both me and Tony. He yelps as we swerve out of the alley and down a steep slope to get to Broadway. We always had fun together, even when he annoyed me. I could never get seriously mad at him because it would be like kicking a puppy.

North Beach and Chinatown rub up against each other and even overlap for several blocks. Without traffic, it's a quick trip through the back streets to Joseph Alley. My stomach tightens as I steer toward the brightly-lit building at the end, the one with green awnings that look like bamboo. I always thought it looked kind of cheesy until I realized that was the point. Above the gated entrance, there's a white marble plaque inlaid with gold characters saying, 'Two Dragon Clan Benevolent Society'. We took the hide-in-plain-sight route, looking like any other Chinatown family association.

We.

See, there I go, already thinking of myself as part of the clan and I can't, not if I want to remain Lennon who walks the

Wayward Way. That's why Tony sent Aaron to fetch me, to get me thinking about family ties, which is also why he wants me to come here, the place that was once my home. Even as I lock up the helmets, I'm tempted to hop back on my Vespa and say 'fuck you' to Tony and his manipulative bullshit.

A strong breeze makes the maze of fire escapes above us rattle like brittle bones. As we approach the stairway, Aaron looks all around before leaning in to whisper, "Tony thinks you're dating Penny."

There's a ton of security equipment surrounding the building, video and audio, and there's a good chance Tony is watching us, so I say in a loud voice, "Dating? Kidding? We're running away to Vegas tomorrow for quickie wedding."

Aaron stops in his tracks, his mouth popping open before his face scrunches up again. "You can't get married. You're only seventeen."

I smack my forehead. "Damn. That's right. And I already paid an Elvis impersonator to perform the ceremony." I grin at his scowl and saunter up the stairs.

A swoosh of fabric cuts through the air. I spin around, leaping from the stairs to the pavement, holding out my palm.

Too late. The Shinobi's already backed up against the opposite wall, his arm wrapped around Aaron's neck in a stranglehold.

He's dressed full-on Ninja from head to toe with his mouth and nose covered so only his eyes are revealed, cold and remorseless as a snake strangling its prey. He has an unhurried expression, content to let his victim panic. Aaron's pupils dilate, making his eyes appear black in a face drained of all color. Snake Eyes twists his other hand so light gleams off the stiletto blade he's holding at Aaron's neck.

Is this how Dad died?

All the oxygen sucks out of me. I want to blink, but in that single blink, Aaron could die. I take a deep breath, trying to focus my *chi*, but the flow stalls as panic jumps all over my nerves. I need to focus so I can aim the Dragon Shout precisely or else it will hit Aaron as well, but my heart is pounding too hard.

I flinch as the door behind me slams open and the guards coming pouring out. Red dots appear all over the Shinobi's body, like puncture wounds, but they can't fire their weapons without risking Aaron's life.

Tony's voice comes from their midst, cold as the Shinobi's eyes. "What do you want?"

Snake Eyes' words slap my face. "Dragon Son, accept Hasaki's challenge or I kill this boy."

Big Brother replies, "You kill him, we kill you, Hasaki, and the entire Kasumi Clan."

Shit is all too real. I gotta stop this now. My swallow barely moistens my cardboard mouth. "I accept Hasaki's challenge."

Snake Eyes shoves Aaron, sending him sprawling across the pavement. The red dots go haywire trying to re-aim. Then he disappears, Ninja-like. Go figure.

A surge of *chi* floods my system with no means of release. I lean against the wall and slide down it so I don't tip over. Son of a bitch. Now what? It doesn't matter. Aaron is safe. He's crouching in the middle of the street, blinking like a startled cat. I almost laugh and bite my lip so I don't because it will come out sounding like hysteria.

Tony reaches out a hand to help Aaron to his feet. Then he tips back Aaron's head to examine his neck. "Did he cut you? Or puncture your flesh at all?"

Little Brother manages a manly shrug. "I'm okay."

Tony grabs his shoulders and enunciates each word. "They use poison. Did he touch your skin with the knife?"

Aaron's face loses what color little it had regained. He whispers, "No."

"This isn't a game. Go to your room."

"But..."

Big Brother's glare cuts him sharper than a Shinobi blade. Aaron turns and sees me on the ground, and his anger scrunches into concern. He comes toward me, so I shake my head to show I'm okay. Then I nod toward the door so he'll go inside. Frustration pinches his face and he stomps up the stairs past me.

Tony comes over to me and holds out his hand. I don't need his help. Not really, even though my legs are still kind of shaky. The idea of Aaron being poisoned makes me sick to my stomach. I take Tony's hand. His grip is how I remember it, firm and steady.

As he lifts me to my feet, I say, "Go easy on him, okay? He's just a kid."

"Did I go easy on you?"

That makes me snort. We both know the answer to that.

"I can't go easy on him, especially during such a time, when we're constantly under threat of attack."

My stomach tightens another notch. I didn't tell Tony about my run in with Hasaki and now it's biting me in the ass in the worst possible way. "We need to talk."

"Inside." He places his hand on my shoulder. My first instinct is to shrug him off, but I can't. I don't want to. I keep treating Tony like he's the asshole, but in this case, I'm the one who fucked up. "Are you all right, Little Brother?"

I suck in my breath and he blinks, making me realize he said the title by habit and not to throw me off. I should refuse to answer to it, but I can't. Losing Tony has been like cutting off one of my hands. The dull ache has grown sharper since I returned. There's only one way to make it go away. "I'm fine. Big Brother."

For a moment, his coal-like eyes go vulnerable, as if he, too, is trying to decide if he can trust those words. I know he wants to talk about it. I do, too. If I'm honest, what I want to do is spill my guts and tell him everything, but I'm not even close to that yet.

Neither is he. He gives that single manly nod of his and we head up the stairs. The guards part before us like water. My stomach ties in knots as we step inside. It's not the home-coming I expected. I hadn't planned to return until my eighteenth birthday and then only to face down the clan and my challengers, and tell them all to go to hell. If I survived, I'd planned to march back out without seeing any other part of the building. Now, Tony and I are heading through the quiet lobby and passing the elevator to take the stairs, like we always did.

With each step, I go over each of my actions in the alley. What the fuck was wrong with me? Aaron could've died because I couldn't get my shit together. I'd thought about Dad and panicked. I've got to learn not to let my emotions overcome me; to be a machine, like Tony and Snake Eyes.

We reach the second floor and head down a dimly lit hallway illuminated by the flicker of candles set on a narrow, rosewood altar table. The sickly stench of rose incense attacks my nose and I want to pinch my nostrils shut, except my hands are clenched into fists. I know who the altar is for and I look away as we pass so I don't see Auntie Sylvia's diamond hard eyes and the unhappy twist of her lips, because if I do, I might knock over the altar and punch a hole in her portrait, and that would be bad.

We pass the bedrooms and the kitchen, and head for the living room, which is weird. As far as I know, no one ever went in that living room or sat on Auntie Sylvia's beige and gold furniture set. The only living things I ever saw in there were huge bouquets of fresh roses, which were replaced weekly. As far as I know, she bought them for herself, which explains a lot. She lived to kill beautiful things.

We walk through the door and I halt because the plush gold carpet has been yanked out to reveal a polished hardwood floor. The fancy furniture is gone, replaced by a blue cloth sectional sofa with a colorful assortment of pillows, a huge, bright orange ottoman, and a plain wood coffee table piled with magazines and random stuff. Across from that is a padded, brown leather armchair that doesn't match anything else in the room. No sign of roses, but living, leafy green plants thrive in every corner.

I didn't realize how tense my shoulders were until they ease back into place as I enter the room. May is sitting on the couch. She reaches for the remote and turns off the TV that replaced the huge, gold framed mirror that had hung on the wall. Then she presses a hand over her mouth to cover a yawn.

I halt again, but this time because I feel awkward. This shouldn't be the first time I'm meeting Tony's wife. I should've been there for his wedding. I hope she doesn't think my absence had anything to do with her. I remember seeing her at the compound and thinking she must be what Fourth Elder looked like as a young woman, plain, warm-eyed, but sort of aloof, like a doctor would have to be. Then she smiles and all her inner goodness lights up her face, and she's beautiful.

"Hello, Paul," she says as she stands, her long, silky hair swishing about her shoulders. "Can I call you Second Brother?"

I don't answer because my mouth has dropped open. She's wearing sweatpants and a T-shirt that displays an obvious baby-bump.

Tony is going to be a dad.

Lennon

It's funny how a single moment can change everything.

Tony's going to be a dad. I'm going to be an uncle. I need to man-up or something. No kid deserves to be born in all this hostility.

My mouth is dry and I have to swallow before I can respond, "Second Brother's fine, um, Big Sister. Um." I clear my throat. "So, how long?"

She and Tony look at each other as if puzzled. Then she smiles and pats her bump. "Oh. Five months."

"Do you know if it's a boy or a girl?"

"It's a girl," Tony says as he steps over to put his arm around his wife. "We're going to name her Chloe Michelle."

My knees buckle and I sink into the armchair. How am I supposed to feel, that the granddaughter of my mother's murderer will share her name? I want to yell at Tony, but I also want to hug him, and I can't make myself do either.

His face loses all its happy warm fuzziness and becomes etched in stone. "You prefer we don't?"

I don't know what to say. Tony loved my mom and wants to honor her memory, but could it also be a way of denying his mother's guilt? Speaking of that bitch, why isn't he using her name instead? Chloe Sylvia doesn't sound as good as Chloe Michelle, but I think it's more than that. Back before everything went to shit, Tony spent most of his time at our place, him and Aaron both, eating Mom's home-cooked meals, asking her for advice, and hanging out in a living room where they could spread out and relax. I always felt bad for them, having to go home to a perfectionist mom always coiled in a tight ball of unspoken bitterness. Tony knows she was jealous of Mom. Subconsciously, he must know the truth, but now isn't the time for me to mess with that.

I clear my throat. "No. I mean, yeah. It's great. First girl in our family since Auntie Cat."

A spark of warmth returns to his eyes. "Boy or girl doesn't matter, as long as it's a healthy baby."

Look at him being all modern. What the hell? Maybe May is making a difference in our family.

Our family. It's become that again. I can't seek vengeance without worrying about the consequences. I need to live and make the world and our clan a safer place for Chloe Michelle.

Tony's arm slides away from his wife as he reaches into his pocket for his buzzing phone. He answers and listens for a few moments before saying, "Don't engage unless they attack first." He looks at me. "Two Shinobi have appeared on the roof. One is Hasaki, head of the Kasumi Clan."

Air whistles through my teeth. "Yeah, about him."

Tony's face goes glacial. "John Walks Long told me about Hasaki's offer to you. He was concerned you might accept. I assured him that you wouldn't."

"Except I just did." I look down and whisper, "Fuck." The Chief is going to be so pissed at me.

"No. He threatened the life of a child to coerce you, an underaged boy. There's no honor in that and we aren't obliged to honor your acceptance of his challenge."

I breath out a sigh of relief. "Why does Hasaki have such a hard-on to challenge me? I mean, I don't remember any Shinobi ever challenging my dad."

"The Kasumi are the smallest and least among the Shinobi clans. That's why they left Japan, to make their name here. If Hasaki beats you, the Kasumi will become preeminent among the Shinobi. I doubt he cares about the rest of the Crossroads."

Tony stares at his phone for a few moments before motioning me over to look at the screen. It shows live video of our roof with two figures dressed in black, surrounded by our guards. Then Tony swipes the timeline so the video goes back several minutes. Two figures land on the roof. One goes directly to the video camera and pulls down her face mask, revealing a teen girl with fierce eyes and a no-nonsense slash of a mouth. She speaks English with a slight accent. "Hasaki-sama of the Kasumi Clan wants to apologize to the Dragon Son."

Apologize. Yeah, right. "I'm gonna blast his fucking apology into the sky."

I start to barge out, but Tony grabs my arm. He doesn't yank, but grips me with enough strength to remind me he's got weight, muscle and years of experience over me. "Think. Why would Hasaki send one of his warriors to attack two underage boys?" Because he's an asshole probably isn't the right answer. "He's baiting you. Getting under your skin."

Well, shit. I scratch the back of my neck. "What do we do? Ignore him?"

"No, we can't. He made sure of that by forcing you to accept his challenge. We go up there. I do all the talking. We're not honoring that challenge, no matter what he says. He's going to try to goad you, but you must remain silent. Can you do that?"

Even though I want to shout that I can speak for myself, I know he's right, so I nod, once, in the manly way.

Tony turns to May and from the concentration on their faces, I can tell they're using the Silent Speech. For a moment, they look so much like Mom and Dad, I turn away.

I try not thinking about that as we head upstairs, but my footsteps slow to a stop when we reach the third floor. I grip the banister as if it's the only thing holding me up. I stare down the hall at the photos hanging on the walls, reminders of a past frozen in time: my school portraits; pictures of family vacations, the three of us, Dad, Mom and me; a large sepia-toned photo of my parents on their wedding day. Each image brings a flash of pain with its particular memory. Each doorway leads to the life I once had, a life that crumbled to ashes in a handful of minutes. I want to open those doors and peer in on that life, but I'm afraid of two things. One, when I open the doors, nothing will have changed, everything will have been left as it was two years ago, waiting for me to return. The other, that everything has been cleared away and the rooms are empty. I don't know which would be worse and I don't want to find out.

"Are you all right?" asks Tony.

I haven't been all right since my parents died.

"Maybe I should talk to Hasaki by myself."

"No. He said he wants to apologize to the Dragon Son. That's..." I take a hard breath. "That's me."

We climb the final set of stairs and enter the roof through a tall, narrow shack. The terra cotta tiles feel familiar under my feet. Nothing has changed. The same wrought iron railing barricades the ledge. Weathered lawn chairs are stacked in the far corner next to the covered grill.

I blink.

It's daylight and my father and Uncle George are standing at the grill, arguing over whether or not the ribs are done. Mom tosses a bowl of cold sesame noodles while Auntie Cat sets out platters of her hand-rolled sushi and Tony slices a watermelon with martial preci-

sion. Aaron and I duck around them to set the table. Auntie Sylvia isn't here. She claims she doesn't like eating outside, but we all know it's because she doesn't like being anywhere near my mother.

I blink again and it's cold and dark. Guards in each corner train their weapons on two figures, who stand amid the fog as if they'd brought it with them. The girl steps forward and bows.

We don't bow back.

"Hasaki-sama apologizes for the actions of Aikuchi-san. Aikuchi-san was insulted by the Dragon Son's disrespectful manners when he refused to accept Hasaki-sama's challenge and wanted to teach him a lesson. That was no excuse for the attack and he assures you that Aikuchi-san will be punished."

Yeah, sure he will. I swallow my gall and let Big Brother speak for us.

Tony fixes his glare on Hasaki. "Tell Aikuchi he's a dead man. No one points a knife at my brother's throat and lives. The Dragon Son's acceptance of the challenge was forced and therefore invalid."

"Hasaki-sama agrees. He wishes to make things right." She squares her shoulders and looks me in the eye. "I am Fukiya. I am seventeen years old. I challenge you, Dragon Son. If you win, Hasaki-sama will kill anyone you name. If you lose, Hasaki-sama will claim the right of first challenge."

So, that's their game. On the Crossroads, challenges between underage opponents are common. It's a way for kids to test their skills. I can't back down without looking like a coward, but as the challenged party, I can name a date after we both turn eighteen. I open my mouth before closing it again since Tony told me not to talk.

He sucks in his breath and I'm sure he's thinking of some diplomatic way to say fuck off.

Fukiya leaps at me. I swerve in time to avoid being kicked in the chest. I duck again as she swings her fist at my face and I almost eat her sucker punch. As I snap my head back, her leg lifts for another kick and I do a backflip to avoid her. I land in a crouch and do a spinning side kick as she comes at me again. I make contact and sweep her off her feet. She lands hard and rolls away before jumping up.

I raise my guard, my hands curled into tiger claws, which are best for grappling, so I can grab hold of her and get her in a chokehold. As we circle each other, someone starts shouting something about the challenge. It's Hasaki and… Wait. What? That motherfucker can speak English?

I glance at him for a split second, and as I do, Fukiya is on top of me. I jump back and block her punch, but her knee connects with my stomach, hard. I fall and manage to roll, but I can't get right back up. She's knocked the wind out of me.

I brace myself, expecting her to jump on top of me and go for the chokehold. I know I can hold her off long enough to get enough air and turn things around. Moments pass. The shouting has stopped and the roof is filled with fog-muffled silence. I sit up and find Tony crouched beside me.

"Are you okay?" he asks with that carved-in-stone expression.

"Yeah, I'm fine. What the hell was that?"

"Hasaki claims you accepted Fukiya's challenge."

My mouth hangs open. I blink before I can speak. "What? No. When?"

"You accepted by fighting back."

I jump to my feet. "Of course I fought back. She attacked me."

"Exactly. He lured us onto the roof for that purpose and distracted you by shouting at me so she would win."

"Win? What win? She took off."

"You fell. You did not immediately get up. Hasaki claimed victory and left."

I'm so mad, I'm trembling. I want to punch the air. I

should've blasted that bitch off that roof and that crazy motherfucker with her. "I didn't lose. I wasn't unconscious. I could still fight."

Tony grabs my arm and hauls me away like an angry child. I want to swing at him and would if I wasn't so angry at myself. Inside, I yank away and kick the wall.

"You're acting like a child. Stop."

"I didn't lose. He's going to tell the whole Crossroads I'm a loser."

"It's only a loss if you take it as such. Being perceived as weak at this point isn't bad from a tactical standpoint. Your opponents will see you as an easy target and be overconfident."

"Yeah, but Hasaki is going to claim that I lost so he gets the right of first challenge."

Tony is silent long enough for my stomach to start twisting into knots. A look of resignation comes to his face. "This is my fault. I shouldn't have allowed you to come on the roof. I should have realized it was another trap. I need to consult with the Elders before making any further decisions."

That means Head Elder will find out what happened and he'll be the one to decide who has the right of first challenge. Bile clogs my throat and my voice comes out like a croak, "But John Walks Long. What about him?"

"I'll call him and explain. Show him the video footage." A cold gleam comes to his eyes. "The best strategy may be to let the Beggars and the Kasumi fight this out among themselves."

I close my eyes and grit my teeth. No. I must lose to John Walks Long or my plan doesn't work. There will be immediate consequences for the Two Dragon Clan if the Beggar Clan takes over the Crossroads. A Kasumi takeover will barely be a blip, especially if what Tony said earlier is true.

God. Damn it. I stalk away without thinking, heading down the hall until I find myself face-to-face with a photo of

Dad. He would be so ashamed. I wait until Tony catches up and whisper, "I lost, didn't I?"

He sighs. "It wasn't a fair fight, but she got in a good enough hit to drop you, so yes, you did. This will make you either stronger or weaker, your choice."

I've got a headful of bees and can't make any choices, except, "I gotta go."

"You can stay in our guest room." The way he says it, like it would mean everything to him.

"No." I suck in a tight breath. "Not tonight. I'm sorry." For everything, but I can't say it.

He nods. I nod back. I manage not to run down the stairs, but I still feel like, once again, I'm fleeing from him and everything.

Penny

1:05 a.m.

Hi. Can't sleep. Are you awake?

3:27 A.M.

Hey, are you still awake?

Yeah. Hi. What's up?

Just got home. Long night. What happened at the Nest? Did your uncle win?

Yeah, he won.

Where was the fight? In the playground?

Lol. No. You should see the Nest since Christy took over. Totally different. He built a gym with a boxing ring.

Sweet. Sounds like a cool guy.

I'm kind of mad at him.

Really, why?

He's trying to marry me off to this guy named Conor.

wtf?

I'm not going to marry some random dude.

Why does your uncle want you to marry this guy?

His family. I mean, Conor's family. They're powerful here in the States. Christy needs allies against Kingfisher.

That asshole's back?

His allies keep challenging Christy, wearing him out so he'll be easy prey for Kingfisher.

That's bad but not your problem. I mean, not so you'd gotta marry some random dude to bail him out.

ikr? I'm pissed, but I also feel bad because it's the one way I can help my uncle. Ugh! Why is family so complicated?

Yeah. I saw Tony tonight. I met his wife. They're gonna have a kid.

You didn't know?

You knew?

Well, yeah. Aaron told us. Your aunt didn't tell you?

When Tony got married, I told her I didn't want to know and not to tell me anything about him ever again. So she's letting news like this bite me in the ass.

Did something happen?

What do you mean? Did you hear something?

No. What would I hear? I just thought it's strange you saw Tony and his wife.

Maybe strange isn't the right word?

It's worse than strange. I fucked up.

Fucked up how?

Long story, but I wound up going to the kongsi. Outside, I get jumped by a Shinobi who pulls a knife on Aaron and forces me to accept Hasaki's challenge.

omg!

So Tony says don't worry that doesn't count. Then Hasaki and some ninja chick show up on the roof. We go up there and she attacks me and I fight back but Hasaki distracts me and she hits me hard enough to drop me.

Hasaki claims I lost and now the Kasumi Clan have the right of first challenge.

What? That's bullshit!

That's what I said. I'm so pissed!

> Wow. But no way any of that counts. They
> tricked you.

I don't know. You know what it's like on the
Crossroads.

I wish I didn't feel like such a loser.

> Hasaki's the loser if he has to trick you like
> that.

Yeah but I'm the loser who fell for his tricks.

> What are you going to do?

I don't know. Tony's gotta talk to the Elders
and to John Walks Long.

> Uh-oh.

Yeah. Tomorrow's going to suck. I mean,
today.

Can I see you today?

> Sure. When?

Don't know yet. Later. After all the shit has hit
the fan.

> Are you going to see Tony again?

Yeah.

> So you two are talking now?

I guess.

> What a shitty night. Both of us got stuck with
> impossible stuff.

Does Bridie want you to marry that guy?

No. She said she'd think of something, which is never a good thing.

Want to run away?

Totally.

Where do you want to go?

Svalbard.

What? Why there?

It's one of the few places on Earth where there's no Crossroads.

Yeah, there's that.

Isn't it covered in snow all the time?

Yeah but there are polar bears so who cares.

I'm in. Let's go.

Packing my bags now.

I'll check the flights to Svalbard.

9:28 A.M.

I fell asleep. Did you check those flights? 😄

1:19 P.M.

Hey, can you talk? I just heard.

2:25 P.M.

Checking in again. Message me when you can.

3:17 P.M.

Sorry. Tony's been here since this morning.

Are you all right?

Did your uncle tell you?

He said John Walks Long and Hasaki will fight tonight to determine who has the right to first challenge the Dragon Son. They need to fight on neutral ground and agreed to use the Nest's boxing ring.

But he didn't say why they're fighting and I didn't tell him anything.

Tony showed the video footage to the clan elders. They decided the Beggars and the Kasumi must fight it out between themselves. If either clan refuses, the right of first challenge will go to another clan.

Have you heard from the Chief?

No. Tony talked to him and showed him the videos. He said the Chief doesn't blame me, but I don't know. I feel like shit. I hate being so powerless.

Will you be at the challenge? I mean, since you're underage.

Yeah. They're waiving that rule so I can attend since I'm… I don't know. The prize? Will you be there?

Yeah. We won't be able to talk or anything, but I'll be there for you.

Thanks.

I gotta do something to stop this. How can the Chief fight Hasaki? He's an old man.

Don't underestimate John Walks Long.

I'm not, but Hasaki's a crazy mofo who fights dirty.

Uncle Christy won't stand for that. If Hasaki fights dirty, he'll call the fight in the Chief's favor.

That's good, I guess. I need to think. I gotta go. I'll see you there.

Lennon don't let that Hasaki guy get to you.

I know. I won't. Bye.

Bye.

Lennon

Riding in the back of Auntie Cat's car, I can barely breathe, so I crack open the window. Dust kicks up from the gravel road leading to the Nest, so I close it again and deal with the pressure on my chest that has nothing to do with lack of air.

The twenty-year rule of the Crossroads is so stupid. How can a match-up between a thirty-eight-year-old and a fifty-eight-year-old be a fair fight? Maybe back in the day, people didn't live that long, so it was never an issue. I don't know.

This is my fault. Fukiya got the drop on me because I got distracted. I know better. I've been trained better. It's not even my training. It's my mind. I was all wound up in personal bullshit when I should have shut that shit down and focused on my opponent. Tony's right; I need to learn from this, but I'm so damn mad at myself, it's hard to think straight. I wish I could talk to Dad about all this. I glance at Uncle Roy in the front passenger seat. I didn't say much to him or Auntie Cat when I got home. This isn't a man-to-man kind of talk. I need to talk to someone who has the entire responsibility of a clan resting on their shoulders. Someone like John Walks Long. He'd get it.

Tony sits beside me like a robot, his mechanical brain

undoubtedly calculating all possible threats and outcomes. It's unfair that he looks so much like Dad and is the last person I can confide in.

My stomach twists as we drive past the Nest's front gate and head down the road toward the new gym. It's bigger than I thought, the size of a warehouse, with exterior floodlights and a parking lot full of cars. Two burly guys dressed in jeans and tight black T-shirts stand outside the front entrance like bouncers at a club. A third man, dressed in trousers, a dress shirt, and a colorful neck scarf, motions for us to pull up to him. Auntie Cat slows the car to a stop and unrolls her window.

The man peers in. He's medium height with broad shoulders, a pale, freckled face and hair as red as Bridie's. "Welcome to the Nest." Irish accent. "Clan?"

"Two Dragon Clan," says my aunt.

The man motions for her to pull into an empty parking spot in front of the building and waits until we all get out. "I'm Jack Finch. My da is the Upright Man. I'll take you to him."

He leads us to a side door and down a long corridor lit with fluorescent lights that blink intermittently. Through the walls, I can hear the shuffling of many feet and muffled roar of voices. As we reach the end, he calls out to an older, balder, thicker version of himself standing at the door. "Oy, Da, himself and his kin are here."

The older man looks us over before asking, "Which of you is Tony Lau?"

Tony steps forward.

"We meet at last. I'm Christy Sparrow, Upright Man of this Nest." He holds out his hand.

Tony shakes it. "Walk in peace."

"Walk in peace. I heard tell the Two Dragon Clan were once wanderers."

"We're Hakka. Our people migrated across China for centuries. We're settled now."

"We're not." The Upright Man lifts his chin. "Strowlers don't settle. Even after all other traveling people have settled, we'll be on the road. That's who we are and proud of it." His gaze sweeps past me to Roy. "And you are?"

"Roy Cheung of the Two Dragon Clan in Seattle. Walk in peace."

"Walk in peace. You're far from home." He raises his voice as if welcoming a response, but Uncle Roy doesn't take the bait.

Auntie Cat steps forward and holds out her hand. "Catherine Lau, the Dragon Son's aunt and legal guardian. Walk in peace."

"Walk in peace, fair lady." He takes her hand and bows his head.

She blinks and her mouth indents, like, 'what the hell?'

He nods toward me. "As his guardian, I assume you know the kind of challenge this is. Could get bloody. Could get lethal. That's why no children are allowed. I'm making an exception in his case, but you have the final say."

All humor drains from her face and she gives a sober nod.

Christy Sparrow looks me up and down and back again. "So, this is who all the fuss is about. Dragon Son, eh?" He clamps my shoulder with his meaty paw. "Mind if I have a word with the lad?"

Tony takes a step toward us. "What about?"

"You're not thick. You know full well."

Yeah, consequences. My family isn't interested in protecting me from them and they back off while Christy take me aside. His voice goes low. "I had a word with Jeremiah Walks Long. He told me you're that same Lennon who saved my sister and her kinchin from that gobshite, Kingfisher. I owe you a debt of gratitude."

Jeremiah ratted me out. Bastard. I manage not to roll my eyes as I stammer, "Um, they helped me, too, so there's no debt."

"I'll be the judge of that." He moves a little closer and seems to expand in girth. "You fancy my niece?"

I want to shove him away, but that won't help things. So, I shrug like it's not a thing. "We're friends, that's all."

"Friends, eh? You know, her mother fancied one of you lot."

Really? He's going there? "You mean Chinese or Two Dragon Clan?"

"I mean both and that's all well and good if Penny plans to live on the Wayward Way with an ordinary bloke, but not you. You're the Dragon Son and you can't take up with her the way Matthew took up with Bridie. I won't have you taking her honor or breaking her heart, so keep your distance, yeah?" He tugs at the short, bright scarf around his neck.

Is that a threat? I'm sick of being backed into a corner, but I can't be disrespectful to Penny's uncle, even though I want to shout that Penny's honor belongs to her and no one can take it away. He wouldn't get it anyway. What would Tony say? Something ancient, but without commitment, like, "I appreciate your concern. I'd never do anything to harm Penny's honor or my own."

"No, you won't, because if you do, me and my boys will be paying you a visit." He grinds a fist into his palm.

Should I act intimidated, like a guy talking to a dad before taking the daughter to the prom? I swallow and say, "Yes, sir."

He pats my shoulder. "Good lad."

Not really, but oh well.

We follow Christy Sparrow through the door and between the bleachers to the boxing ring. Every row is full and everyone quiets down as he escorts us around the ring to an empty bench in the front row. It looks like representatives of every local Crossroads clan is here. Most are dressed in nondescript street clothes, except the Strowlers, who look like they're going to a party. When I lived among them, I learned it's important that they look "flash", that is, well-dressed and prosperous, no matter how little money they might have.

I feel the eyes of the entire room following me, judging me, gauging how easy it will be to beat me since Fukiya was able to knock me on my ass. My face heats and a buzzing sound fills my ears. Emotion. It's the enemy in situations like this. Why do I always react first instead of practicing what I've been trained to do? I take a deep breath and channel the *chi* flowing through my body to cool my thoughts and even my temper. The heat and buzz fade and I manage to mimic the nondescript expressions of my relatives.

We sit and after a few moments, murmurs swell through the crowd until the noise level rises to normal again. Tony sits beside me like he's got a metal rod in his back, looking all high and mighty as befits the head of the Crossroads in San Francisco. A gray-haired couple come over and are introduced to me as the heads of the Tiger Saber Clan. They shake hands with Tony and start to talk. Cat and Roy exchange mouth to ear conversation. I feel awkward, like a freak in a glass cage. I don't know where to look except my lap. Then my phone buzzes. I take it out of my pocket and check the screen.

I'm right across from you.

I look up, through the ropes of the ring, and see Penny sitting on the front bench of the Strowlers bleacher, between Bridie and some tall, skinny guy. My heart lifts at the sight of her and it's damn hard not to smile.

My phone buzzes again.

> That's your aunt? Her head doesn't look
> so big.

And I smile. More like a grin.

> Yeah, that's Auntie Cat. Her head is big,
> trust me.

> Who's the dude next to her? Uncle Roy?

> Yeah, that's him.

> He's the handsome one. I'm surprised she let
> him go the first time.

> She's not letting him go this time, that's for
> sure.

> Smart woman. She must be, with all the
> brains in her big head.

> Who are you sitting with? Your cousin?

> No. It's that guy, Conor 😶

Emotion returns in a hot and cold rush. I don't want Penny sitting next to that douche. I want to run over, shove him out of his seat, sit beside her, and challenge anyone who doesn't think I have the right. Like that would do either of us any good. That doesn't stop me from hating how he's looking at her, like she's already his. He says something to her and I take a deep breath so I don't lose my shit. Penny answers without taking her eyes off her phone.

> What a nob. He asked who I'm messaging 😶

> What'd you say?

> "Your mom"

I snicker and am about to type back when my aunt says, "Who are you texting?"

My shoulders hunch and I turn off the screen so she can't see what we're saying. "Penny."

Her eyebrows raise. "Is she here?"

"Yeah. See, across the ring, the girl in the pink and yellow dress."

Auntie Cat cranes her neck. Worry lines crinkle her face. Her chest rises and falls before she turns to me again. "She's pretty."

"Yeah, I guess. She's cool."

I thought that would cool my aunt's jets, but I'm wrong. She turns to Uncle Roy and they start whispering like crazy. My phone buzzes again.

Was your aunt checking me out?

> Yeah. btw, your uncle knows about us, I mean, that I'm the kid who helped you out two years ago.

I know! Jeremiah grassed. What a berk.

> Your uncle told me to stay away from you.

He said the same thing to me. Ignore him. He can't make us do anything outside the Nest.

"Are you still texting that girl?" asks Auntie Cat.

"Her name is Penny and, yeah, I am."

She gives me a look. "Tell her we'd like to meet her."

We. That's an interesting slip of the tongue. I peek at Uncle Roy, but I don't think he noticed. "Okay."

> My aunt and soon-to-be uncle want to meet you.

> Really? Ok. Is that good or bad?

I'm about to answer when I hear the chatter from a passing guard's walkie-talkie. "The Beggar Chief is prepping now. Thirty minutes to show-time."

I stand without thought. I start to move and Tony grabs my arm. "Where are you going?"

"Bathroom." I say this without thinking.

He motions to the guard and says something. I roll my eyes. That's right. Show the Crossroads that the Dragon Son is still a kid and needs an escort to go potty. An escort who's a Strowler and probably know more about the building than the location of the john. I'm tempted to thank Tony, but suck it in. As the guard leads me away from the bleachers, I ask, "Where's the Beggar Clan?"

He nods toward a door on the other side of the far bleachers. "Over there and the Kasumi Clan are on the other side. We've got plenty of guards between them. No mixing it up until the big fight."

Apparently, Strowlers don't know much about the skills of the Shinobi or the Two Dragon Clan. I drop a little behind him and, using Swift Steps, I sprint for the far door, hugging the wall so I don't run into anyone. Two Beggars guard the entrance, but I'm inside before they notice I got past them. John Walks Long, dressed in a boxing robe, is standing in a corner throwing shadow punches.

Jeremiah draws a gun from his waist and points it at me. Other Beggars surround me, their bodies tensed and ready for attack. I'm not worried about fighting them off, but I don't want to waste time.

Before I can speak, Jeremiah lowers his weapon and raises one hand. He glares at me. "Lennon. What the fuck?"

"Language." His father shakes his shaggy head. "Young people. You don't know how to express yourselves without profanity." He stands before me and sighs. "You want to see me?"

It's weird because I feel like crying and I don't know why. Wait. Yeah, I do. This is all my fault. I shrug to contain the emotion. "Yeah. Hi."

A smile splits his furry lips. "Hi."

"Can I hang out?"

Jeremiah makes a protest noise, but his father cuts him off. "Of course."

He motions me to follow him to the corner. Then he hands me a round, padded punch shield. I hold it midsection and brace myself. He raises his fists, already taped for the fight, and starts landing some powerful blows. Seriously strong, enough to jar my teeth, though I manage not to shift my feet. Maybe he's testing my abilities, trying to figure out how Fukiya got the drop on me.

Between punches, I say, "I'm sorry."

The Chief grunts with a blow before answering, "I don't blame you, son."

"I blame me."

He sighs and lowers his fists. "You and your cousin are young and inexperienced. Hasaki took advantage of that."

"Everyone wants to take advantage of that. Everyone thinks I'm their bitch."

"Then they underestimate you and that's to your advantage."

"Tony said something like that. I wish you and I could fight. I mean, for the challenge thing. I wouldn't mind losing to you." I bite my lip as soon as the words come out. Damn it. Somehow, he always makes me drop my guard. I probably would lose to him.

He drops a fatherly hand on my shoulder and squeezes. "I wouldn't mind losing to you, either."

"Yeah, you would. That's what I don't get. Why are you doing this?"

The hand drops away and he folds his arms. "The Beggar Clan always has the right of first challenge. I won't allow the Kasumi Clan to rob us of that honor."

"Yeah, but if you'd refused to fight Hasaki, he'd be hosed, too. Wouldn't that be worth it?"

"He needs to answer for his treachery."

"But what if he beats you?"

A quick smirk disappears into the Chief's beard.

My phone buzzes. Penny. Or Auntie Cat. I don't have much time, so I can't be subtle. "Did Hasaki offer to kill someone for you, win or lose?"

He motions for me to raise the punching shield again. "What's between us doesn't involve you. Stay out of it."

I position the shield and brace for impact. "Yeah, but you can't trust him. Look at what he did to me."

He raises his fist and before he lands a blow, says, "I don't trust any of my rivals."

The impact jolts me. I get it. He doesn't trust me, but it still hurts. "So, being honorable and being trustworthy aren't the same thing?"

"Not on the Crossroads, son."

"Can't I be both?"

"Are you?"

He knows I'm not. I know I'm not. No one in my family trusts me and I don't trust them, but we're all supposed to be honorable. It sucks. "What's the point?"

"What do you mean?"

"Okay, so let's say Jeremiah kicks my ass and the Beggar Clan becomes the biggest, baddest clan on the Crossroads. So, what? Does it make Jeremiah a better person than me? Does it make the Beggar Clan better than the Two Dragon Clan? Not really, right? So, what's the point?"

"The point?" He stops for a moment to ponder before punching the bag to emphasize each word. "Glory, position, power, territory. The stronger your clan, the stronger your people. The Two Dragon Clan's prosperity is the envy of the Crossroads. All others covet your clan's position."

"I guess I get that. Thing is, I don't care. I haven't cared since my parents died."

The Beggar Chief lowers his guard and sighs. Then he puts his hands on my shoulders and give me a shake. "You don't want to be Dragon Son, do you?"

"No. I wish Tony was the Dragon Son. He'd be way better at it than me." I bite my lip. Shit. I've never said that aloud and barely let myself think it, but John Walks Long squeezes it out of me with almost no effort. Maybe he already knew because he and Dad had talked about it. Did Dad feel the same, wish Tony was next Dragon Son? My stomach squeezes at the thought.

"Choose your destiny, son. Let no one else choose it for you." He pats my shoulders and takes back the punch shield. "I must prepare myself. Come see me later this week and we'll talk again."

It's weird, but I feel a little better. "Okay, thanks. Good luck."

He winks before turning away to hand the shield to Jeremiah. As I leave the room, I look over my shoulder and see him landing powerful punches on his son. He might be old, but he's super strong. All he has to do is land one good punch and Hasaki will drop like a rock. So, why is my stomach twisting in knots?

Outside, the pissed-off guard I slipped away from escorts me back to my relatives.

Tony's icy glare would freeze water. "I would make you leave now if the combatants hadn't requested your presence. If you act up again, you will leave, regardless."

I try not to smirk because he sounds like such an old man. I should probably say I'm sorry, but I'm not. Across the ring, Penny is looking at me with questioning eyes. My phone buzzes. I reach into my pocket, but my aunt grabs my arm. Her glare is sharp rather than cold.

"No more nonsense from you. You sit and be respectful. You and your friend can talk later."

"K. Sorry." And I am, because I don't like giving her grief. I look at Penny and shrug.

She shrugs back.

Christy Sparrow climbs into the ring and snaps his fingers at a red-headed guy, who yanks the cord of the ringside bell. My stomach ties up in knots again. The crowd murmurs to a silence. He speaks in a booming voice, his accent even thicker than his sister's lilt.

"Welcome and well met to all ye who tread the Crossroads. Tonight, the Strowlers have been given the great honor of hosting the challenge between the leaders of the Beggar Clan and Kasumi Clan. The bell will ring only once and combat will begin. It will not end until one man is left standing. The challenge can only be won by physical superiority. No weapons. None of your supernatural-type powers are allowed and if used, the opponent will automatically be named the winner. Death blows are likewise forbidden. However, if fatality results due to fair combat, both sides agree not to hold the other responsible." He turns and gestures to one corner. "In the blue corner, Hasaki of the Kasumi Clan."

The Shinobi enter the ring to a smattering of applause. Being assassins and spies doesn't make you super popular. Hasaki is accompanied by that girl, Fukiya, and a couple of other Shinobi, all dressed in their black ninja gear, completely covered except their faces. I'm tempted to out Fukiya for being under age, but looking at her features in the bright light, I see the resemblance, so strong I wonder why I didn't see it on the rooftop. She's Hasaki's daughter and does what she's told, the way I did before my parents died.

Christy Sparrow gestures to the opposite corner. "In the red corner, John Walks Long of the Beggar Clan."

Almost everyone, but especially the Strowlers, stomp, clap and whistle as the Chief and his entourage enter the ring. My relatives applaud politely, but I'm clapping and whistling along with the rest. Jeremiah helps his father remove his robe. John Walks Long wears long, shiny boxing shorts, padded grappling gloves and laced-up boxing shoes. His powerfully muscled physique seems to glow in the stark lights. I want to feel confident, but his chest full of gray hair makes me want to shout at him to stop.

"Gentlemen." Christy gestures both sides to the center of the ring.

Hasaki bows, as does the Beggar Chief. Then Jeremiah steps forward and hands Hasaki a piece of paper. My stomach drops. Hasaki did offer to kill someone and John Walks Long accepted. I don't know why I'm surprised. He didn't deny it when we talked. I slump down, shaking my head before glaring up at him. Someone's going to die, all because he wants to be head of the Crossroad. All that talk of honor… I snort. He was bullshitting me, like everyone else.

Hasaki's face turns to stone. He shows the paper to Fukiya, who looks it over. Her eyes widen, making her look like a startled child.

Oh shit. No way.

The Beggar Clan's business is knowledge, so they must know who Fukiya's father is, but John Walks Long can't order her death, not when she's only seventeen. Who else would make Hasaki hesitate like this?

"Something wrong?" asks Christy.

John Walks Long's face goes smug, like the cat who swallowed the canary. "Hasaki-san and I had to agree on certain terms before our match."

The contract crumples in Hasaki's fist. Fukiya shakes her head frantically, but he says, "The Kasumi Tribe forfeits this match."

My jaw drops. A stunned silence fills the hall, quickly followed by low murmurs that become increasingly louder. Some of the Strowlers start booing.

Christy holds up his hands. "Quiet." He turns to Hasaki. "You understand that by forfeiting, John Walks Long is declared the winner of this match?"

Hasaki nods once.

"I need a vocal response, please."

"Yes."

Holy shit. No wonder John Walks Long seemed so confident in the dressing room. I need to know whose name is on that contract.

The murmuring and boos start up again. Christy motions the redhead to ring the bell. Then he takes hold of the Beggar Chief's wrist. He motions for Hasaki to join them. Fukiya seems to almost reach for her father. Though her face is blank, I can see the mixture of pain and anger. I know that feeling. If I didn't hate her, I'd feel sorry for her.

Hasaki shows no emotion when he goes to the center of the ring. Christy takes hold of his wrist. "This fight is declared over. The winner, by forfeit, is John Walks Long of the Beggar Clan." He raises the Chief's arm.

The crowd stands and lets loose with an equal mixture of cheers and catcalls. I remain seated. Okay, so Hasaki double-crossed me and now John Walks Long double-crossed him. What next? Do I cheat both of them? Is that how the game of the Crossroads is played?

Christy releases both men. Jeremiah comes over to shake

his father's hand and the Chief pulls him into a bear hug. Hasaki's fingers seems to pinch at something in the hem of his sleeve. He makes a flicking motion at Jeremiah's back. The Chief sees this and spins his son around. I jump to my feet, mouth open, about to shout, when John Walks Long drops to his knees, his hand on his shoulder as if trying to swat away something. Then he grabs his throat as if he's choking. Red foam spews from his mouth before he collapses, face down.

In an instant, the Shinobi disappear.

Everyone around me is exploding in some way or another, running, shouting, gesturing or all three. The noise is so deafening it seems like silence. I'm trapped in this weird bubble where I can't feel anything. My phone buzzes. Penny? I look across the ring, but I can't see her because of all the people milling around. I look at the screen. It's a text from an unknown number and it contains the photo of a contract. I zoom in so I can read it.

I, Hasaki, Leader of the Kasumi Tribe of the Shinobi, agree to the following terms as set by John Walks Long, Chief of the Beggar Clan of San Francisco. If John Walks Long wins our challenge, I agree to kill without hesitation-

There's a line where someone, probably John Walks Long, had written, "*Nobody.*"

If I win, I agree to kill without hesitation-

There's another line, in which John Walks Long had written, "*Fukiya, daughter of Hasaki, Leader of the Kasumi Tribe of the Shinobi, on her eighteenth birthday.*"

The bubble bursts. The noise hurts my ears. I climb to the top of the bleachers so I can see down into the ring. Jeremiah is on his knees, holding something pinched between his fingers. It must be a poison-tipped needle, easily smuggled past the guards. A woman kneels beside the Chief, frantically digging through a medical bag. John Walks Long lays unmoving, blood gurgling from his mouth.

I can't let this happen again. I won't. I was powerless when my parents died, but not anymore. I jump off the back of the bleachers and make my way to the nearest exit. Outside, the air is cold and damp. I suck it in to clear my head before sprinting toward the bay.

Lennon

Memory leads me through the dark tangle of trees to the inlet where Penny and I used to hang out. Pebbles and debris crunch beneath my feet as I head into the cold, still water of the bay. I don't stop until I'm knee deep. Dragons are beings of air and water. I need to channel both if I'm going to have any success.

I take deep breath and send the flow of my *chi* up and out, across the bay, across the Pacific Ocean, in a widening, thinning net.

Ancestor, I need you. Where are you?

Jade Dragon could be anywhere. He could be weaving through the fjords of Norway, circling Mount Kilimanjaro, or swooping across the Gobi Desert. My reach can only go so far. I feel other things. A cruise ship heading for Alaska. A pod of whales on their way to the Channel Islands. Then. Something. Deep, cold, ancient, reptilian resting on the ocean floor. Not Jade Dragon. Another dragon?

Master Stoorworm?

A whip of its tail jolts me and I fall backwards into the icy water. Cursing, I pull myself up, shaking my head against a wave of dizziness. I'm soaking wet, shivering cold, and have expended too much *chi*, but I can't give up.

Ancestor.

Hatchling.

I freeze. Jade Dragon. Distant. So distant, his voice is like a soft echo.

I need your help. He doesn't answer. I suck in more air and reach out to him. *My friend is dying. Can you heal him?*

I gave the healing power of my pearl to my descendants.

He means the Yin Pearl. When Jade Dragon died in his human form, he left behind four pearls, chipped off his own great pearl, that contain the essence of his power. Two of those pearls, the Yang Pearl and the Summoning Pearl, are still with the clan, but the Yin Pearl and the Wisdom Pearl were lost more than 150 years ago, during the Taiping Rebellion.

But the Yin Pearl is gone. I mean, it's missing.

Find it.

I can't. I'm not the one who lost it.

Impatience rolls off him and nearly pushes me back into the water.

Be the one who finds it.

How?

He drifts toward the wreckage of an airplane on the ocean floor.

Do you know where it is?

He's gone.

I slog back to shore and drop onto a smooth boulder. It still retains some heat from the sun, but not enough to warm me. I hug myself as the wind blows through my wet clothes. Fucking dragons, man. You can't understand them, so don't bother trying. I mean, Jade Dragon has helped me, but only when I've done something shiny to attract his attention. A dying friend isn't shiny. I can imagine him saying, *Humans die all the time.* Why should he care?

My phone buzzes. It's Penny, or Auntie Cat, or Tony. It doesn't matter. They all have news I don't want to hear. Instead of answering, I look again at Hasaki's text, studying every pixel of the contract. Maybe it's fake. Yeah, right. Hasaki had plenty of time to whip up a fake contract to justify a murder that keeps him from ever attaining his goal.

Footsteps crunch behind me. I don't need to turn to know it's Big Brother. "Is he dead?"

Tony stops beside me. "Yes. I'm sorry."

A tight pain spreads across my chest. Tears sting my eyes. I bite my lip and choke back a sob.

Tony sits beside me. "You're wet."

"Yeah."

"You were in the water?"

"I fell in." I'd rather he thinks I'm clumsy than crazy.

"Was someone here with you?"

"What?" I turn to face him, but he's not looking at me. He's staring at the bay. "No. Why?"

He shakes his head slowly. "I thought I sensed someone or something…" He sighs. "Or nothing."

I haven't told anyone about my conversations with Jade Dragon. Mostly because I don't want people to think I'm nuts, but also because our talks are private and I don't want anyone else butting in. Still, it's interesting that Tony sensed him. Our fathers were fraternal twins, and if Uncle George had been born first, Tony would be the one having the conversations, not me. Maybe I should tell him, but now isn't the time.

"You got a text after the Shinobi disappeared," he says.

I nod.

"I did, too. So did Christy Sparrow and the other clan leaders."

Of course they did. Hasaki's not stupid. "I don't understand. Why did John Walks Long do something so dangerous?"

"He had no choice. He knew he couldn't beat Hasaki at hand-to-hand combat, so he found Hasaki's weak spot, the same way Hasaki found yours when he threatened Aaron." He sighs. "The Crossroads is a ruthless place. John Walks Long forced Hasaki to choose between glory and the life of his daughter. For revenge, Hasaki wanted the Chief to suffer the loss of his son, though I doubt he cared which of them died."

I rub my temples. "Before the fight, I talked to John Walks Long and he told me how he's doing it for glory and honor and all that Crossroads stuff. Now, he's dead. And for what? Nothing. It's all so pointless."

"It's not pointless, Little Brother. It's who we are. Our way of life. In all the world, there are no other people like those who live on the Crossroads. We live beyond any laws but our own. We test our strength against each other until the strongest prevails. Look at the rest of the world. Everyone lives numb, watching TV, staring at their computers and phones. They get soft and lazy, and allow their governments to run their lives. Not us. Never us. We live on the knife's edge of the world. We hone our physical and mental abilities so we can compete and win."

I study Tony's profile as he speaks. He means every word. I wish I could say something grand like that and believe it, but I can't. "All that Glory Road stuff, it's a cover-up for people to look honorable while they scheme and kill for power." I swallow hard so the anger and disappointment I feel toward John Walks Long can't well up again.

"You're the youngest Dragon Son in more than a century—"

"I know," I interrupt. "That's why everyone wants a crack at me."

"And to get to you, they must go through the Beggar Clan. John Walks Long didn't give up because of Hasaki's trickery. I don't blame him that he used Hasaki's tricks against him."

Tears cloud my eyes. I suck in my breath, but they spill over anyway. I wipe cold hands across my hot face to smear them away. I played the poor orphan boy card so everyone would leave me alone while I made my plans. I didn't care about the rest of the Crossroads and my ignorance made things worse. "What am I going to do now?" I whisper aloud before I can stop myself.

"I can help you if you'll let me," Tony replies quietly.

Like a dog with a damn bone, that's Big Brother. I look at him, at his profile that is so exactly like Dad's, I almost start crying again. I clear my throat. "Remember that day in the Ancestral Hall when my dad made us sworn brothers?"

"Yes."

"We should try to honor that, huh?"

I brace myself for him to blame me for our falling out, but his gaze remains thoughtful and his voice quiet. "Yes."

And that's it. No plans, no demands. We sit and watch the waves lap at the shore.

Penny

"Upon the cross," I say to the bouncer.

He steps aside and I enter Mumpers Hall, a Crossroads pub located in the nether regions of Piccadilly Circus. My family's band, Wild Sky, would play here once a week when we weren't traveling. Panic thuds at my chest. I'm late for the show. I thread my way through the Sharpers crowding the bar. Jeremiah Walks Long and a pack of Beggars stand at the end, drinking and laughing. Why is he here? Shouldn't he be mourning his father? Is this John Walks Long's wake? It can't be. Not in London.

I make my way to the other end of the hall where the tables around the small stage are empty except for one. Bridie and Kai are sitting there, watching Gerry and Matthew onstage. Have they been waiting for me? I glance down at my clothes. I can't dance. Not with all this blood splattered on my dress. I sit at the table. My mother and brother ignore me. Are they mad because I'm late?

Gerry and Matthew put down their guitars and stand together at a single microphone. Gerry's eyes close, but Matthew's remain open as they sing their duet.

"We meet 'neath the sounding rafter,

And the walls around are bare;
As they shout back our peals of laughter
It seems that the dead are there.
Then stand to your glasses, steady!
We drink in our comrades' eyes:
One cup to the dead already —
Hurrah for the next that dies!"

Everything goes silent. I'm alone in the pub with Gerry. He's sitting on a stool with his arms folded and head tilted sideways, his eyes gazing on me with all the love he always poured into me.

The stage becomes a pool of water and he falls in. I run to the edge. The water is clear and I can see Gerry lying on the bottom, staring up at me with the same expression. I fall to the floor and reach in, first with one arm and then the whole upper half of my body, stretching toward him as if trying to embrace him. He reaches back, but he's so far away. My lungs burn as I try holding my breath a moment longer. I open my mouth and suck in water.

I wake up with a sharp gasp, gulping in air with deep breaths. My eyes are crusty and my pillow wet. Tears for Gerry? Tears for the Beggar Chief? I close my eyes and see John Walks Long gurgle and twitch as he drowns in his own blood.

I shudder and roll over before realizing I'm alone in bed. Where's Bridie? We spent the night at the Nest because she was so shaken up. I mean, literally shaking like a leaf at the end of a bare branch. I couldn't have driven us home, either. My innards were twisted in knots and my tears, once they started, wouldn't stop. John Walks Long had been a good friend to my family and my last words to him were snotty and defiant. I rub my aching brow. Would I have been so uppish if I'd known he'd die shortly thereafter? How many near and dear will I vex so I can champion Lennon?

Where did he go when he disappeared last night? I lost track of him in all the fury following the Chief's murder and didn't realize he was gone until I heard about it on a guard's walkie-talkie. I'm almost certain he went out to the point and I was going to follow him there, but Christy ordered Conor to escort me and Bridie back to the house. I would've snuck out the back door, but I couldn't leave my mother in the state she was in. My messages went unanswered until after two a.m. when he sent this:

> I can't talk. I'm a mess. Sorry.

Reading it again stirs my heart and I clutch the phone to my chest. Of course, I'll defend him. I'm not a gentle woman with a pleasing tongue. The Chief knew that. My family knows it and if they want to name me romp, so be it.

My eyes drift shut. How I long to sleep away what promises to be an awful day, but even for a romp, duty awaits. I roll out of bed and glance around for my clothes. The ever-tidy Bridie must've hung them in the closet. We're staying in the guest room, where the curtains and bedding are a-flight with a bird theme, as is every bit of bric-a-brac, including the wall clock. I think the small hand on the Yellow Warbler means it's 8 a.m. The smell of sausages penetrates the door. Bridie must've gotten up to help with breakfast.

I go to the kitchen where I find my aunt and her daughters-in-law, but no Bridie. My stomach twists at the sight of the stewed tomatoes and baked beans simmering on the stove. I don't want to eat. I want to go home.

"Your mum went out a while back," Auntie Joanne announces.

"What for?"

"Said she had to open the launderette."

My brow pinches with irritation. Why didn't she wake me so I could go home with her? "When did she leave?"

"About an hour ago."

The launderette opens at nine. She easily could've waited for me or even messaged Kai to open it before he left for school.

Joanne wipes her forearm across her sweaty brow. "I tried telling her to wait until after breakfast, but she was already out the door." She steps aside in an obvious invitation for me to join her.

This is what Strowler women do when someone dies: they cook. I wouldn't be surprised if Auntie Joanne sends one of her sons to the Beggar Abode with a casserole for Jeremiah. I tie on an apron. I don't want to go near the food, but I can at least wash the dishes.

The front door opens and Bridie trots in, carrying an oblong pink box. "Doughnuts," she announces brightly.

My mouth drops open. What the actual hell?

Joanne gives a gusty sigh. "Oh, Bridie. You are the limit."

"I got them so no one had to cook on such an awful morning."

"I'd ask if you're daft, but I've already got my answer. Did you sleep last night?"

Bridie's head shakes slowly. I look at her more closely and see the dark circles under her too bright eyes. She's not thinking straight, that's it. How can she? The Beggar Chief's death must have brought back awful memories, the same as for me.

Joanne sighs again. "Well, take those out to the table."

Bridie teeters a bit, like a small child who's been mildly scolded and not sure if she should cry. Then she turns on her heel and leaves the kitchen. I finish sudsing a cutting board and rinse it with clean water. Doughnuts. Even for her, that's strange. I can't think of a time when she bought doughnuts. The only time I ever ate them was at school.

We serve breakfast and the whole family sits at the table, except for two: Bridie and Christy. They're in the master bedroom. Joanne taps on the door, but no one comes out. The rest of us set about our meal. Despite my lack of appetite, I crave sugar, so I gnaw on a glazed doughnut and gag it down with coffee. When is she going to be done so we can go?

The door opens and they come out, their faces stone cold sober. They take their places at the table without another glance at each other. Did they tilt? What about? Is Christy pressuring her again to fob me off on Conor? Last night was a game changer and Kingfisher must smell the fresh blood.

Conversation is muted and mostly involves speculation about the contract between John Walks Long and Hasaki. Everyone stoutly defends the Chief, but there's an undercurrent of disappointment. Jack even murmurs he might've done the same if someone handed him a contract threatening his daughter. They don't know the whole truth, about how Hasaki hounded Lennon and forced the Chief's hand, and I can't tell them, not without revealing the depth of my "casual" friendship with Lennon.

Christy pushes his mostly full plate away and clears his throat. "I have an announcement. I talked to Kingfisher this morning. He won't be challenging me any longer."

My stomach twists around the doughnut. The coffee burns in my throat. There's a moment of silence as everyone but Bridie and Christy exchange confused glances.

"That's grand, Da, but why?" asks Jack.

"That's between him and me. I talked to him and he saw reason and said he'd back down. That's the end of it."

The hell it is. It all adds up now. Bridie goes home. Comes back with doughnuts of all things, and then has a private talk with Christy. She's done something, and if it's what I think, it's the worst possible thing.

Auntie Joanne manages a tentative smile. "Good news on a sad day. We can celebrate another time." She glances at Bridie and I know she's wondering what hand she had in this. Everyone must be wondering that. Everyone but me.

The Beggar Chief's death gives me enough excuse not to act overjoyed, especially since I can barely breathe through my tight chest. When, finally, we're in her car, I speak before she starts the ignition. "You gave it to him, didn't you?"

She grips the steering wheel. "We can't talk here. Wait until we get home."

Silence fills the car, so thick that Bridie has to crack a window. I can't look at her. How could she do that? We've already been robbed of our fathers. Why has she put her own life in peril?

Two years ago, Kingfisher had trapped us in this Nest and impoverished us so we had nowhere to go. He'd tried to rape Bridie, but Lennon stopped him by using *dim mak*, a martial art that freezes the body's pressure points. While Kingfisher was paralyzed, Bridie placed a blood curse on him. It involved mingling his blood and hers on a mirror. If the mirror breaks, Kingfisher will die within seven days, and she'll die within seven days after that. Blood curses are serious business and no one casts one lightly. It was enough to keep Kingfisher from harassing us. It didn't extend to Christy, until now. How could Uncle Christy be willing to sacrifice his sister's life so he can remain Upright Man? And how could Bridie offer him such a deal?

Kai is there when we get home, his eyes red from weeping. "John Walks Long is dead?"

"How did you find out?" asks Bridie gently.

He holds up his phone and his gaze becomes accusing. "Aaron. Why didn't you tell me when you got home? And why did you leave again?"

My arms fold. "Yeah, tell him where you were."

A sigh gusts out of her. "It's done, so no hue and cry from the pair of you."

He turns to me. "What's she talking about?"

"She gave Christy the mirror."

His eyes go wide and his mouth becomes an O. He gasps before saying, "No, Mum, you didn't. Did you?"

She nods once.

"Why?" My question is more like an accusation.

Her hands go to her hips. "Because he's my brother. The only one of my family who was decent to me after Gerry and Matthew died. I couldn't sleep last night, thinking about the Beggar Chief, lying there dead and wondering if Christy would be next. Kingfisher wasn't going to stop until he was broken. I couldn't let that happen to my brother." She turns to me. "What would you do if it was Kai?"

My mind blanks. What would I do? Alternatives flit across my mind, but none fit because I know what I'd do. The exact same thing. It doesn't help. I can't stand the thought of what could happen. "What's Uncle Christy going to do with the mirror?"

"We sent a message to Kingfisher. A video, actually, showing me giving the mirror to Christy and telling him to back down or else, if I die before him, no matter how it happens, accident or illness, Christy will break the mirror."

Kingfisher must've cacked his pants when he got that message. Actually, it's brilliant, but I can't like it. "Where's Christy going to keep the mirror?"

"Someplace safe, of course. It's better this way. I didn't like having it the house, always having to worry over what might happen to it."

"You think it's better at Christy's house?"

"I know he'll guard it with his life, same as Kai would if it were you." Her phone rings. She pulls it from her purse and frowns at the screen. "It's Jeremiah."

Penny

Bridie listens with a pensive expression before saying, "Of course, we'll be there. Jeremiah, I'm so very sorry." She hangs up. "Last night, someone put up a memorial to John Walks Long in Golden Gate Park. People have been gathering around it all morning, standing vigil and leaving tokens. He's going there this afternoon to say a few words and asked us to provide some music."

Our final performance for the Beggar Chief. A lump forms in my throat as tears sting my eyes. There's a Crossroads saying: *Death comes. Death takes. He is king of us all.* If that's true, he's a crap king, taking John Walks Long, but leaving the likes of Hasaki and Kingfisher.

After a quick rehearsal, we get changed, leaving off the rum riggings for shabby trim. We've seen Beggar funerals in London and they dress down, way down, their poorest duds, in a proud display of poverty. The memorial is in the Panhandle, a long, thin portion of the park that stretches for about eight blocks, and is close enough for us to walk. We follow a tree-lined path to a large, grassy area and maneuver our way through the motley crowd surrounding a park bench. Some are with the Beggar Clan, but most are the city's humblest, the ones who John Walks Long did his best to protect. Some are weeping. Others are outright wailing and holding each other. A few pass around bag-covered bottles and toast the Chief. When we reach the bench, my mouth drops open and I bump into Kai. He doesn't give me guff because he's staring wide-eyed, too.

A majestic portrait of John Walks Long rests atop a park bench, his leonine glory not diminished by the humble medium of spray paint on a rough, uneven plywood board. I recognize the style of the stencils, the use of multiple colors for texture and depth, and the splattered drops in the background. The lack of "LL" or any tag only confirms that it's the work of Lennon. Handwritten notes taped to the bench flutter in the breeze, as do the flames of the candles on the ground below. Some are tall votive candles of the Virgin of Guadalupe and the Sacred Heart of Jesus, but others are black hex candles printed with skulls and curses for vengeance. In the center lays a pile of five oranges, the top one pierced with three burnt down incense sticks.

This is what Lennon did with his grief last night. He channeled it into his art. I glance around, looking for a round pair of sunglasses shrouded by a hoodie. He should be here to see what affect his art has on the people who loved and admired the Beggar Chief.

A grizzled and red-eyed Jeremiah gives us a subdued greeting. Bridie murmurs her sympathy as she gives him a hug. He closes his eyes and holds on longer than necessary. I've seen how he looks at her when we've performed for the Beggar Clan and feel a reluctant appreciation for Uncle Christy, since his presence keeps Jeremiah from making a move on her.

Bridie steps away and pats his shoulder. "I thought we'd play a couple of Beatles songs. You know how your father liked them."

A smile ghosts across his face. "I always gave him a hard time about that. Said it would have been better for his image if he liked the Stones or Metallica."

"Or the Clash," adds Kai.

The smile becomes a brief grin. "He liked the Clash, but the Beatles are better today. Thanks, Bridie." He leans over and brushes her cheek with his lips.

My mouth puckers. I know I'm technically an adult, but why do adults suck so much? Jeremiah made major trouble for me and Lennon, so why does he think it's okay to kiss my mother? If his father hadn't just died, he'd be in for some major stink eye.

We stand beside the bench and take a few moments to tune our instruments. The crowd quiets somewhat as Bridie lifts the violin to her chin and plays the opening strain to "Blackbird." As she stops playing to sing, Kai joins in plucking the guitar while I strum along on the ukulele. At first, I have my eyes closed to concentrate above the noise of the people and the park. Then I open them as I hear the sniffles that become sobs. Ragged people huddle together, arms around each other as tears roll down their cheeks. My eyes burn and I close them again so I won't get distracted. I listen instead to Bridie sing of a blackbird with broken wings flying into the night.

Our ending is greeted with subdued applause. We look at each other as we sip our bottled water, wondering if we should stop because the crowd seems so overwhelmed. Then we feel it, that sense you get as a performer when the audience wants more even if they don't or can't say so. We share a nod and begin playing "In My Life." Bridie stays on violin, while Kai and I sing a duet as we play. It's easier this time to stay focused, maybe because I'm singing so I need to concentrate more.

We're about halfway through the song when I spot the round sunglasses and hoodie at the edge of the crowd. His head is bowed and I'm not sure it's him until he looks up. I can't see his eyes, but I know he's looking at me. My throat closes and I miss a verse as I swallow and lick my lips. He's wearing worn-out army fatigue pants, like he had during his time with the Beggar Clan. During that time he was my owl boy, the one I could dream with because he was as poor and broken as me. I look away from his solemn face so I can sing again of people and places from times gone by.

The crowd is less broken up by this song and some even join in on the chorus. We end to more enthusiastic applause.

Jeremiah steps forward. "The Beggar Clan offers poor thanks to the Sparrow Family for this gift of song. I offer my own thanks as only a grieving son can." He gestures to the portrait. "My father was a great man. An advocate for the poor and homeless. He knew that princes and principalities hate the poor and he made it his life's mission to defend and care for the impoverished. As his son, I give my oath here and now to follow in his footsteps, inadequate as I might be, and carry on his life's mission."

Already campaigning for Beggar Chief. I'm not sure why he's bothering. I assume he has the election in the bag, but what do I know of Beggar Clan politics? I place my ukulele into the case and edge away from my family to where Lennon is waiting.

"Hi," I say.

"Hi."

I nod toward the portrait. "I can't believe you did that in such a short time. It's brilliant."

He shrugs. "It's all I did since…" He clears his throat. "Since he died. I couldn't sleep or even eat, not until it was done. I put it here because I figured someone in the Beggar Clan would find it. I didn't expect," he gestures at the crowd, "this." He doesn't seem happy about the results. More like overwhelmed. He glances down at my case. "So, you play the ukulele?"

Obvious change in subject, but I'll run with it. "Everyone in the family played guitar, so I wanted to be a little different. I mean, I can play the guitar, but I'm not as good as the rest. The uke adds a different texture to the music. And it's easier to haul around."

Applause bursts out around us. Jeremiah has finished his speech. I expect he's going to chat up Bridie a bit more, but no. He walks through the crowd, making a beeline for me and Lennon. He lays his hand on Lennon's shoulder. "The Beggar Clan offers poor thanks to the Dragon Son for the gift of this portrait."

"I'm not the Dragon Son yet," Lennon mumbles. He ducks his head. "I wish I could do more."

Jeremiah leans in closer. "You've done enough."

Lennon pulls off his glasses to meet his hard gaze. "You think it's my fault?"

"My father took needless risks on your behalf. He never told me why and I don't give a shit anymore. But there are others I blame more, so I'm gonna let you walk away. I don't need your sympathy." He leans in closer. "It's still on."

"I know," Lennon answers without emotion. "I'll piss off."

"Do that." He pats Lennon's shoulder and turns away.

I glare after him, giving him the stink eye he deserves. He's not the man his father was. Not yet, at least. I doubt he ever will be, not with that attitude. I turn to Lennon. "Let's jam."

He looks surprised. "You coming with?"

"If you'd like."

"I do, it's just, I'm kinda the asshole of the hour."

"No, that's Hasaki. Has anyone caught up with him yet?"

He shakes his head. "He's probably in Japan by now. The Shinobi have these villages that no outsiders have access to."

"So the Beggar Clan can't get to him?"

"The American Beggars, no. The Japanese Beggars will be gunning for him."

That's no surprise. The Beggar Clan is the only clan that's truly worldwide. They're loosely affiliated at best, but if you harm one, you harm them all.

"Wait a sec." I take out my phone and message Bridie, who's talking to Jeremiah.

She glances at her phone before looking over at us. I stare back, daring her to disapprove. She gives a little nod. Then she turns to Jeremiah and graciously steps away. A little late to be a good example, but whatever.

We get to the scooter and Lennon says, "I'm heading for the beach. Is that okay?"

"Sure." I'm game for anything that takes me away from here.

We use bungee cords to strap my ukulele case to the back before climbing on. As we head down Fulton, we hit the fog zone, where everything is gray and misty, cool, but not cold. I figure we'll stop at Ocean Beach, but once we reach the ocean, Lennon keeps heading south. We wind along the coast, passing miles of sand dunes that gradually morph into the craggy, perilous cliffs that Northern California is famous for. We pass through Daly City and get off the main highway in Pacifica. Lennon rambles through a suburban neighborhood until I wonder if we have a destination. Then he turns down a road that dead ends at a gravel parking area too small to be called a lot.

We walk along a trail winding like a dirty ribbon through the hairy coastal scrub brush until we reach a weatherworn metal staircase bolted into the cliff. I take the slippery steps slowly, one hand on the rail and the other gripping the handle of my ukulele. Lennon practically glides down, his feet making no noise and causing no vibration in the rickety metal structure. And I thought I was the graceful one. At the bottom, we take off our shoes and start walking across the cold, damp sand.

The fog has lifted off the water, but clings to the cliffs, making everything misty and so quiet, despite the roar of the ocean and the keening bark of distant sea lions. Low tide waves crash in the distance, pushing rivulets of water and foam to shore. I take a deep breath and for the first time since the Beggar Chief died, I feel some of the tension ease out of me.

We walk side by side, but not hand in hand. Am I waiting for him or is he waiting for me? It's fifty-fifty, so we're screwed. My nose crinkles with my smile so I won't giggle.

"What?" he asks anyway.

"Nothing. Just a silly thought."

"I like your silly thoughts." He takes my hand. Our palms slide together and our fingers twine. For several moments, I forget to breathe. When I finally do, I suck in air with a little gasp that sounds like a hiccup. I hope he didn't notice.

We reach a pile of boulders cascading down from a cliff embedded with spiky green ice plants. We stop and roll up our jeans to our knees before continuing on, stepping on slimy, mossy rocks and wading through icy cold tide pools, me clutching my ukulele to my chest. Halfway through the pile, Lennon leads the way up a sandy slope to an alcove eroded into the cliff.

We settle on dry sand warmed by the sun burning through the fog. We sit, knees to chest, and stare the ocean for a while.

"Are you okay?" I ask.

"I am now." Lennon's chest rises and falls. "My family used to come here. It was our beach, so to speak. I've been meaning to come here since I got back. I wasn't sure I could find it."

"Glad you did. It's nice. Quiet."

"My parents didn't like crowds." He glances at my smile. "What?"

"Nothing, really. It's just funny. My parents loved crowds."

"Do you?"

I shrug. "As a performer, definitely, because crowds mean money. Personally, I don't know that I love crowds, but we always lived in encampments with other traveling people, Strowlers and the like, so I'm used to being at close quarters. Our apartment feels like a mansion. It still feels strange to have my own bedroom."

"Do you miss traveling?"

"More than I can say." Tears spring to my eyes and my throat closes with a deep ache. I rest my chin on my knee and let the light breeze cool my cheeks. After a few swallows, I manage to say, "Sorry."

He slips his arm around me. I cuddle close, breathing in that scent of his, a mix of citrus, spray paint, epoxy and something else, something musky that makes my head spin.

He lays his cheek on top of my head and whispers, "I wish I could travel with you."

"I wish you could, too. We could get a caravan and travel across the U.S. When we reach the east coast, we'll sell it and buy plane tickets for London. Buy another caravan and travel across Europe."

His arm tightens around me. He lifts my chin so we're face to face, our noses almost touching. The sunglasses are gone and I can see the intensity in his dark brown eyes. "Let's do it."

My lips part. My eyes close. We're kissing. Not sweet, soft kisses, but deep and passionate, our tongues vying. I sink into the sand as our arms and legs tangle before they twine. He's on top of me and his hard, lean strength makes me press into him, wanting more. We roll to the side as his hands slip under my T-shirt and fumble with my bra hooks. I go a little wild at the cold press of his palms on my breasts.

For a sweet, sharp moment, I want to let go and let it happen. If I believed he'd go traveling with me, I'd do it, lose my maidenhead on this beach with this boy I love. But he won't. He can't. And I can't.

I draw his hands from under my shirt. He draws away. Our eyes meet. He ducks his head. We untangle ourselves and sit side by side, our shoulders pressed together.

He opens his mouth. I interrupt. "Don't you dare say you're sorry."

"It's just… I don't want to hurt you."

"It will hurt me if you say sorry."

He takes my hand and lifts it to his lips before pressing it to his cheek. "I'd go anywhere with you, Penny. Anywhere."

"I know," I say, because I do. He would, if he could, if there weren't an invisible "but" with the weight of the world hanging between us.

"I got there at the end of your first song. Can you play it for me?"

He lays back in the sand as I tune my ukulele. I play "Blackbird" to him, the wind and the waves, and wish we, too, could fly away.

Lennon

And we're back to square one. Or maybe it's square three. What's the name of the square where you fall in love with a girl and it can't work, but you still want to spend all your time with her because she's your best friend?

That's not a square. It's more like a broken toe that doesn't heal. You look all right and go on with life as if nothing happened, but every time you take a step, you're reminded of the pain.

It's been almost a week since we made out on the beach. We haven't seen each other since then. We message every day, saying super witty stuff like, "hey" and "you ok?" and "yeah I'm good." Except I'm not good. I don't have anyone to talk to or make me smile. If my family noticed, they haven't said anything. They're probably relieved. I spend most of my time training with Tony, Cat, and Roy. I haven't gone out tagging or even been to my studio, which sucks. This is not how I want to spend my final days.

It's even worse today. Kai is hanging out with Aaron. They're in the banquet hall, practicing some Irish-sounding song. Faint strains reach the gym, plucking on my nerves as images of Penny, looking like a fairy princess, dance through my head. I dodge Tony's right roundhouse punch and am about to drop into a scissor kick when he comes up under me with a left hook. As I stagger back, he swings his elbow into my face. Then he jumps back rather than get splattered by the blood gushing from my nose.

"Lay down," he commands, so I do. I pinch my nostrils and tilt my head back but that doesn't stop the blood from trickling into my eyes. A slick coppery ooze coats my throat. The ringing in my ears doesn't drown out the music and the pain only intensifies the images of the dancing fairy. I want to see her. I want to talk to her. Maybe that would get the thoughts of her out of my head.

Tony hands me a towel full of ice. I press it to my nose and sit up. He squats beside me, Chinese-style, feet flat on the floor. "I'm pulling my punches." I know that. If he wasn't, my nose would be broken. "Jeremiah won't."

I know that, too. I shrug, but truth is, I'm scared. How could I not be? Jeremiah's got a heart full of vengeance and no one to take it out on except me. He could break my back like a branch if he wants to and there's a good chance he does. I close my eyes so Tony doesn't see my frustration. Everything is screwed up. Originally, I'd planned to show up for the challenge, refuse to fight until my parents' killers confess, and walk away. In my mind, it's a mic drop moment and I look like a badass, but that scenario only worked when I was up against John Walks Long. I can't surrender to Jeremiah. I won't look noble; I'll look like a coward and my family will share in my disgrace. Nobody will take my side and I won't get justice for my parents.

"Don't let him get inside your head," says Tony.

I know he means Jeremiah, but it's Head Elder who's taken up permanent residence there.

"Jeremiah had a better chance of winning when his father

was still alive. Now, he's preoccupied taking over the mantle of the Beggar Chief. He's already taking tribute as if he's the head of the Crossroads. His arrogance will make him less cautious. He's stronger than you, but he's also heavier. You must wear him out while he's running you down and get in the punch that will knock him out."

That's the strategy Tony and Roy have been drilling into me. It's a strategic win, not a power win. It'll make me look smart rather than strong, which is fine until the next challenge. I'll worry about that later.

I take away the towel and tap my nose. It's numb from the ice but it'll start tingling soon. My mouth and chin are sticky with blood. "I'm gonna take a shower and head out."

Tony stands with me. "Not staying for dinner?"

Aaron and Kai have changed their tune, playing 'Purple Rain' by Prince. It doesn't make things any better, since I'm now picturing Penny dancing in purple rain. "Nah, I have stuff to do." I don't look at him when I answer because he knows when I'm lying.

I'm almost out the door when he says, "You're doing the right thing."

Why do people always say that about something that's right for them but wrong for you?

After a quick shower, I wipe the steam from the mirror and check my nose in the mirror. It's swollen and starting to bruise, and I'm going to be a mouth breather for the next few days. I should put some more ice on it, but what does it matter? No one cares what I look like. My phone buzzes. My heart quickens and I hate myself for it. Why am I setting myself up for misery? It'll be Tony, reminding me to hang the wet towel and not put it in the hamper. Or Auntie Cat, asking what time I'll be home. Why even bother looking? But I have to, because it might, it might, it might…

It is. It's her.

Hi. Are you busy? Can you hang out?

My fingers tremble, making it hard to type.

Yeah, sure. When?

Whenever.

Now?

Ok.

Be there soon.

My heart is like a caged animal. If it could pace, it would. Why does my face have to be so messed up? She won't care, though, right? Because we're just friends now. Right.

When I get to her place, she rises from her perch on the stoop. She's wearing Doc Martin boots, tie-dyed leggings and that long, chunky sweater she'd knitted with a bunch of different yarns. God, she's so beautiful, like a piece of art. I want to make stencils so I can spray paint her on a billboard in Union Square and everyone can see how amazing she is.

She skips down the stairs and stands before me with bright green eyes and her mouth a breathless little pucker that I want to kiss. "Hi."

"Hi."

Then she gives a little gasp as her brow furrows. "What happened?"

I almost touch my nose. I shrug. "I was sparring with Tony."

"Are you sure you're okay? We can do this another time."

"No, I'm great. Let's go." I reach behind me and pull out the spare helmet before she can say another word.

As she climbs on behind me and presses her body into

mine, I realize I'm not over her. I never will be and that's okay. I'd rather feel this pain than suffer the empty hole she'd leave in my heart.

We don't say much until we get to my studio, where we don't say anything, but stare at each other like there's a glass wall between us. I want to kiss her so bad, it hurts worse than my nose. I think she feels the same. The way she chews her lip is driving me kind of crazy.

She takes a deep breath before saying, "Do you have any clean rags?"

Not what I hoped or expected, but the distraction is good. I grab an old, reasonably clean T-shirt and hand it to her. She goes to the fridge, dumps all the ice from the freezer into it, and holds out the wadded-up bundle. Our fingers touch and the glass shatters. Her arms slide around my waist and we're kissing and it's amazing. Her lips, her tongue, her breasts against my chest... I almost forget about my nose except for the metallic smell of blood and the ice pack melting in my hand.

Then she steps away and that's okay, too. Kisses are great. They're the best and I don't need more, as long as I can be alone with Penny. She has a funny little grimace on her face. "You got blood on me."

She goes to the sink while I settle in a folding chair. I tilt my head back before pressing the ice pack to my nose. I probably look worse now than I did at the *kongsi*. It's a wonder that she kissed me.

Penny sits beside me, wiping her face with her sleeve. "Are you sure it's not broken?"

I take away the pack and give my nose a test wiggle. "Yeah. It's been broken before. This is nothing."

"For a Strowler boy, his first broken nose is a badge of honor. Is it the same in the Two Dragon Clan?"

"Not really." I'd been twelve years old and it had been Tony who broke it. Dad had looked disappointed. In me, not him.

Penny glances around. "Have you been busy?"

"Busy training. I haven't been here all week. How about you?"

"Dealing with Bridie. She freaked out pretty badly about the Chief's death and..." she chews her lip. "This has got to stay between you and me."

I lean forward. "Yeah?"

"Remember the blood oath she and Doreen made against Kingfisher?"

My eyes widen. "Did something happen to the mirror?"

"Yes and no. I mean, the mirror is fine. After the bout, Bridie gave it to Christy to use as a weapon against Kingfisher and it worked, he backed down, but now Christy has the mirror."

"He'll keep it safe, though, right?"

"Yeah, I mean, I hope so, but power does funny things to people. It makes them turn against their own family."

"I know."

"I know you know, but Bridie's certain she can trust Christy."

I take a hesitant breath. "I'd trust Tony. There's a lot of shit between us, but I know he'd never betray me like that."

"And I'd trust Kai, so I guess I shouldn't fret." She folds her arms. "Anyway, things started to settle down and then yesterday, Jeremiah came over."

"What? To your house? Why?"

She scoffs and rolls her eyes. "Why do you think?"

Bridie is a total hot mom and she and Jeremiah are about the same age and... "No way."

"Way. He came to the apartment without calling first, and with two bodyguards, which had to look weird to our tenants. So, he settles on the couch and waits like a king while we fetch tea and biscuits. Then he tells us the election is this weekend, but he already knows he's the next Beggar Chief, so hoo-rah for him. Bridie was being all polite, but Kai and I were looking at him, like, 'WTF, dude?' Then he says he wants the next Beggars Banquet to be a celebration of his father's life as well as a victory party because he knows he's going to beat you."

"What an arrogant fuck."

"I know, right? So, then, he says he wants Bridie to help him plan the entertainment, which is, like, the worst excuse ever. Luckily, she kept her wits about her and said, 'um, no, not appropriate, since my son's father was a member of the Two Dragon Clan'."

"What'd Jeremiah say?"

"He tried guilt tripping, reminding her of the ties between the Beggar Clan and Strowlers, and how it would mean so much to his father if our family performed for his tribute. I could tell he wanted to put on more pressure, but he kept eyeballing me and Kai. So, he gets up to leave and asks her to walk him downstairs, alone. When she comes back, her cheeks are all red and she tells us he asked her out for dinner."

"Like, on a date?"

"Well, he said it was to talk more about that banquet, but come on. Mr. Stick-to-your-own-clan and he does that."

"Did she accept?"

"She said she didn't. I asked if she's going to tell Christy and she said no; if she does, he'll blow his top and demand we move back into the Nest. Then she said she can handle Jeremiah, which is exactly what she said about Bill and Kingfisher, which I pointed out, and now we're not talking." She collapses back in the chair, arms folded, and grunts out her exasperation. "I hate men." Then she gives me an apologetic glance. "Not all men. Not you."

I shrug. I'd feel the same way if I were her. "I hate the hypocrisy."

"Exactly. They tell us what to do...." Her fingers form quotes. "For our own good. And then they do the exact opposite."

"I know. Why should we listen to them?"

"That's why I wanted to see you, because I don't think we should listen to them. We can still see each other. We can behave." Her mouth crimps. "To a certain extent, right?"

I'm not about to argue over what that extent implies. "Right."

"I mean, we already told them all that I'm here to learn stenciling. There's nothing wrong with that, so we can't let them stop us."

"Plus, I really want to train you in the stealth arts, so yeah, we should definitely keep seeing each other."

"Will training me get in the way of your training?"

"We can work around it."

"Okay, then, let's do it."

We stop talking over each other and smile. I wonder if my eyes betray how much I want to kiss her.

She takes a deep breath and licks her lips. "When do we begin?"

I swallow hard. "Now?"

"Yeah, now."

The last days of my life are suddenly looking a whole lot better.

Penny

It always starts with kissing. As soon as the door to Lennon's studio closes, we're in each other's arms. I mean, immediately. I think about it the whole ride over and can't wait for that door to close. Sometimes, it's a quick snog so we can get to work and other times, it's a bit more… okay, a lot more. It's like we can't stop kissing because it feels so amazing, like a drug that makes your mind and body go warm and fuzzy, but also excited, with every nerve hungry and craving for more. Then, our hands start to roam and we back away because…

Because.

We don't talk about it. The kissing, I mean. It happens like the sun rises or how two magnets click together because there's no way they can't. We kiss because we can't not kiss, so what's there to discuss? Not the future, because it sucks. So, we kiss, and make stencils, and Lennon trains me in the forbidden stealth arts. We don't kiss at the end of day because it's another day gone toward that sucky future. I live for the present, right now, and the time I spend with him.

The future has sucked each day away until there's only a week left until his birthday. Today began with a snog, because we have a lot to do, but I want more. Maybe today we can end with kissing because I need to get as much as I can while I can.

We start by playing our version of hide-and-seek. Lennon waits for five minutes in his studio while I use the stealth skills to conceal myself somewhere in the building. The catch is, I must hide in plain sight because that's what these skills are all about. Strategies race through my mind as I use Swift Steps to race through the building.

Junkyard Metallurgy are hard at work on the ground floor, building a giant spider and web for an upcoming Halloween bash. They offer the best, but most obvious opportunity for concealment. Other options include all the communal spaces, like the art gallery, the lounge, the kitchen, and the bathrooms on both levels. I've hidden in all of them by now, but that can be used to my advantage. He's going to expect me to hide somewhere new. I need to find a spot where I can watch him looking for me. I head for the lounge, which is located on the opposite side of the building from Junkyard Metallurgy. No one is hanging out because of all the smoke and noise, but that's to my advantage. Empty spaces get overlooked. I go to the far corner where I've hidden before, behind an armchair, but this time I turn on the lamp beside it. I've learned that light reveals and conceals, and I move the lamp so that the light creates shadows for me to lurk in.

I take the deep breaths necessary to slow my *chi* and shift my energy from motion to stillness. I feel that now-familiar tingling sensation as my body starts fading from view…

And my phone starts vibrating. Bollocks. I forgot to turn it off and it's too late now. Okay, this isn't a bad thing. I need to learn to use these skills without being distracted. I concentrate on the static hiss of Junkyard Metallurgy's welding equipment so that it becomes one with the buzz of the phone. My energy flows and slows. I take another deep breath and fade away.

Moments later, Lennon ambles into view. He wanders

among the makers, showing interest in the spider even as his gaze penetrates every nook and cranny of their space. Finally, he strolls away, heading toward the lounge, and all I can think is, *don't hold your breath.*

Breathing is the most important element when learning the Two Dragon Clan's stealth arts. As a dancer and musician, I thought I had good breath control, but this is a whole different level that's both physical and spiritual, and involves the flow of energy through my body and keeping it consistent and strong. Being a dancer, I learned the Swift and Silent Steps quickly, but the Shadow Skill is another matter. It involves stillness, not movement, blending into the background so I become like a shadow. If I hold my breath, it will interrupt the flow of energy and I'll become visible.

As Lennon approaches, his eyes scan the lounge. Besides the armchair, there are a couple of well-worn couches, some folding chairs, and a wood pallet repurposed as a coffee table. The only place to hide is where I'm standing and he seems to stare right at me.

I breathe, slow and easy, so my heart doesn't start jackhammering.

He slows to a stop in front of the chair and gives a little shrug and smile.

My breath becomes a huff. "Dammit," I mutter. So much for strategy. I come around the chair and slouch onto the couch. "I suck at this."

"Hey, no, you did good," he says as he sits beside me. "I didn't see you."

I frown. "Wait. So, you thought I might be there and tricked me out?"

"No. I didn't see you. I saw something else. Think about it. Look around."

I glance around the lounge. Did he notice the lamp had moved? Maybe, but it and the chairs are moved around all the time. That the lamp was turned on, but nobody was there? Nothing unusual about that, either. I stare at the lamp and the shadows cast by the light… and I smack my forehead. "You saw my shadow."

"Light. It's a bitch."

"It's a bastard."

"Don't get frustrated."

"Too late."

"I've been doing this my whole life. You've only been training for a couple of months. Considering that, you're doing great." He stands. "Go back to where you were and I'll show you how to stand so you don't cast a shadow."

I jump up. I like this part of training because it usually involves Lennon standing close, touching me, his breath on my neck. My skin tingles as I position myself behind the chair. As he comes up beside me, my phone starts vibrating again. Bollocks. It must be Bridie. She feels it her duty to call me at least once every time I go to the studio. Lennon's aunt does the same to him, making me suspect she and Bridie have coordinated on that. We've been to each other's houses for dinner a couple of times. After the initial inquisition, Cat and Roy were nice enough to me, same as Bridie with Lennon, but there's always this underlying tension and suspicion that he and I are being naughty.

I hold up my hand as I take out my phone. Then I cover my ear so I can hear better. "Yeah, Mum?"

"You need to answer when I call you," Bridie states crisply.

Actually, I don't, but why rock the boat now? "It's hard to hear you. Hold on a moment." I motion Lennon to follow me as I head toward front of the building. "Sorry. We were watching some people build a metal sculpture. What's up?"

Her voice drops to a softer timber. "It's Charles. He's had a heart attack."

I stop in my tracks. "Is he all right. I mean, is he…"

"He's alive. I don't want to discuss this over the phone. I need you to come home now."

"I'm on my way." I hang up and kind of hate myself for how annoyed I'm feeling.

"What's wrong?" asks Lennon.

"Kai's grandfather had a heart attack."

"Kai's. Not yours?"

"No. Matthew's father."

He takes a hesitant breath. "Is he dead?"

I shake my head. "Bridie wants me to come right home."

"Let's go."

As we ride through the city, I find myself holding on a little tighter to Lennon, but not for comfort. It's hard not to feel resentful toward Charles for cutting into my time with him. To be honest, it's hard to care he had a heart attack. Part of me wants to say, 'couldn't happen to a nicer person', but that would be hurtful toward Kai.

In front of my place, I say, "Maybe it's not that bad. I'll try to see you tomorrow."

Lennon nods. We look each other in the eyes. He wants to kiss me. I can feel it like heat coming off his skin. I want to kiss him. Can he feel it? It doesn't matter. We can't, so…

"Bye." I head up the stairs, forcing myself not to look back until I get to the stoop. He waves. I wave back. I want to run back down so badly, I grip the door handle until my knuckles whiten. I wait until he drives away before I go inside.

Bridie and Kai are seated at the kitchen table and he's typing away on his laptop.

"What's going on?" I ask, as I join them.

"Getting airline tickets for us," explains Kai, his eyes glued to the screen.

I look from him to Bridie with widened eyes. "Us?"

She holds up a finger before I can speak. "Charles is very ill. He wants to see all three of us."

For my brother's sake, I swallow a scoff. "Why would he want to see me?"

"I suppose we'll find out when we get there."

"Maybe he wants to apologize," says Kai. "He was mean to Mum and not very nice to you, either."

That's one way of putting it. Here's another. Charles hated Bridie, claiming she lured Matthew off the Glory Road to join her on the Wayward Way. He treated me like a stray cat, worthy of occasional pity, but that's about it.

"Exactly. Why does he want to see me now?"

My brother looks up and into my eyes. "Maybe he's going to die and he wants to say he's sorry."

That's Charles's problem, not mine.

"Or maybe he wants to tell us something about Dad."

That possibility starts my wheels spinning. I always suspected Matthew's parents knew more about his death than they told us. Maybe they know a lot more and a brush with death has loosened Charles's stiff lips. It figures that the break I've been waiting for has come at the worst possible time.

Bridie stabs me with a sharp green glare. "I don't care to see him, either, but I am obliged to do so."

And there it is, the one word that seals my fate. Obligation and honor are the currency of the Crossroads. Charles and his wife, Enid, aided us at our lowest ebb. We couldn't have escaped Kingfisher without them. The law of the Crossroads doesn't hold children accountable for debts of obligation, but personal honor does. I owe them, big time, and that debt has come due. My voice tightens around my words, "When are we leaving?"

Kai looks at the screen. "Our flight leaves at 11:47 a.m."

"When do we get back?"

Bridie's mouth purses and I'm certain she's reading my mind. Her nose gusts before she speaks. "Friday. I explained to

Enid we can only stay for a couple of days. I was barely able to get that much time off."

Friday. Lennon's birthday is on Saturday. I might have a chance to see him then, but probably not. I gnaw my lip, chewing back the words I want to say. I nod instead.

She smiles and pats my shoulder. "Good girl."

Angry, pissed-off, desperate girl, more like.

I go to my room, close the door, and chew my knuckles to muffle a scream. Why must I be the honorable one? What's the worst that could happen if I'm not? Kai would eventually forgive me, right? Unless Charles dies. And what if I later go to London and find that my only source for answers was Charles and he's gone? Shit.

I sit at my desk and pop open my laptop. I have four outstanding orders, three for premade leggings and one for a pinafore that's barely half done. I close my online store for a week, citing a family emergency, and get to work. I spend the rest of the afternoon and most of the evening sewing and getting everything ready to ship, not stopping until Bridie calls me into the kitchen for a quick dinner.

She and Kai have sorted out the building and gave the launderette a good scrub. I swear I'm going to jump down their throats if they try laying on any guilt, but they know better. Afterward, we go to our rooms, supposedly to pack. Instead, I sit on my bed and stare at my phone and the three unanswered messages from Lennon. I don't know how to tell him. I don't want to, especially not in a message or even over the phone. With a huff of frustration, I go into the bathroom and take a shower. Afterward, when I turn off the light, I notice there's no light coming from under the door leading to Bridie's bedroom. She should be asleep soon. I close my bedroom door and turn the lock as softly as I can. Then I pick up my phone.

Lennon

I should've gone to the *kongsi* after dropping off Penny, but I'm not in the mood to spar with Tony, Roy or any of the men lined up to test my strength. I don't know how much more prepared I can be. Maybe that's arrogant, but I need the day off and I message Tony to let him know. He immediately messages back, asking if I'm with Penny, and I can honestly say no.

I go back to the studio, which feels like an empty hole without her. Damn. I hope her step-grandfather is okay. I don't like missing a single moment with her. The only way to get her off my mind is to work, so I start cutting the stencils for what could be my final project. It's a Banksy-style joint, based on a famous photo from the Vietnam War of two men, one holding a gun at arm's length while the other recoils as his brains are blown out. Beneath it, I'll add a proverb, in English and Chinese, "Within the four seas all men are brothers." Yeah, the irony is obvious, but that's the point. I want to paint it someplace Jeremiah will see it. The only reason we're fighting is because our fathers were murdered and now we're carrying on the same bullshit. I don't know if he'll get that. John Walks Long would have.

I close my eyes against the pain and sorrow. I still don't know what I'm going to do if I beat Jeremiah. I'm half-wishing I'd taken Hasaki up on his offer and even doubled-down, demanding that he kill Head Elder and Uncle George. I'm sure he would've agreed to those terms. Thing is, I don't want them dead until I get answers. The only way forward is taking on clan leadership and forging the necessary allies, and that will take years, with no guaranteed results. And no Penny. How am I going to make it through the years without her? Is revenge worth losing her?

My phone buzzes and I practically rip it from my pocket.

Are you awake?

I blink and stare at the clock. It's after eleven. I always lose track of time when I'm cutting stencils.

Yeah. I'm at the studio. What's going on?

I need to see you, but I can't leave my room.
Can you come up here?

My heart starts pounding.

You mean your bedroom?

Yeah. Can you make it up here?

My breath trembles. Alone with Penny in her bedroom. Is that smart? Who cares?

Yeah. I'll be there in a bit.

Stencils and revenge can wait. I dump both and head out. My first impulse is to head directly for Penny's place, but paranoia nudges me. I know Head Elder's spies are watching me whenever and wherever they can. Getting to Penny's bedroom is going to take some finesse. I go home, park my bike, and enter the building like I normally do. Hopefully Cat and Roy are in bed by now. They've stopped pretending, and he's staying in her room instead of sleeping on the couch. There's a service stairway in the back of the studio that goes all the way to the roof. I climb the stairs and slip through the door. A mantle of fog hangs over the city, giving the sky a twilight hue. I breathe deep and spread my arms. *Chi* flows through me and around me and I become one with the fog. That done, I gather what energy I can from the fog and the air to increase my buoyancy. Then I run off the edge and soar through the air, invisible.

The Covert Dragon Skill is one of the clan's highest-level skills, merging the Flying and Shadow skills. It's a *chi* drainer and only good for the short distance. I fly across Golden Gate Park before landing on top of a parking structure at the USF School of Law. After taking a few steadying breaths, I launch again and fly until I land on the roof of Penny's building. The energy I've expended staying in stealth mode drops me to my knees and I become visible. Shit. I wait until the gray haze clears from my eyes before using my phone to do a quick scan for spyware. Nothing registers. I hope there aren't any actual spies nearby. I stick to the shadows and creep to the corner of the building. Then, I slide off the edge and land, soft as a cat, onto the deck of the fire escape.

Penny sits on a lawn chair amidst the tall vines of a potted tomato garden. She recoils, pressing her hand to her heart, before whispering, "Wow."

I want to say the same thing. Her shawl slithers off her shoulders, revealing her breasts straining against the fabric of a thin tank top. That does things to my body that make me shaky in a different way. I glance down at her pajama bottoms and notice her bare feet. Why is that making me feel things? I can't think about anything but being close to her. My knees quiver as she takes my hand and leads me into her dark bedroom.

She lets go to ease the window gently shut. I shrug off my jacket, and slide out of my Vans. Despite the dark, I can see that her room is lined with clothing racks and piled with bolts of fabric. So, this is where the magic happens. I almost say that, until I spot a suitcase beside the chest of drawers. My chest tightens. No way. She can't be leaving. It must be for something else. She slides onto the bed, sitting so she's propped up by the pillows against the wall, and pats the space beside her.

I'm right there, but I don't know what to say or do. I try to think of something. "Um, is this an air mattress?"

"Yeah. We all have one."

"Why?"

She shrugs. "Who knows how long we'll be here or anywhere?"

All those joking talks we had about going to Svalbard or wherever and I ignored the obvious. She's a Strowler and they don't stay in one place for long. I wrap my arms around her and hold her close as if that could make her never leave me.

She twists so she's facing me, her arms sliding around my neck. Her breath caresses my cheeks as her chest rises and falls with mine. All I can think about is kissing her, so I do, and it's amazing. Her mouth tastes like a strawberry and her tongue touching and probing my mouth makes me wild. Our hands are all over each other and when we break to take a breath, our shirts come off. The air mattress doesn't betray our sounds as we roll and slide among the pillows and plushies until I'm on top of her and her legs are wrapped around mine. Her breasts against my chest is the most amazing thing I've ever felt. My kisses travel down her neck and when my mouth closes around her nipple, I feel even more amazing. Her light scent has gone musky. My head spins. Her soft moans make me grind my hips into hers.

And then we stop and draw away, facing each other, our huffing breaths vying between us, my heart pounding so hard, I can barely hear. Her fingertips brush my tattoo. I tremble. I want to take her back in my arms and lose myself in those plump lips, gorgeous breasts, hips, thighs… every secret part of her.

She whispers, "Matthew had the same tattoo."

I stiffen. Not in the good way. Is that why she pulled away, because she thought of her stepfather? Oh wait. Shit. Her grandfather. Or step-grandfather. Whatever. He's sick, maybe dead, and we're making out.

Then she taps the pearl inked at the throat of my dragon. "He told us all men in the Two Dragon Clan have identical tattoos, except the Dragon Son."

No, this isn't about her grandfather or even Matthew. It's about us. If I were an ordinary clansman like Matthew I could run away with an outsider, like Bridie, to the quiet disgrace of my family, but I'm not. I'm the Dragon-fucking-Son and if we go any farther, it will ruin us.

We sit up and put our shirts back on.

She rests her cheek on my shoulder. "I wish I didn't love you, but I'm glad I do."

She loves me. I guess I'm supposed to be surprised, but I'm not. I know she loves me. I don't want her to wish she didn't. "I love you and I don't care what anyone thinks."

"I know. Sorry. That didn't come out right. I love you and I want us to be together. I hate that we can't be, but I don't want to stop loving you. I can't."

I feel her sigh with my whole body. I want to kiss her again. I slide my arm around her waist and she snuggles close. I'm about to turn my head when she speaks, "I have something to tell you." That never ends well, and this time is no exception.

Her step-grandfather is super ill and she has to go with her family to London. "I don't want to go," she finishes. "But I don't have any choice."

The selfish part of me wants to say she always has a choice. She can choose not to go, to stay here and be with me, really with me, and alienate her family. I have a choice, too. I can tell the entire Crossroads to fuck off, I'm not the Dragon Son, and they can stick their challenges where the sun don't shine. Then Penny and I can run away together and leave our families to face the consequences of our actions. I wonder what Jade Dragon would think of that? He'd probably find it interesting, as if his favorite TV show had an unexpected plot twist.

She nudges me with her hip. "Say something."

"Is he really that sick?"

"I guess." She gusts out a sigh. "Apparently, he had the heart attack a few days ago, but Enid didn't call us until today because she didn't want to worry Kai. He's in a care home now and he can have visitors."

"You'll be back Friday?"

"Yeah, but late. I doubt we'll be home before midnight."

"So, all we have left before my birthday is tonight."

She nods.

"Can I stay?" I kiss the top of her head. "I can behave."

Her smile brings me back to life. "Me, too."

We lay back down, nestling into the pillows as we spoon together. That grinding feeling comes and goes, and is finally gone as her musky scent fades into something softer. All I want to do now is sleep with my arms around her, so I do.

"Oh, Penny." Bridie's voice jolts me awake. The room is bright with morning sunlight. Penny and I rolled away from each other in the night and are back-to-back, which is a slightly better way to be caught.

"Mum!" Penny bolts upright and rubs her eyes before

glaring at her mother. "I'm not a child. You can't unlock my door like that."

"I can if you're living under my roof, committing such folly."

I roll off the bed and to my feet. Great. Bridie was already ambivalent about me. Now, she must think I'm her daughter's evil seducer.

Penny comes to her feet beside me. "That's where you're wrong. We haven't done anything. We know the consequences." She says "we" in a way that makes her mother's eyes narrow.

Bridie's arms fold. "You expect me to believe nothing happened last night?"

"I expect you to believe my word."

"You give your word?"

"Yes."

They share a glare. Bridie blinks and huffs out a sigh. "Well, regardless of what did or did not happen, Tony called." She turns to me. "He said your aunt is worried, that your scooter is home, but you're not there. He asked if you're here and I said of course not, but I decided to check for myself." She jabs her finger toward me. "And here you are. Lennon, what are you thinking? Are you thinking?"

I duck my head. The last thing I want is to cause the Sparrows any more grief or to damage Penny's reputation. "I'm sorry. I'll go."

She sighs. "No wait." Before I can reply, she takes out her phone and taps the screen. "Hello again, Tony. I found Lennon… I'm sorry, Paul, asleep on our couch in the front room, so he was here after all. He'll be on his way soon, after breakfast. Well, I can hardly turn the boy out without feeding him. Yes, I'll tell him. He's to go straight there. No, it's quite all right."

As she hangs up, Penny bounds over and kisses her cheek. "You're the best, Mum."

"Don't take that as approval." She stands by the open door and nods for us to go through.

Kai stares at us from the kitchen table, a forkful of sausage halfway to his mouth.

"Lennon spent the night in my room. Nothing happened. My word."

He blinks and seems to decide Penny's shorthand version of events is acceptable since the fork makes its way to his mouth and not my throat. Then he not-so-discreetly takes out his phone and starts messaging.

I ladle a bowlful of Bridie's oatmeal, cooked with fruit and nuts, topping it with a couple of sausages before sitting beside him at the table. "What's Aaron say?"

Kai holds up his phone so I can see.

Duuuuuude...

"Tell him Tony was told I spent the night on the couch."

Kai nods and messages. It's a little sad that I can trust him and Aaron with my secrets, but not Tony. I want to trust Tony. I want to tell him everything, but I can't. There's no world for him outside the clan and Crossroads, and no gray areas, either.

Breakfast is over too soon, with Bridie pointedly reminding us that they need to leave for the airport in an hour. She follows Penny and me to the front door and steps ahead to hold it open. "Goodbye, Lennon, and good luck. On your birthday, I mean."

I can't say 'have a good trip' and I don't feel very lucky, so I shrug and mumble my thanks for the breakfast.

Penny steps past her and joins me in the hall. "I'll walk you down."

I can feel Bridie's eyes on us all the way to the stairwell.

After going down the first flight, I look over my shoulder, expecting to see her glowering down at us, but she's not. We stop at the landing between the first and ground floors. It's the most privacy we're going to get. Penny's hands slide around my waist and tugs me into an embrace that makes my head spin. She smells like breakfast in bed. I want to devour her, but I don't want what could be our last kiss to be horny and gross. I keep it soft and sweet, and so does she. She strokes my cheek as she steps away.

I take hold of her hands. "I hope your grandfather makes it."

"Thanks." She takes a breath. "I know you'll win."

And after I win, I'll be the official adult Dragon Son and it'll be even harder for us to be together. I don't say it and neither does she. Instead, she nods and squeezes my hands before letting go. It's so much like our last goodbye two years ago, tears come to my eyes.

Her eyes glimmer. She blinks and quickly wipes her cheeks. "Bye."

She's running up the stairs before I can reply.

I lean against the wall and take deep breaths so my tears don't spill. Win or lose, this isn't a final goodbye. I will see Penny again.

Penny

We exit the tube at Paddington Station where the sky is pissing rain, which suits my mood and my suspicion we're about to get shit on. Charles had the heart attack while on his rounds at St. Mary's Hospital and was later moved to nearby Kensington Care Home, where he also works. Is it me or does that seem a little too convenient? Or maybe it's me being a selfish cow who hates being separated from her best friend.

Speaking of best friends, I turn to Bridie as we begin our trek. "Can we please see Helena and Gareth this time?"

Bridie's face pinches as I say the name of her best friend, Helena, also known as Mad Maud, chief of the London Beggar Clan, and Gareth, Helena's brother, the man Gerry loved.

"Yeah, can we, please?" wheedles Kai. "Please?"

Anger chases sorrow across Bridie's face. "No, and that's the end of it. You know full well we can't. It's too dangerous."

I bite my lip to keep from snapping back that I'll see them when I return on my own. They were like family to us. No, they were family. Gerry and Gareth were going to be wed…

Pain sears my chest, filling my eyes with tears. I can't think about that right now. It has to wait until I return with Lennon to seek my revenge.

It's a short walk to the Hyde Swan Hotel, but we're dripping wet by the time we enter the posh lobby. The clerk doesn't bat an eye, but his lip curls at the sound of Bridie's working class Irish accent. While he double, and then triple checks our reservation, Bridie sends a text to Enid.

Her brow pinches as she reads the response. "Enid expects us at the care home in half-an-hour." She rolls her eyes. "So typical. I'll tell her we need more time to settle in."

Kai's face scrunches with alarm. "What if we need to see Granddad right now? Maybe he's dying. I don't want to sit around. I want to see him."

"Of course, of course," Bridie soothes. "Let's go to our room and freshen up quickly so we don't look ragamuffin." She blinks with surprise as she signs the paperwork. "We're booked into a two-room suite. That's very kind of Enid."

Not really. The kindness is meant for Kai and includes me and Bridie because we're with him. If it were only me and her, we'd be staying in a hostel at our own expense. The suite has a shabby elegance with fraying furniture and plush beds. It's stopped raining and I have enough time to step out onto the balcony and breathe in the cold, wet air. We're on the top floor with a view of Hyde Park. I can't help hoping we have a chance to take a walk there. One of my happier memories is wandering its grassy meadows with my family and feeding the geese and swans at Round Pond.

I glance over my shoulder. Bridie's still in the loo, so I take out my phone and type.

> Hey, we're here. In London at our hotel.

I chew my lip. Maybe he's asleep already and won't answer.

You ok?

I'm fantastic. Lennon stayed awake, waiting for my message. I keep my back turned so Bridie and Kai can't see my smile.

Tired. Jet laggy. Wish I could go to bed. How are you?

Tired, too. Tony's been working my ass all day. He's still sore about me spending the night at your place.

Does he believe you slept on the couch?

I gave him my word nothing happened with us, without saying where exactly I slept, so I guess so.

Bridie taps on the window of the French door and gives me a stern look. Damn.

I gotta go.

Hope Kai's grandfather is better.

Thanks. I'll message you in the morning. Your morning. Lol.

Message me whenever. I'll have my phone with me.

Warmth spreads across my chest. I stretch my face muscles to remove any trace of happiness before rejoining my family.

We cross the square, passing through a small park with dripping trees and enthusiastic pigeons, and enter the Kensington Care Home, where we queue up at the front desk behind a family who came in before us.

"No, no," a strident voice calls out across the lobby, startling everyone, including the other family. High heels skitter across the marble floor as Enid Wong barrels toward us. "No need. I've signed you in already."

I smell a rat. Her eyes aren't red-rimmed from tears or dark-bagged from lack of sleep. She's wearing a tasteful amount of makeup, with her sparse eyebrows penciled dark brown to match her hair, which is neatly swept above her high forehead and sprayed into side-parted submission. She's dressed in pressed wool trousers and a silk blouse buttoned to her neck. Even those heels have a polished perfection. Not at all like a woman whose husband is in the hospital and possibly dying.

Kai doesn't seem to notice. He steps forwards, arms spread. "Grandma, are you okay? How's Granddad?"

Enid's tense frown cracks into a brief smile as she shares a brief hug with her grandson. "You should come see us more often. That's what we need to keep us healthy." Her frown returns as she glances at me. "Hello, Penny."

I greet her with equal warmth. "Hello, Auntie Enid."

Matthew's parents don't care for me. It's not a case of like or dislike. They hate my parents, but hating me isn't fair, and they know it, so I'm more like an appendage attached to their grandson. They both have PhDs. Charles is a Cardiologist and Enid is an historian. She works as a curator at the Victorian and Albert Museum. Calling them both Dr. Wong doesn't work so, with tight-lipped reluctance, they settled on me using "auntie" and "uncle."

Enid turns to Bridie with that tweaked-off look she saves for her. Her voice drops below freezing, "Bridie."

There was a time when that look would've withered Bridie. Now, Mum keeps her head high and her tone kind. "Hello, Enid. We got here as soon as we could. How is Charles?"

Enid's eyes go anxious. She blinks and licks her lips before her usual uppish look reappears. "He's on the top floor." She motions us to follow her to the lift. Once inside, she hands us each a stick-on badge.

Kai starts to laugh. "Grandma, you took the wrong badges. This says I'm Rupert Smith."

Mine says I'm Emma, while Bridie's has the name Maggie, all of us Smiths. My nose twitches as the stench of rat grows stronger.

Bridie frowns at her tag. She isn't buying it, either. Then she sticks the badge on her jumper without comment, so I do the same.

Kai's face scrunches with dawning realization. "Did you give us fake names?"

Enid won't meet his gaze. "I'll explain when we see your grandfather."

We exit the lift to the acrid scent of bleach and pain. It's hushed and noisy at the same time with the hum and beep of medical devices. Most of the doors are open and all have single beds and simple, posh furnishings, meaning this place is only concerned with the care of toffs and not the general public. Exactly the kind of place Charles would stay if he were ill. Maybe I'm judging Enid too harshly. She's the type to keep up appearances with a stiff upper lip and even so, worry could make her scatterbrained enough to take the wrong name tags. She leads us to a closed door the end of the corridor, which she opens and steps aside.

I enter first and stop in my tracks, mouth wide open. Then I gag, sickened by the sight before me. I smelled a rat, but I didn't think it'd be this big.

Charles Wong sits in a chair beside a hospital bed surrounded with white curtains. Next to it stands a beeping medical monitor, its screen lit up with jagged vital signs, but not his because he's not connected. He's wearing trousers and a white lab coat, like a doctor on his rounds. There's a healthy color to his square, jowly face, the eyes behind his glasses are bright rather than dull, and his sparse gray hair is neatly combed.

"Grandson." He stands with his arms wide open.

Kai backs away, shaking his head.

Enid closes the door and stands in front of it like the Queen's Guard, emotionless and unmovable.

Un-be-fucking-lievable. I could be home right now with Lennon, but no, I had to be honorable and this is how I'm repaid.

Bridie sucks in a tight breath before she speaks, "You're not sick?"

Charles clears his throat. "I had a mild heart attack last week and have recovered sufficiently to resume part-time duties here."

"Really?"

"It's what all the records present. I went through certain motions to make it seem real, but it was actually a ruse to get you here."

I want to shout, 'Why did you include me in your bull-shit?', but the rigid fury of Kai's expression stops me.

"Not. Cool." His words hang in the air like icicles. "How could you do this to me?"

"Forgive us, Grandson, but it was necessary. You'll under-stand soon."

"Is this some kind of joke?" demands Bridie. "I can't go on holiday at the drop of a hat. If my boss finds out, I'll be sacked and we'll be homeless. Kai is missing school. Not to mention the classes I had to cancel with my students. That's money I'll never get back."

Enid rolls her eyes. "We'll pay all expenses incurred, Bridie."

A strangled sound emits from Bridie's throat. "That's it. That's the limit. Let's go."

Sounds good. Out of here and back on a plane to San Francisco and Lennon. I don't care what justification the Wongs have for luring us here.

Enid doesn't step aside. "It's about Matthew."

Of course it is. Everything is about Matthew and how the grotty pikeys stole him away from his fine family and clan.

Bridie's eyes shoot daggers. "You're going to sink that low?"

"I apologize," interjects Charles, "but there's a great need for discretion. Please, sit." He gestures at the couch next to the tinted window.

"What about him or her?" Bridie nods at the bed.

"One of my patients. He's in a coma."

"So, we're hijacking his room?" She glares at Enid. "I assume the Smiths are this poor man's family."

Enid doesn't even blink.

"And you say I have no class." Bridie looks from me to Kai. "Children?"

Kai doesn't answer. He eyes his grandparents like they're strangers.

I give a tight shrug. I'm hating them so hard right now, but we should stay on the off chance they have useful information about Matthew and Gerry's deaths.

Enid waits until we're seated before leaving her post. She opens the briefcase on top of the small dresser and pulls out a binder. I sneer. They certainly made themselves at home in Mr. Smith's room. I hope the real Emma shows up and kicks us all out.

Charles manages a strained smile. "Kai, you're friends with the Dragon Son's cousin?"

My brother's eyes pinch with suspicion. "Yeah?"

"Do you see the Dragon Son much?"

"Sometimes."

"Are you friendly with him? I mean, friendly enough that he would do a favor for you?"

"Maybe." He glances at me. I give my head a slight shake. I'm not about to tell them I'm in more of a position to ask the Dragon Son for favors. "Why?"

"Is that why you lured us here?" interrupts Bridie. "All you had to do was ask instead of putting us through this load of bollocks."

"That wasn't the reason," says Enid. "Have you heard of the Taiping Rebellion?"

Okay, that's random.

Bridie's brow furrows. "The typing rebellion?"

Auntie Enid smirks. I want to thump her, for this and for all the times she looked down her nose at Bridie's lack of education.

"It was a rebellion in southern China in the mid-nineteenth century," I look Enid in the eye. "By some loony who claimed he was the younger brother of Jesus Christ. Why?"

The smirk becomes a glare. "Hong Xiuquan stood up to the Manchu invaders and the European colonials. Although his religious tenants were questionable, he implemented radical changes, such as declaring men and women to be equal."

Oops. Have I insulted her bestie? I can't stop myself from goading her. "Didn't twenty million people die?"

Uncle Charles raises his voice to interrupt his wife's reply, "The Taiping Rebellion is of particular interest to our clan. Hong Xiuquan was Hakka, and the Hakka people rose up to join his rebellion. The Two Dragon Clan ordered its members to avoid the conflict, but half the clan deserted to join the Heavenly Kingdom, including the Dragon Son and his wife. They and their children ran away from the clan's stronghold, absconding with five clan treasures."

Auntie Enid opens the binder and turns it toward us,

revealing a drawing of an antique pendant shaped like a dragon, coiled around a huge pearl. "This is the Yang Pearl, the symbol of the Dragon Son. It contains the essence of the power given him and descendants by our founder, Jade Dragon." She turns the page to a drawing of a similar amulet, except a phoenix coils around the pearl. "The Yin Pearl is its companion, worn by the wife of the Dragon Son. Its main property is healing." The next page is a jade pendant with a smaller pearl set in the middle. "The Wisdom Pearl, worn by Head Elder and his descendants."

I lean forward, interested despite myself. These must be the pearls Lennon told me about, the ones left behind by Jade Dragon, except I'd thought he was speaking metaphorically and not about actual pearls.

The next drawing isn't jewelry, but a sword. "The Moonlit Dragon." She turns the page to another sword. "The Moonlit Phoenix. These had been forged by Jade Dragon and were to be wielded by the Dragon Son and his wife. The Dragon Son knelt before Hong Xiuquan and offered him the Wisdom Pearl. One of the primary powers of this pearl is persuasion." She flips another page and shows a photo of a man dressed like a Chinese emperor. Her manicured fingernail taps at a pendant around his neck. "This is the only known depiction of Hong Xiuquan wearing the Wisdom Pearl. Using its power, he persuaded rich and influential people to join his forces."

Kai squints before asking, "Are those pearls supposed to be magic or something?"

His grandmother's frown becomes a scowl. "Those pearls were given to us by Jade Dragon. They are part of his great pearl and contain his power."

"So, they are magic."

His grandmother looks offended. "Did they teach you nothing at the *kongsi* in San Francisco?"

"Not that."

"Jade Dragon gave us the pearls to cultivate our internal

energy and make our clan the most powerful on the Cross-roads. There's nothing magic about it." She sneers. "Magic is for ignorant people."

That's a dig at Bridie and me, and Strowlers in general. I'm about to pop off with some ignorant profanity, but my mother's fingers dig into my forearm. I bite my lip instead. I know that for Matthew's sake, we need to be Enid's toad eaters awhile longer.

Enid continues her history lesson. "The Dragon Son and his wife wielded their pearls and swords to bring further power and glory to the Heavenly Kingdom. In the end, even they couldn't hold back the might of the Manchu forces. Before they died, they placed their children with Christian missionaries who were fleeing the conflict. The clan tracked the two boys to Guangzhou. The oldest boy, who became the Dragon Son on the death of his father, had the Yang Pearl in his possession. The rest of the treasures had disappeared. It's believed a girl, their eldest child, had been given the Yin Pearl, but she, too, had disappeared. The boys said their sister had been taken by a different family of missionaries, but they didn't know who, only that they spoke English."

"The search for her and the Yin Pearl, along with the other treasures, has gone on for over 150 years. Were the missionaries British or American? Or did they speak English, but come from elsewhere? No one knows. That's why the clan pays for the education of historians like myself, so we can search for these treasures."

"I had little hope of finding them, but I never gave up. Perhaps my enthusiasm waned as I grew older. Then, an auction house I deal with through the museum alerted me to an estate sale in Vancouver that contained Chinese artifacts collected by a 19th century missionary. I didn't get my hopes up. I've looked at such collections before and found nothing. I saw photographs and one piece in particular caught my eye: a large pearl set in a gold ring, surrounded by tiny diamonds. The ring base was obviously twentieth century, but the estate insisted the pearl was from China."

"Without the original setting, the pearl's price was significantly less. I decided to take a chance and buy it. Clan historians are allowed to handle the Yang Pearl and trained to tap into its energy, to prepare us should we ever find the missing treasures. When the pearl arrived, I tested it. It was genuine. I had found the Yin Pearl. You can imagine my excitement. Immediately, I called Head Elder and told him of my discovery."

Head Elder. Lennon's grandfather. My stomach tightens. This isn't going to end well.

"He was skeptical. He told me to stay silent and he would send experts to test the pearl. That night, men dressed as Shinobi broke into our home and stole the Yin Pearl."

Auntie Enid turns to Uncle Charles, who takes over the story, "We fought them off as best we could, but we were overpowered. I allowed them to believe they'd disabled me. As they left, I shadowed them, following them through the city. To my surprise, they entered a building in Chinatown, one very familiar to me, the *kongsi* of the Two Dragon Clan. We didn't know what to do. Had Head Elder ordered the Yin Pearl to be stolen? Or had it been the Dragon Son? There were rumors the two were at odds. We had no way of knowing and couldn't ask for help without jeopardizing ourselves and our position in the clan. We had to get the Yin Pearl back and for that, we needed a thief."

Bridie gasps. "Gerry and Matthew. You asked them to steal that thing, didn't you?"

Charles looks down. Enid remains unblinking.

I take a tight breath. My body feels like a taut wire, ready to snap, ready to scream at the people who sent my fathers to their deaths.

"How could you?" whispers Bridie. Her voice rises as her cheeks redden, "How could you? You knew they had children." She points at Kai, who stares at them with shock in his eyes. "Your own grandson. He's an orphan because you wouldn't do your own dirty work."

"We didn't want to involve Matthew," admits Enid, "but we were desperate. The disgrace for losing the pearl would fall - has fallen on our entire family. We only wanted to hire the gypsy."

Really? Even now, they're being assholes about my father? "His name was Gerry," I snap.

"We offered him ample compensation for his efforts."

Bridie's eyes blaze. "The funds you've been giving us, your so-called generosity, it's blood money, isn't it? The money you never paid Gerry."

Enid remains sour. "Matthew insisted on accompanying him. Unlike Gerry, he'd been inside the building and could follow my directions to where the pearl was possibly being kept."

Her husband licks his lips before speaking. He still can't look at us. "That night, I drove them to Chinatown. A football match had ended and a pack of hooligans was rampaging through the streets. We used that as an excuse for me to take refuge in the *kongsi*. Matthew and Gerry snuck in after me. I left soon after and returned to my car to wait." He takes a long breath. "I heard shots fired and saw them jump out of a window. Matthew had been trained to survive such falls, but he'd been shot. I ran to help them, but I was pushed aside and then held back as their bodies were stripped naked and searched. They gave me Matthew's body and told me to leave."

I bite my lip to hold back tears. Bridie sucks back a sob and a tear slips down my cheek. I don't want to look at my brother or I'll break down.

"Leaving Gerry behind," Bridie chokes out.

"They gave his body to the Strowlers, did they not?"

She doesn't answer.

I taste blood, thinking of those hellish days. No one told us shite. Bridie had to call Enid, who coldly informed her that Matthew was dead. She and Charles had claimed no knowledge of what happened to Gerry. We had to wait three days, until I was able to contact Gerry's family. His oldest brother, Oren, cursed Bridie for a whore and me for a bastard, before telling me Gerry had died on that same day. As if determined to make it worse, none of them would tell us how or why they died.

I glance at Kai. Tears shine off the glare in his eyes. "Why didn't you tell us before? Why did you wait until now?"

"After I brought Matthew home, Head Elder called. He demanded I give him the Yin Pearl. I told him what happened. He said the Yin Pearl wasn't in the *kongsi*. They couldn't find it. Matthew and Gerry had landed on a grate. Nothing was found in the alley and the sewers were being searched with little hope. The Yin Pearl was lost again and Head Elder blamed us. As punishment, we were banished from the clan. We didn't want the disgrace to fall on Kai as well, so we encouraged you to leave London."

"How very kind." Bridie wipes her cheeks with the back of her hand. "That doesn't explain why you're telling us now."

Auntie Enid looks at her grandson and her cold demeanor thaws. "Kai, we want you to know, to understand, that we had no choice, for your safety as well as ours. Please forgive us."

I get a sick feeling in the pit of my stomach that another shoe is about to drop. What could be worse than what they've already said?

"Despite Head Elder's words, he suspects we still have the Yin Pearl. Our house has been broken into several times, but the so-called thieves took nothing. And the truth is, we do have the Yin Pearl. It's been hidden in a place they'll never look."

Charles and Enid's eyes stray to the white curtain. No way. They hid it with a coma patient? How is that possible? Wouldn't his family notice?

I freeze.

No. He can't be. They wouldn't…

Oh, yes the hell they would.

I jump to my feet and rip aside the white curtain. I blink rapidly, my eyes suddenly too dry. Blood rushes to my head and I feel like I'm going to puke.

Bridie rushes past me. Her hands fly to her mouth to cover her scream.

It's Matthew.

Penny

The world tilts. I grab hold of Kai's hand so I don't fall over. He squeezes hard enough to hurt, which is good. The pain helps me focus.

Matthew is alive. He's been alive all this time, and his parents didn't tell us. They let us - no, encouraged us - to move to another continent, give up our way of life, to suffer and mourn. They hate Bridie and don't care about me, but how could they do this to Kai? And having done it, why are they telling us now?

Bridie reaches out with trembling fingers to touch Matthew's brow. His eyes remain closed. She strokes his hair. He moans and shifts. She collapses into the chair beside the bed and lays her head on his chest, weeping.

My heart pounds, more pain, more anger.

Kai lets go of my hand. He looks as if he's aged ten years in ten seconds. "He's in a coma?"

Uncle Charles takes a hesitant breath. "No. He's in a minimally conscious state. He responds to touch and sound, but he can't speak. We don't know how aware he is of who we are. The bullet wound was minor, though he lost a lot of blood. He landed on Gerry, which softened the impact on his body, but his head hit the concrete."

Landed on Gerry. He says it so casually, as if Gerry was there for that purpose.

"I took his body home, thinking to prepare him for burial, and discovered he was still alive. I smuggled him into hospital and forged an identity for him, Xavier Smith, the adopted Chinese son of elderly, deceased English parents. His brain had started swelling by then and he had emergency surgery. His surgeon was surprised he'd survived. No one could figure out what saved him, until several days later, when he relieved himself. We found the Yin Pearl in his stool."

He'd swallowed it. I almost smile. I'm surprised Gerry hadn't been the one to do that. It sounds more like him.

"After he recovered sufficiently, we put him in this long-term care facility where I'm on staff. Unfortunately, he's made little progress over the years…"

Bridie spins around, tears streaming down her cheeks, her voice hoarse. "Years we thought he was dead. I married a man I didn't love and moved my children to America. If I'd known he was alive, I never would've left his side."

"Precisely," snips Auntie Enid. "If you hadn't left, if you'd visited here for no plausible reason, Head Elder would have realized Matthew is still alive. You did your part, unwittingly, yes, but we're grateful." She says the word in a grating tone. "We're only sorry we had to keep our grandson from his father."

To them, I don't matter. They don't care Matthew was my father. Not "like a father." My actual father, every bit as much as Gerry. My legs feel like rubber as I approach the bed. It's tilted so he's sitting up, head resting against the pillow, his face smooth and peaceful, as if he'd fallen asleep while watching telly. I slip my hand into his. Matthew stirs and seems to clasp my hand. It feels so much like I remember, warm, calloused and alive. Tears spill out of my eyes and drip down my chin. I swallow the lump in my throat so I can speak, "Ba, it's Penny. Can you hear me?"

His fingers twitch. I motion Kai to join me. He moves slowly as if walking through thick, churning water. His eyes have gone luminous and he's biting his lip. I take his hand and lay it over his father's. "Ba, it's Kai, your son. We're all here now."

Matthew's chest rises and falls. His eyes open.

For a blessed moment, it feels like one of the miracle recoveries, like on the telly, until Auntie Enid calls out, "It's a reflex. He can't see you."

It's true. Matthew's gaze is unfocused. His lids flutter and close.

Bridie covers her mouth with her hand. Her tears stream as if from a well of unending sorrow.

I notice a red silk cord around his neck and gently tug on it, pulling out a small, polished wood gourd with an intricate knot on top and a beaded tassel below. It's inscribed with Chinese characters and a yin-yang symbol.

"It's a *Wu Lou* gourd," explains Uncle Charles. "A *Feng Shui* symbol that absorbs illness. The Yin Pearl is hidden within. We placed it in a cheap, sentimental setting no one would want to risk losing their job over stealing."

Damn, they're good at conniving. What they're not good at is having feelings for other people. "Why are you telling us now, after all this time?"

"We've been waiting for the right time and it's finally come." Guilt creeps across his face again. He looks at his wife.

Auntie Enid has no problems with guilt. "Bridie, we encouraged you to marry that man for one reason, because he lived in San Francisco. Our banishment didn't include Kai. We wanted him to meet the future Dragon Son and hopefully become friends. Unfortunately, the young man left San Francisco after his parents died. However, we became encouraged when Kai befriended the Dragon Son's cousin." A tight smile stretches her mouth.

Kai doesn't smile back. "That's why you told Mum to marry Bill? That guy was an asshole. He was bad to her. Do you even care?"

"Of course we cared. We helped you after she left him."

"Because you wanted us to stay in San Francisco."

"Well, yes. We knew the Dragon Son would return to the city for his eighteenth birthday. We want you to ask him to heal Matthew in exchange for the Yin Pearl."

Kai's face scrunches. "What?"

Bridie gives an exasperated gasp. "You can't be serious."

Can't they? I've seen Lennon do some amazing things, but… "Heal? You mean, like, Jesus kind of healing?"

"Don't be ridiculous," snaps Enid. "I'm talking about the transfer of *chi* between two bodies. When the wearers of the Yin and Yang Pearls combine their *chi*, it becomes the Dragon Touch, which can heal mortal wounds."

Wearers. Two people. The Dragon Son and his wife. My heart starts pounding hard. The thought that Lennon must get married to save my father is ludicrous beyond words, yet here we are.

Bridie gnaws her lip. She glances at Matthew, hope glimmering in her eyes, and chooses her words with obvious care. "The Dragon Son isn't married yet and he's quite young. Does the other person need to be his wife?"

Charles and Enid exchange glances. She speaks, "The Yang and the Yin pearls can only be wielded together by a man and a woman who are bound spiritually and physically, which is to say," she clears her throat, "through sexual intercourse."

Heat rises from my neck and spreads over my face, which must be bright red. I can feel Bridie and Kai making an effort not to look at me.

Enid continues, "We realize the Dragon Son is young, but a marriage has no doubt been arranged for him. We need you to return to San Francisco, ask him when he'll be wed and if he's willing to heal Matthew."

"We're sure he will be," interjects Charles, "for the return of the pearl, but you must be certain he won't tell Head Elder any of this. That's why we needed you to gain his friendship."

Kai's eyes dart at me before he speaks, "Yeah, I can ask him, but he and Head Elder don't get along so good."

"Ah, perhaps he's carried on his father's quarrel. Since we've been banished, we know little of what's happening within the clan. We hope the return of the pearl will also mean our reinstatement."

Of course there's something in it for them beyond healing Matthew. I chew my lip to keep from blurting that I can make sure the Dragon Son never reinstates them.

Bridie sucks in a hard breath. "I need to speak to the children about this privately."

Charles nods, though he has to tug on his wife's arm to get her to move. Her face looks like sour milk as she leaves with obvious reluctance.

The door closes and we're alone, but Bridie and Kai still won't look at me. My sigh is tight. "No, Lennon and I haven't shagged." Though I'm wishing now we had, because that would've made this a whole lot easier.

I can see the conflict on Bridie's face, stuck between relief and disappointment. She sits on the bed and takes Matthew's hand, twining her fingers with his.

Kai covers his ears and groans. "Don't talk about shagging." He turns to our mother. "So, what are we gonna do?"

A tear rolls down her cheek, which she quickly wipes away. "Matty wouldn't want his daughter to sacrifice her reputation to save him." She looks at me with glimmering eyes. "Has Lennon spoken to you of his marriage arrangements?"

"No." I grit my teeth. The idea of him marrying anyone else fills my head with steam. He's mine! I exhale to release some of the pressure. That's stupid. He's not mine and we can't possibly get married, but I still can't stand the thought of him being with someone else. "Look, we're assuming Enid and Charles know everything about those pearls. Maybe Lennon knows more. I mean, he is the Dragon Son. We should wait and talk him about all this."

Bridie nods, though her eyes remain doubtful. "That's the best course of action. There's nothing else we can do right now." A long sigh quivers out of her. "I'm so angry, and yet so happy. I can barely think."

Kai squeezes his father's hand. "I'll never forgive them."

I lean against the door so the Wongs can't barge in and ruin our time with Matthew. How different our lives would've been if we'd known he was alive. We never would've left London. Bridie would've found a way to scrape by if it meant staying near him. The only thing I'd regret is never meeting Lennon, though maybe our lives have always been on some sort of collision course if those magic pearls are the only way to heal Matthew.

Bridie tugs off her shoes and lies down on the bed, resting her head on Matthew's chest. He shifts and stirs until she's cuddled up against him with his arm around her. She closes her eyes over an expression of pure bliss. Some part of him must be awake and know who we are. We've got to break him free of his mental prison and dependence on his odious parents.

So, how do I tell Lennon we need to shag so we can save my father's life?

Lennon

9:45 pm PT

Hey, I'm back from dinner. Are you still stuck in Denver?

Hi! We finally boarded the plane. Just got our seats.

Hope you got the window seat.

No. Kai gets that or he whinges.

Whinges?

Whines.

😶 Him and Aaron both.

10:20 PM PT

Taking off now. Text you in a few.

10:45 PM PT

Well that was intense.

What was?

The turbulence. We're flying over the Rocky Mountains now and it's all good. That's what the pilot said. It's too dark to tell. I'm so bummed.

About the mountains?

Lol. No. About not seeing you today. Also being stuck in Denver for 4 hours. And Heathrow for 2 hours. And being on planes and in airports for what feels like my entire life.

That does suck.

So hard. I really wanted to see you.

Yeah, me, too. What time does your plane land?

Midnight. We went through customs in Denver, so don't have to worry about that in SF, but it still sucks.

I know.

I know you know. I need to vent.

Lol. Go right ahead

That's ok. It's not all about me. How was your birthday dinner?

Ok, I guess. Or weird. I mean, it's not my birthday, but I get that we had to do it today because tomorrow will be "busy."

May's a good cook and everything was... I dunno. Nice? I guess it's still weird for me when my family gets together and my parents aren't there.

We had cake. I blew out the candles.

Did you make a wish?

Oh yeah.

What for?

Can't tell you.

Presents?

Mostly clothes. Tony got me a watch.

A watch watch?

Yeah, with hands and everything. It's even engraved on the back.

What's it say?

It's some Chinese proverb. The English translation is a 'tiger father begets a tiger son'. Literally, it says a tiger father can't have a dog son.

Wow. No pressure.

From Tony? Never.

I got you a present.

No way! What?

Can't tell you

Lol.

Maybe I can come over and see it?

Tonight?

Yeah.

We won't be home until after 1.

That's ok.

No, it's not. You need to sleep.

I sleep better with you.

Just kidding.

Are you still there?

Yeah. It's just, I want to see you. So much. But
we need to wait until after the fight.

I know. Wishful thinking. I want to see you so
bad. You're the only person who doesn't want
something from me.

Hey.

Are you still there?

Yeah. Sorry. Bridie's being grumpy and nosy.

When is she not?

Lol. Yeah.

Is she trying to tell you things will change between us after tomorrow?

Something like that.

Tony and Auntie Cat tried telling me that tonight. Again. They're all wrong. Nothing changes between us, win or lose.

I hope not. I don't want to lose you.

That'll never happen. Ok?

Ok.

I love you.

I love you.

See you tomorrow. After the fight. I'll come get you and we'll go to the studio.

That would be amazing.

Will be amazing. For sure. Ok?

Ok.

12:01 AM PT

We've landed at SFO. Happy birthday!

I wake up to a message from Lennon, sent about two hours ago.

> Sorry. I fell asleep. Thanks. See you soon 🤍

His heart makes me press my hand to my heart. I scroll up and look at our conversation from last night.

> You're the only person who doesn't want something from me.

Except now I do. Will he hate me for it? I wish I'd known he thought that way about me, though what difference would it have made? Well, for one thing, maybe I wouldn't have gone to the chemist next to our hotel and bought a pack of condoms. I didn't tell Bridie. When she wasn't sitting at Matthew's bedside, she was pacing our suite, chewing her nails to bloody nubs. I couldn't get her to talk about the next step, so I had to deal with it myself. I got tired of her looking at me like she's the ewe and I'm her sacrificial lamb. I mean, yeah, first time sex is a big deal and purity is highly valued among our people, blah-blah-blah, but fretting isn't making it any better for me.

I roll over and look at Lennon's gift, which I'd set beside my pillow. After going to the chemist's, I went to the charity shop across the street. It had cardboard boxes full of old LPs. I thumbed through them until I came upon a dog-eared Clash album, 'Give 'Em Enough Rope', with the signature of the lead singer, Joe Strummer, scrawled across the front. I held my breath when I took it to the cashier, but she barely glanced at it as she said, "Two quid." The record has scratches, so maybe that's why. I hope Lennon likes it.

With a gusty sigh, I haul myself out of bed and rub my crusty eyes. It's 8:30, and I took a bullet for the fam and volunteered to open the launderette. I'm sure I smell as good as I look, but since I'm planning to roll back into bed when I'm finished, I pull on a T-shirt and yoga pants, and leave the apartment without bothering to wash my face.

Whoever filled in for us did a crap job and I grumble as I pick up used dryer sheets, food wrappers, and empty bottles. The vending machines are nearly empty, so I refill those as quickly as my bleary mind allows. My phone rubs against my thigh. My fingers itch to dig it out of my pocket and message Lennon, but I don't want to distract him. His bout with Jeremiah is at 1 p.m. My heart starts pounding. No way I'll be able to fall asleep again, not until I know the results.

The front door rattles, followed by a series of impatient raps on the glass. It's an old man teetering under the weight of a heavy laundry bag. I glance at the clock on the wall. It's five minutes until nine. He shifts from foot to foot, his wrinkles and gray hair reproaching me. I'm almost done anyway. Might as well let him in so I can leave early. I open the door and he trundles past me, muttering in Chinese, and dumps the entire contents of his bag into the nearest washer. I go back to the vending machine and finish loading the last row with little boxes of laundry detergent. He comes up behind me and I roll my eyes. Of course, he doesn't have supplies.

He jabs my neck. Once. Twice. Pain. I gasp and try to turn, but my legs become liquid. I clutch the vending machine door to break my fall. It starts tipping over, so I fall toward it and the little boxes come spilling out. Everything spins as I slide to the floor, my exposed skin scraping against the machine's sharp edges. Someone catches me. The old man. I try screaming, but my mouth feels full of cotton. I try focusing on his face, but everything fades and finally goes black.

I awake with a gasp, sucking in air as my heart pounds in my throat. I lift myself on my elbows, wincing as pain shoots through my left arm. Dizziness overcomes me and I lie flat, swallowing back on nausea until I can open my eyes again. I'm on a couch in a windowless room. There's a water cooler in one corner and a TV in another, and a coffee table spread with magazines. Wait. Am I in a doctor's office? I lift my arms. There's a bruise forming on my left elbow. My right forearm has a long scrap and smells like it's been treated with antiseptic.

I gasp with relief. I must have been rescued and now I'm being treated. I lift myself carefully to avoid putting weight on my throbbing elbow and glance around. I'm alone and there's no reception window. I ease myself up to a sitting position, kneading the pain lingering in my neck. My chest tightens as I glance at the covers of the magazines. They're all in Chinese. My heart starts pounding again. I reach for my phone, but it's gone, along with my keys.

The door opens and I flinch before gripping the edge of the couch. A man walks in, handsome in a slick, middle-aged way with deep-set eyes, rugged features, and thick black hair receding at the temples. He's wearing a stiletto tie and the edges of his sharkskin suit are sharp as daggers.

"Good. You're awake. Are you thirsty?" His voice has an odd affectation, as if he's trying to sound English.

Should I trust the water? If they wanted to poison me, they could have done it while I was passed out, so I nod. He pours a cup and hands it to me. I drain it and some of the ache in my throat eases. He pulls a chair in front of me and straddles it so his forearms rest on the top. His smile brings a gleam to the malice in his eyes.

I set down the cup and fold my arms. "Where am I?"

"The Two Dragon Clan *kongsi*."

At this point, I'm not surprised, but it doesn't make me any less scared. I take a shaky breath before asking, "Where's Tony?"

"Not your concern."

"I want to talk to him."

"You can't."

"Is he still in charge?"

The man laughs as if I told a bad joke.

If Tony's no longer in charge, that can only mean one thing. I'm being used to trap Lennon. I lick my dry lips and try swallowing the tremble from my voice. "My uncle is Christy Sparrow. When he finds out you kidnapped me…"

"I'll tell him you're lying, that you're making trouble because you snuck off with your boyfriend."

"Lennon isn't my boyfriend."

His smirk becomes thoughtful. "Interesting my nephew named himself after John Lennon."

Nephew? Is this Uncle George, the one who murdered Lennon's father? How much worse can this get?

"Honestly, I'm impressed. I didn't think he had it in him to be so rebellious. I thought his father had smothered all the spirit out of him. I'm glad I was wrong. Too bad I was kept away from him. I could have helped channel that rebellious streak into more acceptable endeavors. My brother thought I was a bad influence. He thought he could run Paul's life and mine. Everyone idolizes my brother, but I'm his twin and I can tell you, Michael wasn't a good man. When you see Paul, tell him I said so."

That sounds like he's not going to kill me. I try to gain what confidence I can from that and shrug.

"I need you to answer a few questions."

I scoff. I'm not going to tell him shite.

"Why did you and your family go to London?"

Ice water runs through my veins. Bollocks. What if this isn't about Lennon? What if it's about the Yin Pearl? I manage another shrug. "Family stuff."

He gives a sympathetic nod. "I heard Dr. Wong was ill. Such a shame. He hasn't been the same since his son died. It must have been hard for you and your family, being outsiders, shunned, on the Wayward Way. Dr. Wong must regret how he treated you." His voice is soothing. He doesn't want to harm me. He wants to help. "There was something he wanted to tell your family, right? Or something he wanted to show his grandson."

Charm. Or a Two Dragon Family version of it. That's got to be what's compelling me to speak, and yet it's something more, as if a hook has pierced my will, making me respond to George Lau's tug. "Yeah, there was something he wanted to tell us." Shit. Stop. I know the drill. The only way to fight Charm is with more Charm. "When he had the heart attack, he thought was a goner. All he could think about was apologizing for treating us like rubbish. Like your brother did to you."

George's laughter scrapes like a rusty nail. "Did you accept his apology?"

"No. Did you accept your brother's apology?"

The mirth in his face turns off like a light. "No. He took something from me I can never get back." His eyes narrow. "Your stepfather also took something from me."

"What are you talking about? You knew Matthew?"

"We met in passing."

I blink with surprise and in that moment between my lids falling and rising, his will floods past the wall I'd built. "He took something of mine. I want it back. His parents must've told you."

I'm nodding. I can't stop myself. Words well up. I dig deep and dredge up enough Charm to hold back the surge. "Matthew took a lot of things from a lot of people. He was a thief. If he stole from you, I'm sorry. Can you tell me what he took? Maybe I can try getting it back."

He leans back and stares at me with eyes like razors, trying to cut me open and see what I'm made of. "I can see why my nephew likes you. You play dangerous games, little girl."

"I'm not a little girl and you're the one playing games." I fold my arms so he can't see my trembling hands. "You're forgetting the Dragon Son is my friend and he's going to be pissed that you kidnapped me."

"We kidnapped you to ensure his cooperation. You're nothing more than a bargaining chip, little girl."

I grit my teeth. He wants to use me against Matthew and Lennon. I can't let that happen, but what can I do? "You're wrong about my uncle. When he finds out I'm here, he'll come after you."

George sputters. "What are the Strowlers compared to the Two Dragon Clan? You gypsies have little unity and no power base. What is your uncle going to do to me? Tell my fortune?"

"I'll tell your fortune." I mean it as a threat, but he cocks his head.

"Can you?"

"Of course. Give me your palm."

Suspicion glints from his eyes and something else, too. That which earns Strowler women their gelt: superstition. He covers it with his smirk as he holds out his hand, palm up.

I'm loathe to touch him, but I need to buy whatever time I can. I press my thumb into the center of his palm. Using Second Sight, I sense his essence and feel the white heat of his anger. It's a slow boil that's never stopped. His soul is evaporating in a toxic steam, because… I give a little gasp.

"What?"

"Someone betrayed you. Someone close to you…" I press deeper and there it is. "Your brother. He…" Oh wow. Oh no. No wonder… Maybe I'm wrong. The only way to find out is to say it. "He slept with your wife."

George snatches back his palm and jumps to his feet. "How do you know that?"

What can I say, except, "It's there."

His hand balls into a fist. Is he going to punch me? I flinch, raising my arms to defend myself.

"What else did you see?" he whispers.

I shake my head. "Nothing." Though that's not true. I felt an old anger still burning bright, not quenched by murder.

There's a knock on the door. George opens it and speaks to another man in Chinese. Then he turns again to me. "My nephew has arrived. If you both cooperate, you'll be out of here by the end of the day. If you don't… your fate is in his hands, and his in yours. I'd call it romantic, but I wouldn't know. As you pointed out, I've been betrayed." He strides out.

My stomach drops as I hear the door being locked from the outside. I'm trapped. I cover my mouth to keep from hyperventilating, but breath spurts from my nose. It takes all my strength not to jump up and run around the room in frantic circles.

Stop. Don't panic. Think.

I close my eyes and slow my breathing. I have to find a way out of here and warn Lennon.

Lennon

Today is the day I step up and become the Dragon Son for real. Happy birthday to me. My first present is this text from Jeremiah:

I snort at this clumsy attempt to psych me out and text back:

Will he see through my attempt to disarm him with my callow youth? He's not the man his father was, so probably not. A sharp pain stabs my heart. If John Walks Long were still alive, I'd hand him the Crossroads on a silver platter and walk away. Instead, I'm going to fight his tool of a son and, win or lose, be the Dragon Son. In any case, I'm not going to lower my guard in case Jeremiah changes him mind.

Penny hasn't sent any messages since last night, probably

because she has hella jet lag and is dead to the world. A chill prickles my skin. No, not dead. Asleep. Why can't I shake this feeling something is wrong? Probably because I was passed out cold with jet lag while my parents were being murdered.

I look up from my phone at Uncle Roy and Auntie Cat in the front seat of the car. I'd be pissing in the wind if I asked them to swing by Penny's place so I can check on her. Besides, we're almost in Chinatown. My stomach flops around the piece of toast I ate so it wouldn't be empty. I'm not sure what to expect. If we were at the clan compound on Chisel Knife Mountain, there'd be a big ceremony, followed by the first challenge, and then a feast. Since I refuse to go there, Head Elder has gone silent. I'm supposed to be getting the Yang Pearl today, but I'm certain he's withholding it so he can dangle it like a shiny toy, forcing me to come get it.

Oh, I'm gonna come get it all right, and then he's gonna get what's coming to him.

I close my eyes and reach out to Jade Dragon. I sense him way out in the distance, barely in range. He's made himself small enough to fit into a nautilus shell and is messing with an octopus. I sigh. Most people don't realize dragons are playful, or at least my ancestor is. Maybe he's the weird one.

Hey, Ancestor, you got a moment?

Nothing. He's too preoccupied, weaving past snaring tentacles and a snapping beak.

Just so ya know, today's my birthday and I'm officially the Dragon Son now, so woo-hoo.

Woo-hoo? Of course, that caught his attention.

It means I'm excited, but not really. Sarcasm, you know?

He either doesn't know or doesn't care because he's now bopping the octopus on its head.

Anyway, I have to fight this challenge and I might die, and if I do, can you talk to my cousin, Tony, like you do to me? He's going to need your help.

Your brother?

Cousin, brother, must be the same in Dragonland. *Yeah, him. The older one.*

You're not going to die.

A vote of confidence. *Gee, thanks.*

Sarcasm will not help you. Wisdom will. He breaks off contact as he attaches himself to a dolphin for a free ride, I guess. Like ya do when you're so damn wise.

The car pulls up in front of the *kongsi* and the first thing I notice is the guards, two at the door and two in the street. My aunt and uncle exchange wary glances before looking back at me.

"I don't recognize them. Do you?" asks Auntie Cat.

I shake my head. The toast becomes a hard ball in the pit of my stomach. I bite back on saying it's a trap. Of course, it is. It'd be stupid for any of us to say we didn't see it coming. And the only way to escape this trap is to step into the middle of it.

We go inside and are immediately surrounded by more unknown guards, who pat us down and take our phones. Who are these people? Maybe Head Elder sent his goons to keep us in check. My aunt and uncle start demanding answers, but the goons ignore them.

Little Brother.

Tony. He's standing next to the stairs with two men obviously shadowing him. At first glance, he looks as expected, neatly dressed in black, but not in a suit because he doesn't do suits or ties, or anything that gets in the way of being combat-ready. It takes a Tony expert to see past his impassive expression to his rigid jaw and tense gaze.

Big Brother. What happened? Who are these guys?

Head Elder is here.

Shit. He never leaves Hong Kong, so I'm allowed to be surprised. Okay, then, he must've brought the Yang Pearl to be the cheese that baits this trap. Little does he know Jade Dragon gave me the ability to use the Dragon Shout to its ultimate power without it. I almost smirk, but there's something about Tony's expression that stops me.

What else?

My father is here, too.

Cold fury ices my veins. Both murderers here, together. Why wait to learn whatever truth there is to their actions? Who cares what their reasons are? I can kill them now and it will all be over with.

They have Penny.

Her name freezes me. *What?*

My father kidnapped her. She's here, locked in a room, under guard.

No no no no no. First they kill my parents and now her. No, not her. Never her. I'll raze this whole damn building, burn it to the goddamn ground before I let that happen. Hot energy burns through the cold too fast, messing up my *chi*. A reddish-gray haze covers my eyes.

Stop. Tony uses the word like a slap in the face. *Listen. Panicking won't help. She's heavily guarded and your rescue attempt could result in her death. I've taken steps to ensure her safety.*

I take a deep breath to balance myself again. He's right, but it's hard. The thought of her in my uncle's hands makes my heart pound. *What steps?*

I called Christy Sparrow. He'll be here soon to demand her release. By then, Jeremiah and the Beggars will have arrived and they'll join forces. Head Elder will be forced to release her.

If they hurt her…

They won't, not unless you make a move. They need her as a hostage. Paul… Lennon. Think. You're the Dragon Son now. This is about strategy, not power. Play the long game, like we practiced during sparring. Don't focus on what you can't do. Work on what you can. I'll be with you. I won't let anything happen to Penny or you. Be strong.

Tony's with me. He's taking my side against Head Elder and his own father, and by doing so, put his own family at risk. How could I have ever seen him as the enemy? He's been with me my whole life and pledged himself to me, as I did to him, that day in the Ancestral Hall. *We will rescue each other in difficulty; we will aide each other in danger.*

Big Brother's eyes glow. *We ask not the same day of birth, but we seek to die together.*

I nod. If we die saving the people we love, so be it. We'll have kept our pledge to my father.

Tony's face stiffens as the goons part to let Uncle George swagger through.

My father's killer. A surge of energy zig-zags through me. If Penny weren't in danger, I would fry his ass here and now. Anger clutches my throat and burns through my body. It meets the energy and sickens me. I start to tremble. Shit. I better calm down or I'll drain my power before I have a chance to use it. Tony's right. I need strategy before I start racking up a body count.

Auntie Cat pushes free and steps in front of her brother, hands on her hips. "What the hell is going on, George?"

He shakes his head. "I don't have time for you, Cat." He starts to move away.

She steps so he can't get around her. "Make time. You haven't spoken to me in two years. You won't answer my calls, texts, emails, nothing."

"Your messages were full of false accusations. You always chose Mike over me and listened to his lies."

"That's not true."

"It is true, whether you choose to believe it or not."

"All right, fine, believe what you want. We're here. I'm listening."

He breathes out an impatient sigh. "What do you want me to say?"

"Did you kill Mike?"

Everything goes silent. Nobody moves. My breath stops. It feels like time has stopped and can't move forward until he answers.

"No."

"Did you order him killed or hire the Shinobi?"

"No."

The world spins again, though the tension in the room feels wound tighter than ever. No one believes him. How could they? So why are these men obeying him?

"Anything else?" he asks.

Cat's eyes are like a raw wound. I know she doesn't believe him. "Why are you here?"

"Why wouldn't I be here? It's a big day."

"That's not an answer."

"All will be revealed." He winks.

Auntie Cat's face goes blank. She glances at me and Tony before looking away quickly. She whispers, "I won't let you hurt our nephew."

"Our nephew." Uncle George smirks. "I won't hurt our nephew. I've never blamed him. I only blame the guilty."

What the hell are they talking about? Why would he blame me for anything? The only guilty people here are him and Head Elder.

He turns to me. "Paul. It's been too long. Such a shame we've been kept apart by lies."

I spit in his face. "Fuck you, murderer. You killed my father."

His eyes deaden as he wipes his cheek with his suit sleeve. "I'm sure your Big Brother has told you that I have your girl-friend. Let's have no more outbursts. We wouldn't want anything unfortunate to happen to her."

Damn. I need to suck it up, but it's so hard with him standing there alive and well while Dad and Mom are dead. I grit my teeth and swallow back all the bile wanting to pour out.

Uncle George motions the men surrounding me and I'm herded away from my family.

"Where are you taking him?" Auntie Cat calls out. "George, answer me."

He strides along from behind without saying a word. *All will be revealed.* What did he mean by that? Am I finally going to find out what happened between them? Is he going to try and blame Dad? Is it possible that Dad, maybe, did something wrong?

Am I about to find out Dad's sin?

My stomach tightens and churns. Dad wasn't perfect, and maybe he did something bad, but nothing justifies murder. No way I'll believe any of my uncle's lies, regardless of what happened.

I'm led down the hall to Dad's office or, more accurately, the Dragon Son's office. Tony was using it in the interim, but it becomes mine today. What the hell? Am I supposed to sign some paperwork or something? We stop in front of the closed door and a couple of goons grab my arms. Before I can react, Uncle George jabs a vital point in each of my shoulder blades. Pain zings through my body as the flow of my *chi* is disrupted and my arms dangle at my sides, useless. The goons yank back my arms and slap handcuffs around my wrists. Fucking bastard. He's kept me mobile while preventing me from using the Dragon Shout.

The door is opened and I'm shoved inside. I stumble and almost fall, but manage to catch my balance because I'll be damned if I'll kneel before the man who caused all my suffering. Head Elder looks exactly the same as when I last saw him. Steel gray suit, steel gray hair, reptile eyes, and a mouth that only smiles in the face of misery.

The door closes and I'm left alone with him and Uncle

George. Head Elder stands and allows my uncle to take the seat behind the desk. What the actual fuck? Then I notice the framed portrait on the wall above the desk. It's supposed to be the previous Dragon Son watching over his predecessor. When Dad was alive, it was a photo of his father. After he died, Tony hung Dad's photo there. Now, Dad's photo has been replaced with the previous one of his father. It's like Head Elder and George hated Dad so much, they want to wipe out all memory of him.

I bite my tongue to keep from raging. *Play the long game.* I can't strike out at them, yet, but I can focus what power I have. I take deep breaths, calming my heart, and directing the flow of my *chi* to restore the pressure points Uncle George disabled.

Head Elder eyes me like a speck of dust he wants to brush away before demanding, "Where is the Yang Pearl?"

I did not expect that. "What?"

One of his reptilian eyes twitches. "Where is the Yang Pearl?"

I repeat myself, too, but more emphatically. "What?"

Uncle George speaks in this bullshit-friendly tone. "The Yang Pearl was not on your father's body. He gave it to you for safekeeping when you left the compound."

This weird feeling comes over me, like a compulsion to agree with him. I muster my *chi* to fight it off, which weakens my attempt to release my arms. "No, he didn't."

"He knew he was in danger and wanted to keep the Yang Pearl out of the hands of Head Elder, should he die, so he gave it to you."

That pressure returns, making me speak without thinking, "Why would he do that? I was fifteen years old. I don't have it and I don't know where it is." I blink hard to shake off the compulsion. Then it hits me. Holy shit. "You lost the Yang Pearl?"

Uncle George's friendly expression hardens. He and my

grandfather exchange looks, and Head Elder is the one who looks nervous. He blusters, "We didn't lose it. Your father, he had it."

"Wasn't he supposed to have it?"

"He concealed it so we couldn't take it."

I almost smile. Good work, Dad. I hope with all my heart that's what happened, although another scenario seems more likely. "What about the Shinobi? You said they killed him. Maybe they took it."

Uncle George shakes his head. "No."

"How do you know?"

"I was there. I would've seen them take it."

The same way I saw Auntie Sylvia attempt to strangle my mother to ensure she was dead. Unless she wasn't trying to strangle her… what if she was actually taking something from around Mom's neck… shit. I know my expression must betray some knowledge, so I say, "That's why you tore apart Auntie Cat's house. You were looking for the Yang Pearl."

They exchange shifty glances. I expect them to deny it, but they have bigger fish to fry, namely me. Uncle George's sharp eyes skewer me. "Tell us where it is."

The pressure returns with double force. I counter at the expense of my arms, using my *chi* to block the compulsion, but my words come out unfiltered. "I don't have it. I would've already used it against you murdering assholes if I did."

Head Elder's lips flounder at my disrespect. Uncle George tilts back in the chair and steeples his fingers. His lips twitch in a near smile. "We'll kill your girlfriend if you don't give us the Yang Pearl."

Shit. Don't panic. Call his bluff. "And piss off the Strowlers? I don't think so. Besides, killing Penny isn't going to make it magically appear."

"Enough," says my grandfather. "The Beggars will be here soon. This can wait until we're done with them." There's no softening is his eyes, but his tone loses its bluster. "I didn't kill your mother. She was my daughter. I won't allow you to be harmed, either, but you must obey me."

Notice the omission? I sure do. "But you killed my father, is that what you're saying?"

"The Shinobi killed your father."

"Shinobi don't kill without being paid."

"You'll learn the truth shortly."

I'd spit in his face if I could. "I know the truth."

"You know nothing." He shakes his head, his eyes bleak with disappointment. "You're not the dragon."

Okay, that's random. One of the legends about Jade Dragon is that a Dragon Son will someday manifest as an actual dragon, the way he did on his fifteenth birthday. I figured it was just a story because how is that even possible? Then again, I am descended from a dragon, so maybe it is. Not that it matters because I'm not a dragon, so I shrug. "Am I supposed to be?"

The disappointment becomes something palpable. It radiates off him. I can taste it, harsh and bitter as hell. "A comet appeared in the sky the year Jade Dragon died in his human form. That same comet reappeared the year you were born."

I know all this. Dad said it meant I was born lucky, which I later found out is bullshit since the Chinese consider comets to be bad luck, and signs of chaos and change.

"You." He jabs his finger at me. "Everything I did was for you. My daughter, I married her to your father so that you, the next Dragon Son, would be conceived and born that year, when the comet returned to manifest another dragon in human form. I was to be the grandfather of the new family dragon. You would have been guided by me and followed your destiny as you should. Your fool of a father ruined everything."

My mouth drops open. Holy shit. For real? I almost want to

laugh, except… "Wait. Is that why you killed my dad? Because a comet didn't turn me into dragon?"

Head Elder waves an impatient hand and turns away. Is that a denial or show of anger because I'm not on Team Comet?

Uncle George opens the door and his goons enter and grab hold of me. As I'm dragged down the hall, it hits me. How can they expect me to fight Jeremiah if I can't move my arms? There's only one answer. They don't want me to fight him. If that's true, there's only one reason.

I'm no longer the Dragon Son.

I'm shoved into the banquet hall and at first glance, everything looks as it should. The tables and chairs have been taken away and the huge altar at the end of the room has been set with fresh fruit, flowers, and newly-lit candles and incense. There's even a thick coil of rope on the ground, to be used to form a makeshift ring for my fight with Jeremiah.

Except there is no Jeremiah, or any other leader of the local clans, who should all be present, waiting to witness our bout. Instead, there are a handful of Two Dragon Clan elders, all of them dressed in their finest and looking bewildered. Wariness marks their faces as they watch me being dragged to the center of the room to stand with Tony, Aaron, Auntie Cat and Uncle Roy. The goons let me go and join the men who ring the room, guarding the doors and shuttered windows. Smoke from the altar clings to the ceiling in a sweet miasma that makes my head ache. I'm dying for a drink of water, but I don't bother asking.

I turn to Aaron. "Worst birthday party ever."

His fear-pinched mouth spreads into a grin, which disappears the instant his father and Head Elder roll in. They stand near us, not with us, so we're not all one big happy family. Well, we would be if the ground opened and swallowed those two. Divine intervention. Now, there's a thought. I close my eyes and reach out, far and wide, deep and high, searching for that cold, scaly presence. *Come on, Jade Dragon. Are you going to disappoint the birthday boy?* It's no use. My *chi* is too weak.

Another presence brushes against mine. Tony. *They harmed you somehow. What did they do?*

Maybe Jade Dragon won't help, but Tony will. *They froze my pressure points to disrupt my chi.*

He lays his hand on my shoulder as if offering support. *Chi* radiates off his palm, its warm flow easing the chill at the affected points.

Big Brother, no. This will weaken you.

I can be weak. You can't.

There's a quicker way to do this, with a couple of jabs to the pressure points, but that would be too obvious and the shock to my body would still leave me weakened. The transfer of *chi* will return me to full power, but slowly drain Tony of his vitality.

I glance around. *Where are all the other clans? Their elders should be here by now.*

Head Elder told them not to come.

What? Is Jeremiah here yet?

The Beggars are amassing outside.

Amassing? Jeremiah should be showing up with two, maybe three Beggar Clan officials. He challenges me. I accept. Then we fight and winner takes all.

Christy Sparrow must have called Jeremiah.

That's good news, except… *How are they going to get in?*

I don't know. My people would have let them in, but Head Elder's men have blockaded the front door.

I have a bad feeling about this.

Really?

Did Big Brother actually make a joke? The loss of *chi* must be going to his head. *How can Head Elder expect me to fight like this?*

He doesn't reply.

Isn't it obvious? He can't. I think he's about to boot me out of the clan.

No. Why would you think that?

Because he just told me this bullshit story about a comet…

"Son," Uncle George calls out sharply. "Step away from your brother."

Damn it. Trust him to figure it out. Tony's hand slips from my shoulder. His *chi* strengthened me, but not enough to release my pressure points. If I can stay calm and balanced, I should be able to release myself in a few minutes.

Uncle George holds up his hands to hush the murmuring elders, who eye him with suspicion. Then he nods to Head Elder, who turns to address the crowd.

"Twin sons were born to our previous Dragon Son. The firstborn immediately had a red string tied around his ankle. The boys appeared identical, so the string wasn't removed. Or so everyone was told. The next day, while bathing the boys, a nurse accidentally washed off the string. She tied it back on without knowing which was the firstborn and told the doctor, who chose not to tell the parents. This was kept hidden for many years until the doctor, on his deathbed, confessed to me. By then, it was too late. Michael had already been declared the Dragon Son. I kept this hidden, hoping fate had chosen the right child. Fate was against us. The wrong twin was chosen. The one named Michael led a life of sin and besmirched his innocent brother, George, accusing him of gambling and other sins to hide his own crimes."

Calm and balance fly out the window as the flow of my *chi* is interrupted by the hammering of my heart. I think of those words I heard my grandfather yell at Dad two years ago. *I will not allow your sin, your dishonor to ruin us.*

"Michael was lustful and immoral. He seduced his brother's intended wife, Sylvia, before she and George wed. She became pregnant and they tried to pass the child off as George's. Guilt hounded Michael and he eventually confessed his sin to his brother. A paternity test revealed the child, Tony, is actually Michael's firstborn son."

A collective gasp bursts out, even from the goons, before the room fills with a mushroom cloud of toxic silence. It chokes me so I can't speak. Neither can Tony. He's frozen to stone. Aaron's mouth hangs open while he blinks rapidly. Auntie Cat and Uncle Roy are staring at the floor. Then they look up and exchange looks, hers angry, his sad, both resigned, as if what they'd heard didn't surprise them.

This was Dad's sin. A son he had no right to. No. It can't be true. I won't let it be true. I shout, "That's a lie!"

Except I know it's true, because it explains so much. Dad couldn't live with the guilt anymore and told Head Elder that Tony was his first-born son. Head Elder refused to acknowledge it and had Dad murdered, with Uncle George's enthusiastic aid.

Uncle George takes an envelope from his coat pocket. He goes to Tony and hesitates, looking down before handing it to him. "I'm sorry, son. I would have told you sooner, but I was forbidden. I never blamed you."

Tony yanks out the document and unfolds it so we both can read it. Aaron crowds in so he can see, too. The top of the page has a company name, DNA Diagnostic Center. Beneath that is the document's title, Final Certificate of Analysis.

Alleged father: Michael Lau
Child: Tony Lau

Mother: Sylvia Leung

Results: Michael Lau cannot be excluded as the biological father of Tony Lau.

Probability of paternity: 99.9991%.

Tony turns to the next page, which contains tables of data and signatures of authentication. His arms drop. The document flutters to the ground.

My throat constricts and I can't breathe. I try concentrating on my *chi* to stabilize myself, but anger and anguish move through me like a howl, making it impossible.

Uncle George picks up the document and hands it to one of the elders. While they crowd around and stare at it, Head Elder continues.

"I learned of this when Michael came to me, demanding to replace his true born son, Paul, with his bastard. I refused to allow this travesty. Jade Dragon would not accept a bastard born of an incestuous relationship. I remained silent, hoping this sin had not tainted my grandson. He was born the year of the comet, heralding the rebirth of a new dragon for our clan, but he didn't manifest as a dragon on his fifteenth birthday. I waited, hoping the manifestation was somehow delayed. Now, he is an adult and I must face the truth. He will not become a dragon because his father was not the true Dragon Son. Righteousness dictates I must relinquish favoritism of my own blood. Therefore, from this moment forward, our new Dragon Son is George Lau."

And there it is. Head Elder can't control me or Tony so he found a new tool. They must have been planning this moment for years, ever since they killed my dad. No wonder Auntie Sylvia killed Mom. She stood in the way of Tony becoming the Dragon Son.

Shit. Tony. My brother. I turn to him. His face is like a blank piece of paper with knife-sharp edges.

Big Brother?

He blinks once, but doesn't answer.

Dad did this to him. To us. To our clan. And all because he was thinking with his dick. And with Auntie Sylvia of all women. Nausea clenches my throat. If I keep thinking about it, I'm going to puke. Uncle George has drawn Aaron away and is whispering in his ear. Lies? The truth? Both are equally bad at this point. Or maybe he's using the compelling skill to turn Aaron against us. The situation is way beyond my control. I need help. I gather what I can of my *chi* and use its power to broadcast far and wide.

Jade Dragon. Dude. I'm not being basic. He's ancient and wise, but something shiny can grab his attention.

Somewhere off the coast, a cold scaly presence moves through the ocean depths. He's left the nautilus and returned to full size, and is now circling the wreck of a ship he'd last seen over a century ago. Its deterioration fascinates him, until he hears my summons and rears his head.

I am a dude?

See? *If that's okay with you.*

A dude is a young male. By dragon reckoning, I am young, there-fore, yes, I am a dude.

I'm in a shit ton of trouble and I need some answers.

Jade Dragon swishes his tail, already losing interest. I've been in trouble before and it hasn't impressed him.

Was I supposed to be the next dragon?

His presence grows stronger again. *Why would you think so?*

There was a comet passing the Earth when you died. That same comet returned the year I was born.

Humans. Bubbles snort from his snout. *You place great impor-tance on things that have no real bearing on your lives. A comet is a comet, nothing more. The gravitational pull of the sun decides its trajectory. My death and your birth are mere coincidence.*

Okay, but my birth was basically engineered to coincide with the comet so I'd be the next dragon. Since that didn't happen, my grand-father has decided to punish me.

The same grandfather I told you to kill.

Yeah.

Why don't you kill him now?

I can't. I'm tied up.

Get untied and kill him.

It's not that simple.

The bubbles appear again. *It never is with humans.*

You were human once.

At first, I think he's not going to answer. Then he swims upward, bursting out of the ocean and into the air, flying closer to San Francisco. *Dragons do not aid their young. After spawning, the eggs are left alone, as are the hatchlings. Only the strongest can survive. And the strongest of those continue through the years. I understand humans are different, so I speak with you. Even so, you must become strong on your own.*

I know, but this is something I can't find the answer to.

Nor will you. The new dragon cannot know his destiny. It must come upon him, like birth, and he must accept it. When this happens, I will offer some help because he is still human.

I could use some help right now.

He's silent and for a moment I think he's done. Then he speaks and his hissing tone sounds softer, *Your mate is in danger.*

He thinks Penny is my mate. I'm not about to tell him any different. *Yeah, she is.*

Dragons once had mates, long ago. We lost the ability. That is why I mated with a human. I was close to my mate. Are you close to yours?

She's my best friend. I love her.

I will help her. As he says this, he flies higher, away from my reach.

Hey, wait. How are you going to help her?

His presence recedes as he plunges into a thick bank of clouds.

I hate it when he does that. Okay, if he helps Penny, that will probably help me, but how? All I can do is be prepared for anything.

Penny

The water cooler sloshes and scuffs as I drag it across the hardwood floor. I stop every few feet and wait, staring at the door, which doesn't open. If there's a guard outside, he either doesn't hear or doesn't care what I'm doing.

After testing the cooler's cord to make sure it's long enough, I go to the TV and unplug it. The cart's wheels squeak as I roll it next to the cooler. I wait, dry-mouthed and heart pounding. The door remains closed. I'm locked in and seemingly pose no threat, so maybe there isn't a guard, or he's down the hall. If no one comes, I'll be out of water and entertainment, but it's a risk I'm willing to take.

I tie the TV's cord around the base of the water cooler. Then I take hold of the end of the water cooler's cord and stand beside the door. I take deep breaths, as Lennon taught me, reducing my presence and visibility until I've blended into the background. Then I yank on the cord as hard as I can.

The cooler tips into the TV, which falls first, smacking the floor with a boom followed by the crack and shatter of broken glass. The cooler thuds as it hits the TV. Its top pops off and rolls, spraying water everywhere, including onto me. I press against the wall and stay still except for my thudding heart.

The door opens and the guard rushes in. He stands in the middle of the room and stares at the wreckage. I slip out behind him, close the door and lock it.

Using Swift and Silent Steps, I rush through the hall. I make it to the lobby and sidle along the walls. The front entrance is blocked by guards. Even the stairs and elevator are blockaded. I huddle in a dark corner and bite my lip to keep from panting aloud. Fuzziness overcomes me and my feet feel like they're buried in quicksand. Lennon warned me that *chi* powers are tricky, even for experts, but especially for beginners like me. I'm paying the price of switching between skills so rapidly. I reach deep within, trying to pull out what power remains so I can reach the stairs, but it's no use. I'm nearly drained and seconds from becoming visible. All that for nothing. What if I've made things even worse for Lennon?

Something surrounds me. Another presence, powerful and so cold, yet warmth fills me and my *chi* is bolstered, keeping me invisible. Is it Lennon? No, it can't be. The presence is ancient and scaly with a scent of sea and sulfur…

Oh God. A ghost? No. A dragon? Bile fills my throat. Fear rushes through me like ice water, but before it can affect my visibility, I'm gently slid along the wall to the corner beneath the stairs. Whatever is doing this is sheltering me, but why?

The front door starts rattling and shaking, like the top on a pressure boiler. The guards all turn their attention to it, wary-eyed and nudging each other. A few reach for their weapons.

The door blows open and off its hinges. Wind gusts into the room with tornado force, swirling around, lifting the guards and tossing them into air. I can barely hear their screams of terror as they're slammed into the walls, their weapons dropping from their hands. Then the wind ends as abruptly as it came. The men slide off the walls and crumple onto the floor.

Everything goes silent, except for my heart pounding in my ears.

I felt none of it. The presence shielded me. As it slides away. I grasp after it. "Wait. Who are you?"

No answer. Did I imagine it? If I did, how was I protected from all this... whatever this is. My first thought is a bomb, but there were no flames, and other than the door, nothing is damaged. Not the furniture, the carpets or even the security equipment at the front desk. I should do something, run, call for help, but my legs are shaking too badly. The *chi* from the presence remains and I pull from its power to gather myself together. As I step away from the corner, someone enters from the outside.

"What the hell?" Jeremiah Walks Long glances around at the men lying scattered on the floor. Then he turns and makes a motion out the door.

A guard rolls over, groaning, and sees Jeremiah. He reaches for his gun. Jeremiah leaps forward, swinging his staff. As it makes contact, the guard squeals and rolls into a ball, clutching his damaged arm.

The Beggar Clan come pouring in, weapons drawn. Most, like their Chief, are dressed in ragged military fatigues, and I'm sure they've had plenty of experience subduing the enemy. In less than a minute, the guards are disarmed and kneeling with their hands on their heads, while the Beggars call out, "Clear."

A female Beggar spots me and runs over. "Are you Penny Sparrow?"

Who else would I be in this situation? I nod. She places an arm across my shoulders and shuffles me across the room, hollering, "Chief, the hostage has been recovered."

I want to tell her we're in a building in San Francisco, not Kabul, but I don't think she'd listen.

Uncle Christy and his sons stride through the door. That

presence I felt and that wind, maybe it came from him. Growing up on the Wayward Way, I didn't learn about the more powerful Second Sight skills, reserved for men of status on the Glory Road. So much for George Lau's words about gypsies having no power.

I run to my uncle and hug him. "I'm so glad to see you."

He holds me at arm's length to look me up and down. "You're all right?" I nod. "What happened in here. Some kind of explosion?"

"That wasn't you?"

"What? No. We thought it was a bomb."

I turn to Jeremiah. "You didn't do that?"

"No." He rubs his unshaven chin. "I saw something like this once, though, in Afghanistan. A nest of insurgents had booby-trapped the entrance to their hideout, but it backfired, literally, and blew them all away." His eyes narrow in on me. "Were you sheltered somehow, Penny?

"Yeah, I was hiding behind the staircase."

"Two lucky breaks," says Uncle Christy. "I don't think we can count on a third."

Do I tell them about the presence? How do I even begin? Maybe it was Lennon somehow trying to protect me, except if he can do all that, why hasn't he broken free and kicked ass? I head for the stairs, but my uncle grabs my arm.

"Where do you think you're going, missy?"

"Lennon, we have to help him. His uncle and his grandfather are trying to take over the clan. They kidnapped me to use as a hostage."

Uncle Christy smacks his fist into his palm. "There's hell to pay and I'm the Devil."

A Beggar soldier leans over the banister from the stairwell. "Sir, we have secured the perimeter and surrounded hostile forces."

My nerves ratchet up. This isn't over by a long shot. I wish I could warn Lennon or let him know we're coming. Maybe that presence will help me again. I reach out mentally, trying to gain some sense of it. Nothing. It's gone.

"Lies," Auntie Cat calls out. "My brothers looked similar when they were born, but Michael had a birthmark on his shoulder. There was no red string. His parents always knew, from the moment of birth, which boy was which. Michael was the true Dragon Son, not George."

I hold my breath, begging her to say the paternity test is fake, too, but she doesn't, because it isn't and I know it.

Uncle George shakes his head with mock sorrow. "I must remind everyone that Catherine is the daughter of my father's second wife. She doesn't know the truth, only the lies our brother told her. The mark on Michael's shoulder appeared later, not at birth. Isn't that right, Sister?"

Auntie Cat's face goes blank. She blinks several times before nodding. "Yes. Of course. I only know what Michael told me."

Damn it. Now he's using that mind control thing on her. I want to shake her out of it using the Silent Speech, but that will hinder any progress I've made with my pressure points. I've got to speak up in my father's defense. "Jade Dragon. He's the proof. He communed with my father. We all saw it. Why would he do that if my father wasn't the Dragon Son?"

Everyone turns to Head Elder, including Uncle George, who says softly, "What did we see?"

"A trick of the eyes," claims my grandfather. "Easily manipulated. Our ancestor never spoke to him. Michael made us believe so to hide his dark secret."

"No." Uncle Roy takes a step forward before a guard pushes him back. "We all saw it. I saw it."

"Ah, the best friend," says Uncle George. "He told you it was fake, remember? You know it is."

Uncle Roy gets that same blank expression as he nods along. "Yes. Fake."

Auntie Cat tugs on his arm, trying to shake him out of it. "No. You told me you saw Michael commune with Jade Dragon."

Interesting. Uncle George can only control one person at a time. What the hell is he doing? I want to call him on it, but I can't put a name to it, and will anyone believe me, considering the position I'm in? I need to stall him while Jade Dragon helps Penny. "I saw it. And felt it. Jade Dragon spoke to me."

Head Elder shakes his head sadly. "He even manipulated his son, forcing him to tell me that Jade Dragon wanted me dead."

"That's not true," I yell.

Satisfaction gleams in those reptile eyes. "Did you or did you not tell me Jade Dragon ordered you to kill me?"

Why was I so stupid when I was fifteen? I'm not that stupid anymore. If he can lie, so can I. "I never said that."

Head Elder's lips thin. He's probably digging deep into his sack of shit, searching for something else to smear me with…

A booming sound explodes through the building. The walls start shaking and the floor trembles.

Earthquake.

I brace myself, like you do when you're from San Francisco, gauging if it's strong enough for you to take cover or weak enough to shrug off. Tony and Aaron brace me with their bodies as if I'm still the Dragon Son and they must protect me. Auntie Cat and Uncle Roy clutch each other and stand tight. Panic fills Head Elder's eyes and he starts to run, until Uncle George grabs hold of him with an impatient yank. The Hong Kong goons look like they want to run like panicked chickens. On the altar, candles tremble and offerings rattle, while on the wall the framed pictures of the lineage of Dragon Sons sway. Just as suddenly, it's done. One of those short, sharp jolts that's over before doing any real damage.

Could that have been Jade Dragon? Back in his human days, our clan believed dragons cause earthquakes. Maybe this was his way of helping. I need to work it in my favor somehow. Then one of the framed pictures falls off the wall. The one on the end.

Yeah. Mine.

I'd smack my forehead if I could. I reach out for Jade Dragon. *Dude, was that you?*

He swishes his tail before diving into the ocean, his way of waving goodbye.

Head Elder points an accusing finger at my fallen photo. "Jade Dragon has spoken. Paul Lau is not the Dragon Son."

I shake a mental fist at that dragon. "If that's true, then why didn't my dad's photo fall, too?"

"You dare question this omen from our ancestor?"

"No, I dare question your bullshit."

His face blotches dark red and I can almost see steam pour out of his ears as he comes at me like a freight train. I flinch, but stand my ground, until he raises his hand and smacks me across the mouth. His wedding ring tears into my lip and I recoil into Tony, who clamps me with both hands to hold me up. There's no pain, yet, though the bottom of my face tingles and I taste blood.

"Silence." Head Elder leans in closer so only Tony and I can hear. "You will obey me or I will have you, your brother, and that girl put to death."

I bite my tongue and taste more blood as I bottle up everything that wants to pour out of me in a red rage. Then his face contorts as his eyes soften and mouth goes slack, and somehow, I know he sees his daughter in my face. I can almost feel Mom's touch on my shoulder and her voice in my ear, whispering, *please, don't hurt him.*

My breath shakes as I inhale and he backs away. I can't kill him and, despite his abuse and threats, he can't kill me. We'll always have my mom standing between us.

"I will finish what Jade Dragon has begun," announces my uncle. He snaps his fingers and motions at two of his goons.

One picks up my picture and takes Dad's off the wall. The other hangs a framed photo of Uncle George, who preens like a goddamn peacock.

Tony presses both his palms into my back. I tamp down my anger and concentrate on the flow of my *chi* joining his *chi*. This is what Dad wanted, us working together, fighting for our family. I can deal with his sins later. Right now, I need to be…

Released. The points unlock and power flows through my limbs, loosening and strengthening my muscles and core energy. I still can't perform the Dragon Shout. The energy flows from my hand, not my mouth. Tony's hands stay on my shoulder as if he's leaning on me. That final push must have drained his *chi*.

Big Brother?

I'm all right.

But he's not. I can barely hear him, as if he's struggling to use the Silent Speech. The emotional toll alone must have messed up his energy. He shouldn't have weakened himself further, especially since my hands are still bound.

Then his internal voice comes back stronger and more determined. *I can pick the lock on your cuffs, but not without being seen. We need to create a distraction.*

Do we? Uncle George is being plenty distracting as he struts over to the altar and stands before it, waiting, while his goons gather up the elders.

"You will now swear obedience to the new Dragon Son," orders Head Elder as he joins him.

"No," protests the first elder. "This isn't right."

Uncle George hones his concentration onto him. "Yes, it is. You know it is. I am the true Dragon."

The elder's eyes lose focus. His lips tremble before he gibbers, "Yes, yes, the true Dragon Son."

He'll do that to each of us if we don't act now. We need to get Aaron, Auntie Cat and Uncle Roy to provide cover. I reach out to my aunt using the Silent Speech and encounter a barrier of sorrow and guilt. I push past it until I touch her consciousness. Her eyes flicker and she glances at me as she reaches back.

Nephew. Lennon, I'm so…

The doors burst open, breaking our connection. Then a ragtag paramilitary force comes pouring through. The goons raise their handguns, but they're no match for the semiautomatic rifles pointed at them. They fall back with raised arms and red laser beams on their vital points. I want to jump for joy. That earthquake must've been Jade Dragon helping the Beggar Clan break in.

"Drop your weapons," booms a burly Drill Sergeant kind of guy. As the guards comply, he shouts, "All of you, on the floor. Kneel. Hands on your heads. Do it."

I never thought I'd be so happy to drop to the floor while a badass woman points a gun in my face. She motions me to put my hands on my head and I show her the handcuffs.

"How dare you?" blusters Head Elder. "Who is responsible for this outrage?"

Jeremiah comes striding in, carrying the Beggar Chief's staff rather than a rifle. He's wearing camouflage pants, combat boots, and a black muscle shirt that shows off his burn scars and tattoos in equal measure. He's accompanied Christy Sparrow and his sons, all wearing their bright Strowler scarves. Then Penny steps around them.

For a moment, it seems like she's bathed in a silver glow. Everything else, all sight and sound, disappears and all that exists is Penny, my mate, feisty as hell, her fists clenched and battle ready. Her eyes meet mine and her face lights up as she shouts my name.

A painful smile splits my face, widening the bleeding crack in my lip. Sight and sound return as I notice her messy hair, dark-circled eyes, and bruised arms. My fury at Uncle George redoubles. Maybe I can't kill my grandfather, but nothing will stop me from ending him.

Penny takes a step toward me and her uncle clamps her shoulder. "What are you doing here, girl? I told you to stay downstairs."

"I want to see Lennon." She tries twisting away, but he keeps his grip while staring her down. She bites her lip and I know she wants to say more, but can't challenge her Upright Man in front of rival clans.

Christy turns to his sons. "Casey, Brendan, take her home."

Our eyes meet again and I wish I could break my shackles, run to her, run away from all this bullshit with her, but justice is so close, I can taste it. I'm not going anywhere until this is done. She gives a little nod as if she understands and mouths, *Later*. I nod back as her cousins escort her out the door. When all this is done, I'm going to train her in the Silent Speech. That way, if anything like this happens again, we can communicate. Not that it will happen again. Not on my watch.

Head Elder glares up at Jeremiah. "You are the new Beggar Chief?"

Jeremiah nods.

"I am Head Elder of the Two Dragon Clan. How dare you invade our sanctum? This goes against all Crossroads laws."

"How dare you kidnap a Strowler woman? This isn't an invasion, it's a rescue and fully sanctioned by the laws of the Crossroads."

"Who's the dunghill that trepanned my niece?" asks Christy, rubbing a fist into his palm.

I nod toward Uncle George.

Christy snorts as he strides forward. "I'll rip out your spine and piss in your skull, you piece of shite."

Uncle George doesn't flinch. "Is that your way of challenging me?"

Christy grabs him by the collar, hauls him to his feet and shoves him away before raising his fists.

Uncle George folds his arms with a sneer. "I don't have time for your nonsense." He nods toward Jeremiah. "My first challenge is with the Beggar Chief."

"What shite are you talking?"

Head Elder raises his voice. "Step back, Strowler Chief, and show respect for the new Dragon Son."

"What? Him?" Christy jabs his thumb toward me. "I thought it was the kid."

"Paul Lau has been deposed. The true Dragon Son is George Lau." Head Elder turns to Jeremiah. "You interrupted our proceedings. Leave now and we shall continue. When we are ready, you will be called to challenge the Dragon Son."

"What the hell?" Jeremiah looks from Head Elder to me. "You going along with this?"

I give him a look before gesturing with my cuffed hands. "That's why they kidnapped Penny, to make me cooperate."

"I don't give a damn about clan infighting. Last I checked, you were the Dragon Son, hostile takeover or no."

"He is not the Dragon Son," counters Head Elder. "I have declared it so."

"So what? I thought the Dragon Son was head of the clan, not you."

Score one for Jeremiah. If Head Elder says he's head of the clan, the elders will dispute that. If he says it's the Dragon Son, then he's giving his tool, George, permission to rule over him.

"The Dragon Son rules with the advice and consent of the Head Elder."

"Bullshit," I call out. As if consent had anything to do with what's going on.

Jeremiah holds up his hands. "I'm here to fight the Dragon Son. That's him." He points at me. "My father died for this. I'm not leaving until I do. Uncuff him."

"I don't have the key," says Head Elder.

"Who does?"

"Him," I nod at Uncle George.

He shakes his head with that damn smirk. "No, I don't."

"Search him," orders Jeremiah.

Drill Sergeant grabs hold of my uncle and starts roughly digging through his pockets. Then Uncle George starts whispering to him and he slows down. Shit.

"Don't listen to him," I call out. "He's got this power to convince people about things."

Drill Sergeant glares at me. "Power, my ass. He doesn't have the key."

Damn it.

"Banks," Jeremiah hollers. A woman with full military gear, except for her bobbing dreadlocks, comes trotting up and salutes. "Get to work."

She pulls a lock pick kit from a pouch on her belt and motions me to stand. While she works on my cuffs, I size up the situation. Uncle George and Head Elder are keeping Aaron between them. I know this is intentional since I can't blast them without hurting him. I need to get rid of the Beggar Clan and the Strowlers and I can only do that by fighting Jeremiah.

He steps in front of me, blocking my view. "You look rough, kid."

I shrug. "Shittiest birthday ever."

"You wanna wait and rest up a few hours? My people will clear your enemies out of the *kongsi*. The Beggar Clan backs you, not them, whatever that Head Elder guy was saying."

Of all times for Jeremiah to decide to be a good guy. "Nah. I want to get this over with."

"You know, for a while there, I blamed you for my father's death. Now that I see all this, I think something else is going on."

"Like what?"

"You think it's a coincidence that both our fathers were killed by the Shinobi?"

I did, but now that he says it like that, it makes me wonder. It seemed like a poor excuse that Hasaki wanted to elevate his own tiny clan. What if he'd been paid to challenge me and maybe even kill me if I accepted the challenge? That would be a convenient way to get rid of me. "I don't know. Maybe not."

"Maybe?" He gives a dry laugh and shifts around to stare at Banks. "What's taking so long, soldier?"

"British-issue cuffs, sir. They're harder to pick," she replies.

Uncle George must have gotten them in Hong Kong… Uncle George. Where is he? I twist away from Banks and turn in a circle like a chicken with clipped wings, searching every face in the room. My heart starts pounding even harder when I realize Drill Sergeant is gone, along with Head Elder, Uncle George, and…

Shit. No! I do another turn to make sure.

Jeremiah grabs my shoulder. "What the hell are you doing?"

I yank free. "They escaped. They took Aaron."

He gives the room a quick scan before getting on his shoulder remote.

I look for Tony and he's already sprinting out the door, Auntie Cat and Uncle Roy on his heels. Beggars aim their rifles at them and Jeremiah hollers at them to let them go. I try standing still so Banks can finish picking the lock, but I feel like I'm going to vibrate out of my skin, which I know is making it harder for her. I close my eyes, take a deep breath, and find the center of my *chi*, concentrating on its power to calm and strengthen me despite all the frantic noise and movement going on around me. The cuffs come loose and my hands are free. I open my eyes and give myself the luxury of rubbing my wrists before taking off. I'm halfway across the floor when Tony enters, his arm supporting a limping and wincing Aaron. He leads him to a chair and sets him down.

I stop in my tracks as relief drains some of the energy from me. "What happened?"

Tony kneels and rolls up Aaron's pants leg. His ankle is twisted and gashed, and the sock is soaked with blood.

"Medic," Jeremiah hollers. A man with an EMT shoulder kit rushes to join Tony on the floor.

Aaron grimaces as they start working on his wound. "I don't know," he says through gritted teeth. "My dad was talking to a Beggar and then they started herding me and Head Elder toward the door. I thought the Beggar was taking us somewhere else in the *kongsi*, but he escorted us all the way out of the building and into a car. That's when Tony, Auntie Cat and Uncle Roy showed up. The car started to drive away and they chased after us. I opened my door and tried to get out, but Dad started talking to me, convincing me to stay. The car slowed to turn the corner out of the alley and Tony grabbed me and dragged me out, but my ankle got caught…" He hisses and bites his lip as the medic starts swabbing the wound.

Tony stands and addresses Jeremiah, "Cat and Roy are still in pursuit. I ordered our guards to join the chase, but the Beggars won't let them go."

"I'll give the orders," says Jeremiah before talking into his shoulder mic.

A shamefaced Drill Sergeant reenters the room, rubbing his forehead.

"Torres," yells Jeremiah. "What the hell did you do?"

Drill Sergeant shakes his head. "That… that evil bastard. He started talking to me and…" His chest rises and falls as his eyes become bewildered. "I don't know. He somehow convinced me that he was in charge and I had to follow his orders. It wasn't until he was in the car that I realized I'd been tricked."

Jeremiah looks at Tony. "What the hell is that? Some kind of Two Dragon Clan skill?"

Tony shakes his head, "None that I know of."

I don't say anything, but he's kind of lying. It is a skill we know, but it's been lost for over a hundred and fifty years. Damn, that's a scary thought. Is it possible Uncle George found the Wisdom Pearl? Or maybe he found some lost manuals and studied them to learn the power without the pearl. His expertise is in scholarship, not physical strength.

Jeremiah turns to me, "You said your uncle has some kind of power like that."

Christy Sparrow gives me a sharp look. I know he's wondering if Penny told me about Charm. Not that he's going to say anything. We have our clan secrets to keep, even in the face of all this. I shrug. "Yeah, he tried it on me. I don't know what it was."

We wait in tense silence for what seems like forever. All the while, Jeremiah is listening to his headpiece and talking into his shoulder. Finally, he says, "The car was stopped by the cops for speeding on Stockton Street. When your aunt and uncle caught up with them, George convinced the police to hold them at gunpoint and block off the entire street. Then the car drove away through the tunnel. We're still in pursuit, but if they get to SFO, there's nothing we can do."

Shit. I thought I'd be getting justice and instead I got played. They'll return to Chisel Knife Mountain and set up Uncle George as the new Dragon Son. Even if I fight Jeremiah and win, I'll be as powerless over them as ever. The Two Dragon Clan is a worldwide organization. Who knows how the different chapters will side with two different Dragon Sons in contention? We're not in any position to assault the main compound and seize back control, especially not until Tony and I figure out things between us. We need a powerful ally or even enemy to challenge them for us. I look at Jeremiah, chomping at the bit to fight me.

"Are we still on?" I ask.

He blinks. "You don't want to wait?"

"No, let's get this over with."

Tony stands. *What are you doing?*

What I need to do so we can survive.

Beggars grab hold of the coil of rope to form a makeshift ring around Jeremiah and me. Tony hesitates before grabbing a hank so I'll have someone in my corner, so to speak. He keeps nudging at my mind to continue the conversation, so I cut off contact. There's a small commotion as Auntie Cat and Uncle Roy return. I see their faces, discouraged and concerned, and for a moment I waver, thinking of the years they'd spent training me for this moment. Then I think of what they've kept from me. If I'd known Tony was Dad's son, I never would've run away or moved away. All that hatred and resentment I'd felt for him... it's hard not to transfer it onto them right now.

My head aches and my stomach quivers, so I take a deep breath to stabilize the flow of my *chi*. I need to be clear-headed and strong for this. No one speaks. The rules are simple. We fight until one of us drops.

Jeremiah raises his fists. I raise mine, signaling the beginning of the fight. He comes at me, about to attempt an obvious sucker punch, but I'm not the sucker here. I drop my guard and lower my head, signaling that I accept defeat.

Silence.

Gasps.

"What the hell?" says Jeremiah, fists still raised as if expecting a feint.

I look him in the eye. "You win. You're the head of the Crossroads. Congratulations."

Silence fills the room, except for the buzzing in my ears. My stomach folds on itself and I want to puke. The Elders' mouths gape before flapping with protests, but the sound is overpowered by the Beggars, who lift their weapons in the air with their warrior cries.

Jeremiah's eyes stay locked with mine. He might be a sucker, but he's not stupid. He knows what I did. Head Elder and Uncle George will protest the results and insist the Two Dragon Clan remains in command. The entire Beggar Clan will dispute that. They'll have to fight it out among themselves, leaving Tony and me to regain what power we can.

Jeremiah nods slowly. "You're taking a big risk, kid. We're not going to let the Two Dragon Clan take back control of the Crossroads, no matter who the Dragon Son is."

I shrug. "The Beggar Clan should be in control. You fight for the people, against injustice. We used to do that, but not anymore. We don't deserve to be the head of the Crossroads."

His eyes soften slightly. "My father always told me you were different, that I shouldn't judge you so harshly."

A lump forms in my throat and I can't answer. It doesn't

matter because a swarm of Beggars are lifting Jeremiah on their shoulders while cheering and jeering at the sullen members of my clan.

Tony stands beside me. *Well done.*

I'm glad you think so, because it should've been your decision, not mine.

No. His face is like a blank piece of paper with knife-sharp edges. *You are the Dragon Son. Not him. Not me.*

No. You…

No. You.

I can feel his weakened state, drained of *chi* to save me. I know what this has done to him. His righteous core has become a dark pit of shame.

The Beggars parade out of the banquet hall, followed by Christy Sparrow and his remaining son. He shoots me a final warning look over his shoulder as he leaves. I roll my eyes. Penny's an adult. It's up to her if she wants to see me again, though after all this, maybe she'll be done with me. That thought leaves me numb, like I don't have any emotion left to spill out.

Roy and Cat gather our forces and stop Head Elder's men from leaving the room. Then everyone looks at me and Tony. He's gone stone silent. Well, shit. I don't know what to do with those guys. There's no point in keeping them prisoners, right? I walk over to where they're standing in sullen silence. "If you stay, you're with us. If you leave, you're with the traitors. Your choice."

"I have no choice," says one of them. "My family lives in the clan compound."

Okay, first lesson of leadership, there's no such thing as a cut and dry. "Then do what you have to do."

As if that's any easier, because I don't have a fucking clue.

Lennon

Tony pulls himself together enough to issue the orders necessary to secure the *kongsi*. The elders clamor at us, insisting we need to talk right this very moment, like that's even a good idea. We leave them to discuss among themselves, since neither of us are in the mood to win anyone's loyalty. Either they're with us or they're not, and if they're not, better to know now.

We head upstairs, taking each step slowly, trying to delay the inevitable. As we head down the hall, we pass the shrine to Auntie Sylvia. Tony stops, blows out the candles, snuffs the incense, and continues walking without a backward glance. Why does it feel so shitty? Maybe because he lost both his parents today and unlike me, he can't feel good about at least one of them.

In the living room, May and Cat are patching up Aaron while Uncle Roy paces in front of the fireplace. He stops and stares at us, his face brimming with regret. Do I even want to know what his excuse is? I suppose I do, since I perch on the ottoman while Tony collapses into his armchair. I lean forward on my elbows and look from Roy to Cat. "You knew."

They both nod.

I expected this, but a burn still spreads across my chest and fills my throat. My fists pound my knees, releasing some of my fury so I can speak. "How could you do this to me?"

Tears brim in Auntie Cat's eyes. She mouths, "I'm sorry."

I grit my teeth as tears fill my eyes. No, I'm not going to cry. I want answers, not apologies. "How could you keep the truth from me. You, of all people. I thought you were on my side. You've been lying to me, like everyone else."

She licks her lips and swallows. "I wanted to tell you. I wanted to tell everyone."

"She did," says Roy. "She fought with her brothers. She fought with me." His head bows. "We ended our relationship over it. That's why I moved back to Seattle."

"That's why you didn't get married?" asks Tony. "Because of me?"

Auntie Cat wipes away a tear. "No. None of this was ever your fault."

"Mike was afraid that if word got out of your paternity, Head Elder would have you killed," explains Uncle Roy. "He had all of us, me, Cat, George and Sylvia, swear an oath that we would never reveal the truth."

Auntie Cat glares at him. "I'd told Mike it's better for the truth come out. That such a secret could destroy our clan. I told him he couldn't marry Michelle with this over his head."

My mouth goes dry. "So, my mother didn't know?"

"I don't know. I kept my word and never spoke to her or anyone about it, until now. I didn't know Michael had planned to make Tony his heir, if that's even true."

Tony's head raises. "It's not true. If my father wanted me to be the next Dragon Son, he would have made it so. Paul is his heir. He is the Dragon Son."

I suck in a harsh breath, thinking of all the things I saw and overheard those last days at the clan compound. I'm convinced

Dad wanted Tony to be the Dragon Son and Head Elder stopped him. And there's something else I'm even more convinced of. My glare stays fixed on my aunt. "Why didn't you believe me when I said Auntie Sylvia killed my mother?"

She blinks before shaking her head. "I didn't disbelieve you. I told Head Elder what you saw. Maybe her cancer kept him from punishing her. Or maybe, like me, he's unsure because what would Sylvia have gained by killing your mother at that moment?"

I'm on the verge of spitting it out, but one look at Tony stops me. He's done. Shock and grief have hollowed him out. He used all his energy to help me, only to get punched in the gut again and again. This would be the final blow and it can wait.

I'm done, too. I stand and nod to Tony. "Let's go."

He blinks and stands without question. I feel the eyes of the others as we leave the room. From the closet, he hands me a leather jacket and a helmet, probably May's. It's a tight fit, but it'll work. We head downstairs and walk wordlessly through the lobby. The security crew is trying to figure out how to reattach the front door. The Beggars must have blown it off. Damn slick work since there aren't any scorch marks or signs of an explosion…

Unless it wasn't the Beggars. Jade Dragon. He let them in and saved my mate.

Thanks, dude! I call out.

He doesn't answer. Typical.

We climb onto Tony's Ducati and he roars out of the alley. I don't ask him where we're going. That's up to him. He takes to the steep hills of California Street with a vicious abandon and I grasp his waist to keep from falling off. My heart pounds my throat, and for those moments, I can think of nothing but gravity and the coefficient of friction. Finally, we glide into the avenues. He steers off California and meanders through the residential streets until we reach Sea Cliff, and he pulls into the parking lot for China Beach.

On a sunny weekend, this place is crowded with locals. Since it's a foggy, windy weekday, we've got the place to ourselves. We head down the trail until we get to the beach, still damp from the receding tide. Tony stops and his legs seem to give way as he sinks to the sand. He takes a deep gulp of air before his head drops to his knees.

I sit beside him, balled up in my own misery. I thought I had nothing left to lose except Penny, but I do. Faith in my father. Gone. He fucked his brother's fiancé, conceived a child, and denied them both. That underlying tension I always felt between our parents is finally explained. Why did Uncle George and Auntie Sylvia live in the *kongsi* instead of some-place far away? Maybe because they didn't want to get over it. They wanted to rub it in Dad's face every day, and he let them, because he wanted to be close to his son.

Tony. My role model. Everything I aspired to be when I was still a *Xia* on the Glory Road. Dad made him into his own image, except more righteous. I can't imagine Tony trying to sneak into Penny's pants. I grab a handful of sand and hurl it toward the water. The wind picks up the granules and blows them back on us. Tony lifts his head and gives me a look.

I wince. "Sorry."

He raises his eyebrows, like he always does when tolerating his pain-in-the-ass Little Brother. Then he studies the waves as if the answers he seeks will wash up onto shore. Since that's never going to happen, he sighs. "All my life, since I can first remember anything, I wanted Uncle Michael to be my father. You don't know how I envied you. I didn't care about being the Dragon Son. I wanted a father I could respect and admire. Dad… or whoever he is. Uncle George. He was never there. I always wondered why. I mean, I knew he and Mother didn't like each other, but I thought he could at least be there for his sons. Now I know why. And that man I admired so much, he rejected me, too. Didn't want me to be his son. Wished I'd never been born."

Pain squeezes him into something tight and fragile. I've been there. I know how that feels. You ball up into a hard shell so you can't be cracked, but it doesn't help. I lay my arm across his shoulder and squeeze. He flinches, but some of the tension eases.

"You don't hate me?" he asks.

"What? No. Why would I hate you?"

He stares at the waves. I chew my lip, wanting to ask if he still thinks his mother didn't kill mine. That's gotta wait until I can come up with the final proof. I take a deep breath. "There's something I've never told you or anyone. That last summer on Chisel Knife Mountain, I overheard Dad and Head Elder arguing about something to do with Uncle George. Head Elder kept mentioning Dad's sin. I didn't know what he meant, until now. From what I heard, I can tell you, Dad wanted you to be the Dragon Son."

"No. If he did, he would have named me his heir. He brought you before Jade Dragon, not me."

"Yeah, because Head Elder forced him to. Anyway, forget them. I'll tell Jade Dragon you're the new Dragon Son."

"It's pointless to discuss this. The time of the Summoning Ceremony has passed and you don't have the Yang Pearl."

"I don't need it. I talk to Jade Dragon all the time."

He turns to me with narrowed eyes. "What?"

"Well, not all the time. I reach out to him, you know, like, with the Silent Speech, and if he's in the mood, he answers. Speaking of which, first thing you need to learn, dragons are moody as hell. Anyway, I talked to him while we were being held captive. He's the one who blew the door off the hinges and let the Beggar Clan in."

Tony shakes his head with an almost smile. "Everyone

always underestimated you, even our father. Especially him, but now I understand why. It was because of his guilt over me." All trace of humor disappears and his eyes burn like coal. "I never underestimated you. I always knew you had the capability to be a great Dragon Son."

Uh-oh. Not where I want this to go.

"I was right. You speak to Jade Dragon at will, without the Yang Pearl. No other Dragon Son has accomplished this. He even rescued you, his true son."

"No, no, you don't get it. He talks to me because he's bored. I'll explain the situation and he'll talk to you, too. I mean, he probably already knew and was waiting for us to figure it out."

"If Jade Dragon thought I was the true Dragon Son, why didn't he reveal it at the Summoning Ceremony? It's because he accepted you as his heir, not me. I'm nothing to him but the product of sin and unrighteousness."

I rub my forehead. How do I convince him? I study his tense jaw and bleak eyes. Now is not the time. He's got to get over it and that's not going to happen anytime soon. I pick up a handful of sand, but this time I let it sift through my fingers. "I always thought of you as my brother, never as my cousin. I think we both always knew, we just didn't know."

That came out lame, but he nods. "Yeah."

"I'm glad we finally know the truth, despite everything."

"Me, too." He stands and brushes himself off. His expression has become impassive again, the unbreakable Tony that I've always known and looked up to. Now that he's cracked open and I've seen inside, I admire him even more. He'll make a great Dragon Son, once he gets it through his thick skull.

I stand, too. "Can you drop me off someplace?"

"Penny's?"

"Yeah."

He nods. Talk about progress. Too bad we had to suffer so much to get here.

Penny

Uncle Christy sits in our front room, locked and loaded, and full of shite. He points a thick finger at me and I grind my teeth so I don't roll my eyes. "If she'd married Conor, she'd be settled now and not made a disgrace of herself."

Bridie stands, hands on her hips. "My daughter will marry when and who she pleases, Christy, and that's the end of it."

My heart swells at the regrowth of her backbone. She's a right world beater now she knows Matthew is alive.

"You think any proper lad will want her now that she's been kidnapped and used as a pawn because the Dragon Son's sweet on her?" His finger now wags at me. "Stay away from him, you hear me? Any further congress with him will be the ruin of you."

"That's enough. It wasn't Penny's fault that she was kidnapped."

"It's her fault for running wild with that boy. I wouldn't let a son of mine marry a romp, even if she still has her virtue. Someday, she'll want to return to her people, sadder and wiser, like you did. She won't find a catch like Conor waiting to wife her. She'll find rakes like Kingfisher waiting to make her a convenience."

My mouth pops open, ready to cry bullshit, but Bridie beats me to it in a voice as cold as ice. "I won't be talked to like that, Christy. I'm not a toad eater anymore. You might be the Upright Man, but best remember who and what are keeping you in place."

Her brother's startled blue eyes tighten into a hard squint. His mouth opens, but he sucks in his words and his hands slap his thighs as he stands. He stalks out of the room, yanks open the front door and slams it behind him.

Bridie presses her hand to her chest. She stares at the door with pensive eyes and chews her lip before saying, "I suppose that was a poor way of thanking him for saving you."

He didn't save me, but I can't tell her that, not until I figure out what it was that caused the explosion. "Mum, you've been kissing his feet and thanking him since we came home. Besides, Uncle Christy couldn't have done shite without the Beggar Clan. You should be thanking Jeremiah."

"You're right, I should." She picks up her phone. Her lips twist. "I wonder if he'll even bother with me now that he's king of the Crossroads. I'll text him first."

I leave the room before allowing my own wry smile. If Jeremiah wants her for his queen, he doesn't have a chance in hell anymore. I pass through the kitchen where Kai perches on a chair while thumbing away at his phone. The little sod got excused from our uncle's tirade, but lingered close enough to hear everything. He doesn't miss a tap on the screen as he says, "So, the marriage with Conor is off?"

"The marriage with Conor was pants from the get go." I lean against the counter. "Tell Aaron I said hi."

"Okay." He taps some more and stops for a moment. "Aaron says hi. He says Tony just came home, but Lennon isn't with him." He gives me a look. "You going out?"

I shake my head. The kidnappers took my phone and my keys and I have no idea where they are. Even if I go to the studio, I have no way of getting in. My best option is to message Lennon from my laptop. I head for my bedroom with the intent of doing exactly that, but stop in my tracks when I reach the bathroom. I haven't showered since London, which feels like a month ago. Almost without thinking, I strip and step into the shower. The hot water eases my tense muscles and the steam clears my head. As I dry off, there's a knock on the door. From my room, not Bridie's. I freeze.

"Penny?" says Lennon through the door.

My heart leaps into my throat and I wrap the towel around me as I say, "Don't come in here."

"I know. I heard the shower, so I'm letting you know I'm here."

"Okay. I'll be out in a moment."

"Sorry. I don't have my phone. They took it from me."

"It's okay. They took mine, too." I unwrap the towel and rub it through my wet hair. "Good thing it's me in here and not Bridie or Kai."

"Yeah, I know. If it was one of them, I figured the worst they'd do is kick me out, and even then, I'd still see you."

I pick up my clothes, stained and stinking of fear sweat, and wrinkle my nose before putting them back on. Then I leave the bathroom, locking the door behind me. Lennon is standing in the middle of the room, his back turned. I'm torn between relief, caution, and this sort of frantic love where I want to throw myself at him. My arms fold. "Hey."

He turns around and looks at me with those warm brown eyes that always catch my soul. "Hey."

A bruise discolors the left side of his mouth and chin, accented by the deep gash in his lower lip, which must be where the blood on his shirt came from. I'd been hustled out of the banquet room so quickly, I didn't see that he'd been hurt.

I'd noticed his hands seemed bound behind his back and now I see the proof of it in the red welts encircling his wrists. With a little gasp, I run to him and wrap my arms around him. His arms encircle me and it doesn't feel like we can hold each other tight enough, so we keep trying.

"Are you all right?" I whisper.

"Yeah," he breathes into my hair.

We release each other enough to be face to face. His expression is one of hungry desperation and I wonder if mine is the same. I want to kiss him, but I don't want to hurt him. Then he's kissing me and not gently, but with that same hunger that makes me respond in kind. I taste his blood and my head spins because I don't care. We stop, sucking in air, our foreheads still pressed together. Then he lifts his head and touches his bleeding lip. I break away to grab a handful of tissue. He presses them to his lip and we sit on the bed, close enough our legs touch. His arm slides around my waist and his head rests on my shoulder. He inhales deeply as if the stink of my clothing is perfume.

A tingling sensation starts between my legs and spreads through my body. Fear, stress, weariness all combine to make me want to forget there's a world outside my door, but I don't want him to think I'm using him. We need to talk, but how to start? With something simple. I reach back and dig out the Clash album that had gotten wedged between my pillows. "Happy birthday."

Despite the tissue, his mouth drops open. His thumb reverently rubs the signature on the cover. "Strummer himself," he whispers. "This must've cost a fortune."

"Nah. I got it at a charity shop for two quid. I don't think they knew who Joe Strummer was. Sorry it's not in good shape. I mean, the record. It's got scratches."

"Kidding? It's the best gift I ever got." He can't mean that, but I allow myself a moment to enjoy his pleasure as he turns the album over to examine the back. Then he looks at me and the glow in his eyes makes my heart skip a beat. "Thanks."

"You're welcome."

"You got it in London?"

"Yeah."

"How'd it go there?"

I suck in a hard breath. "I found out what happened to Gerry and Matthew."

The tissue drops from his seeping lip. "Really? Can you tell me?"

"Yeah. It's…" I search for a word. The best I come up with is "Complicated. And it involves you."

"Me?" His eyes become wary. "How?"

I tell him the whole wonderful, awful story of learning Matthew is still alive and how he can be healed. I leave out the sexual part about the Yin and Yang pearls. He probably already knows. I hope. I don't want to be the one to tell him. My heart sinks at his grim expression. Have I joined the ranks of those who want to use him?

Then he takes my hands and squeezes. "I'm glad Matthew's alive. I'll do everything I can to help, but like you said, it's complicated."

"I know. And your uncle has made things worse."

"How?"

I tell him about being kidnapped and questioned by George Lau. "I'd swear he was using Charm, except no Strowler would teach him how."

"The Two Dragon Clan doesn't have that skill. I'm not sure how he learned it."

Speaking of skills. "So, was it you who did that explosion thing?"

He won't look me in the eye. "Sort of. Not exactly."

"Can you tell me exactly?"

He shakes his head.

"Clan secret?"

"Sort of."

I hate it when he's evasive like this. I mean, I know I have to respect his clan's secrets, but I have a million questions, like why he was able to cause an explosion, but still remained a prisoner. It's also a reminder of what will always come between us.

He changes the subject, but not in a good way. "About the Yang Pearl, it's more complicated now."

My heart thuds a little harder. Uncle Christy told us that Lennon's clan leadership was in dispute. "Yeah?"

"Yeah."

Hope fades and turns to ash as I listen to his story. I keep it to myself, since I can't imagine how awful it must be to find out your dad cheated with your aunt. Poor Tony. Those are two words I never thought I'd put together. The selfish side of me rages silently against fate. If Tony is the true Dragon Son, then he and his wife could have used the pearls to heal Matthew, but now the Yang Pearl is gone, too.

I chew my lip. With all that's going on, he doesn't need this, but it can't wait. "I'm sorry. I know you just went through a lot, but I've got to bring this up. Since there's a big power struggle in your clan right now, what kind of threat is your uncle to Matthew and his parents?"

"A big threat. That's why we can't afford to sit around and cry over what happened. We gotta act now."

I suck in a sob, but my eyes still fill with tears. My head drops. So damn close.

"Penny?"

"I'm sorry. I don't mean to dump this on you. I don't expect you to risk your life for Matthew. I was hoping we could use the pearls to heal him, but if the Yang Pearl is gone…"

His fingers curl around mine. "We can do this."

I lift my head. He's got that heartbreaker smile, the one that names me his co-conspirator and belies the always deep sadness in his eyes. I believe him because he is my partner in crime and has never let me down, but I've got to ask, "How?"

"I know who has the Yang Pearl."

"Who?"

The smile fades and the sadness deepens. This doesn't dilute the resolve in his voice as he says, "Tony."

Next in Series

The story continues in Scion: Dragons of the Crossroads Book 3. When Penny and Lennon set out on a quest to find the lost dragon pearls, they unleash unknown powers deep within them. They are the human descendants of dragons, but are they becoming something more?

To find out more about Dragons of the Crossroads and to purchase more books in the series, please go to loriwriter.com.

Acknowledgments

Heartfelt thanks to my editors and proofreaders: Jennifer Gagliardi, India Cale, and L.J. Redding.

The following song lyrics are all in the public domain.

- Chapter 1, song lyrics, "The Unfortunate Lad"
- Chapter 1, song lyrics, "Red is the Rose"
- Chapter 17, song lyrics, "The Revel" by Bartholomew Dowling

About the Author

Lori Saltis left her heart in San Francisco. She goes to visit it whenever she can afford the bridge toll. She's been an indie author since 2016. She's very passionate about the themes of alienation and found family. Her favorite genre is fantasy because who doesn't want to believe they'll look up in the sky one day and see a dragon?

To find out more about the world of the Crossroads, check out her website loriwriter.com.

www.ingramcontent.com/pod-product-compliance
Lightning Source LLC
Chambersburg PA
CBHW020746310726
48969CB00002B/444